The Bones of a Season

Paul Breen

* The feisty northern lass from
South Shields bears no semblance to
anyone real or re-imagined when she
appears in the uncut version, pint in hand,
managing the whole bloody show!
(must be read in Geordie accent)

Also by Paul Breen

The Charlton Men

To Donna,
All the best
Paul Bree
X

To Chris Harrison, Steve, Sarah, and Charles amongst others for their invaluable information, stories and suggestions along the way. Thanks also to Chris Dunn and Ken Sinyard for the cover image, and to David Ramzan for his advice as a fellow author. A special word too for Rick and all those at Voice of the Valley, for Charlton Athletic Supporters' Trust, and for all other publications or platforms that have given me support and publicity over the past couple of years since writing my first novel *The Charlton Men*. Thanks also to David and Kelly for their assistance and guidance in the process of bringing this book to fruition. Lastly, a note of thanks to all my readers, reviewers, critics, and prospective readers of this new work.

1. Lyric of the Valley

$\int$tanding by the apple tree in his garden on a late spring morning, Fergus Sharkey could see history tattooed on the flesh of South East London. One of those tattoos that people get in places where the needle hurts, and they know that if it goes wrong they're going to suffer. But he had accepted suffering as his fate from the moment he first got caught up in true love's cataclysmic affliction. Not so long ago he had been listening to the vintage crackle of love songs, with a rhythm free as jazz running through his system, when the room shuddered in the wake of a dawning truth.

All at once the record player shook violently, and the needle slipped. Originally nothing more than a surface wound, the damage magnified over days and then weeks, into a haze, a London tea-bag fog that was impossible to see through. He may as well have been walking around with his head buried in the apple blossom that foamed off the tree at his side, and would soon be transformed to the soft green of the parakeets that rode the blue highways of morning in the distance. Once the green leaves came, a wealth of apples would follow, bending the bough, and shining in summer's sun.

Those bitter sweet spheres of memory would grow blood red as the stadium he could see beyond their branches. Down in a valley, the ground tormented him insistently as silence at the end of a love affair. A growing silence, like the needle on a record player turning to a scalpel and shaving flakes of vinyl off the most precious parts of a man's record collection. Maybe one of the songs from the decades before he was born, given by his father in the days before he crossed the sea to Beatles country.

Sometimes he could hear echoes of past music down in that stadium in the valley, carved out of Charlton's chalky soil more than a century before. They sang an adaptation of a Paul McCartney song for their anthem—*Mull of Kinytre* melted down and remoulded into *Valley Floyd Road*.

When he heard that song, shivers went through him, as in one of those moments where wine and lyrics strike your feelings at exactly the same time. But these days the love ballads had faded out on a grey horizon. Some days the image of that football ground stalked his doubts like an Irish banshee—a white ghostess crying at his window, in a voice shrill as a mating parakeet.

When he lost love, the records stopped playing. He hadn't taken such a punch as this since his days in the boxing ring as a teenager. Then he supported a different football team and lived in another country. He was going to be the champion of the world like his countryman Barry McGuigan, walking into the ring to the sound of *Danny Boy* on a summer's night at Loftus Road Stadium in a place called Shepherd's Bush. The date remained stamped in Fergus's memory—Saturday 8th June 1985—three months and thirteen days before Charlton left The Valley, punch drunk and reeling.

Back then he hadn't known much about Charlton.

None of their stories had filled his dreams like McGuigan's heroics. He'd grown up far away from the urban rush of England's capital, and supported Liverpool Football Club with a child's unquestioning passion. That's what all the Irish did back then.

A dagger of irony stabbed his thoughts. 'We followed the winners.'

And now he felt like a loser, punch drunk and reeling from the absence of someone's voice. In his heart he could feel their songs and stories gone, as hopelessly fucked as a cheap cassette eaten up in the jaws of a car stereo.

This was never how the journey was supposed to end for the boy who was going to be champion of the world. Born ginger, he'd grown up a fighter on account of teasing in the playground. Though of medium build, featherweight proportions, he'd learned to channel his rage into the confines of a boxing ring. But as a teenager he made one fatal mistake. He'd stolen a car and gone on a joyride that killed his passenger and ended his hopes of standing on an Olympic podium or fighting professionally.

But that happened before Fergus came to London, finding the woman not just of his dreams but of his destiny, and adopting a new football team with the passion of a convert to a religious cause.

His team was Charlton Athletic and his *home* ground The Valley, with a capital T, more than a common noun, more than a common ground. This was land worth fighting for in the heat of a match day, when the red and black dye of his team's colours smothered the streets of south London.

That was what she had never understood—the woman he grieved for, even though she remained alive, but out of reach like Ireland across the sea. With her at his side, this place became the home he'd never truly found. Like those men a century before who had sweated a football stadium out of a dying industrial valley, he'd fashioned new life out of nothingness.

This place on the edge of London had become a small planet of memory tattooed in the back of his mind alongside songs listened to, conversations shared, and secrets unshelled.

Wine and cheese, walks in Greenwich Park, and boat rides upon the Thames mapped out the back channels of his memory. But now the scene had changed, even though of course it had always been there.

Rusting ships and abandoned warehouses mapped out the terrain along the side of the Thames, a couple of hundred metres beyond The Valley. Downstream the brown-brick edifice of Woolwich solidified the sense of decay. Long ago, furnaces roared. Factories fed an empire. Ships had risen out of the dockyards planted there in King Henry's reign. But those days were dead and gone, with King Henry in the grave.

Brutal man for brutal times. The stadium had known its own brutality too, battered from the sufferings of history, and a period of exile. Fergus had known nothing of Charlton in this time of suffering. He had heard those stories of agony second hand from his friend Lance who passed them on stark and plain as Catholic Stations of the Cross.

Like the apple tree, Lance had his roots in local turf. He had spent his whole life in London aside from a brief exile in Afghanistan, fighting a war that left half a leg missing. The right leg, the wrong one for any explosion to steal—the shooting foot of his favourite player of all time, the great Clive Mendonca, another convert to the Charlton cause.

'Maybe that's the perfect name for your prosthesis,' Fergus sometimes suggested in the drunken banter of a match day.

'Men-donc-a,' Lance extended every syllable of his hero's name.

It sounded different in their respective accents. There were a lot of differences in England and Ireland, though they shared such close geography.

As a child, Fergus could never have imagined crossing the water. Nobody does, he supposed. And yet he'd made his life in Charlton.

He used to joke with Katy about their first born son becoming the 21st century Barry McGuigan or Georgie Best, wearing English colours instead of his father's Irish.

Fergus could end up as a parent to the kid who scored the winning goal in England's first World Cup final since 1966.

Perhaps a penalty kick in the dying moments of the game.

The whole of Ireland and Scotland screaming for Georgie Sharkey to miss, and you're there, in a drunken haze, unsure of your loyalties.

Come on you little bastard put it over the bar.

But he'd never know whether his kid struck the target or not. There wasn't going to be a little Georgie—at least not with Katy Prunty. His dark headed Yorkshire Rose had buried their love and fled to the coast.

He'd lost her as a team loses a Cup final, perhaps a play off at the end of a season when they've come within touching distance of promotion. Players know the chance has gone but they stay haunted by the knowledge of what might have come to pass in different circumstances.

Once upon a time Fergus might have been a boxing champion. But that was blood and sweat not yet spent. It was life played out in a future conditional tense. Katy, on the other hand, had once existed in the present. He'd gone to bed at night with echoes of *'Love you Fergus'* receding into the urban darkness, set against the last whispers of a record player.

'Tree words,' Fergus played upon the loss of love.

Right here in this garden, they'd stood beneath the tree and picked fallen apples from the ground, red and bruised as the distant Valley.

Katy would carry them inside on the first steps of an

expert journey. Through the window of his memory, he could picture her working. First she took a sponge to their red shirts and then stripped them bare. She'd cut the bruises from their flesh, leaving them pure white as her own milky fingers. Then, with the skill of Mendonca, she'd sway and swivel against the oven, perhaps humming songs to herself, those lullabies mothers sing to daughters as they pass on the knowledge of baking. But Katy was always alone in her craft, blue eyes dazzling as she focused on acts of love.

If she baked you something it came from the heart. He could watch her for hours, with her every action intense as a penalty shoot out. Surrounded by the tools of her trade, she set gas purring and dough rising. Fragrances of the garden would slowly fill the small kitchen as she sweetened, stewed and boiled the flesh of apples to a living, breathing feast.

Yes, he could see her as a blue eyed ghost peeping through the white smoke of apple blossom, looking sexy in her apron. Smeared too in the pitch of battle, smudged and stained in sugar, butter, raisins, and cinnamon. And her dark hair, smoky grey in traces of flour, so that just for a second you can imagine her as an old woman, baking by the very same gas fire.

He used to wonder then if he would love her just the same when her head turned silver, and the dough of mid-life rose behind her apron strings. Yes, he would have the very same urges then—to kiss her floury head, and fantasise upon making love in a treehouse in the garden.

But like the harsh winter just passed, their love had turned cold.

This had been the bitterest March since the keeping of records. Killer of lambs in the English countryside, and migrants frozen to death in container trucks on the high seas as they sought refuge in a cold land. Winter's chill had been a destroyer of football's match day experience too. Sometimes Fergus felt like he was watching games from inside an ice-box, instead of The Valley's East Stand in Lance's company.

He blamed the weather for what had happened in the slow decaying of his romance with Katy too; the end of three small words proclaiming love. Words you waken with and sleep upon. Words that stay in your heart like lines of poetry or codes of the periodic table from your school days.

But there was nothing he could have done to keep Katy. She gave him a choice between two things that he loved equally, two forms of maddening desire. He'd have killed and died for both, but had to make a choice.

He selected the one that would always be there, wedded to his side, even though Katy professed that it was Charlton Athletic playing the part of mistress in their love triangle.

'Love triangles lie at the heart of every story,' she often poeticised, and theirs was one of the oddest love triangles in history.

'Sometimes it feels as if I hold second place in your heart,' she would drive her words so forcefully across the garden he could imagine them as daggers piercing the stadium's wine-red shell in the distance. 'If you enjoyed another woman's company as much I'd be very worried.'

She whisked up terms like football widow in every argument. Even when such conversations started as a joke, they ended as a fight. She made a competition out of matches, giving him choices and ultimatums.

Everything had come to a head on the night of a game against Cardiff City, one of the top teams in Charlton's division. That same night, Katy wanted to attend a poetry event. Suddenly Fergus had a choice to make between the two forces at play in his heart. He could select a cold stadium warmed by the presence of fifteen thousand people or choose the snug of a room inside Greenwich's Old Royal Naval College. In his heart he wanted both, but in his head had to make a selection so that the requisite tickets could be booked.

'Wife versus mistress,' he joked with Lance in the days before.

'Cardiff are strong,' his friend reminded him. 'They're at the top of the division and we're at the bottom. We'll probably lose by two or three goals.'

'Yeah,' he'd settled on his choice. 'When you've a season ticket you can afford to miss a couple of matches here and there.'

Katy, thrilled by his decision, wore her favourite black dress for the event—the one he thought of as a paradox. Inside the dress she looked the most beautiful woman in the world and yet every time she wore it, all that he wanted to do was to get it off her body, and get inside the layers beneath. That night, as they caught the bus into Greenwich, passing The Valley along the way, he regretted nothing.

'I made the right choice,' he told her. 'I'm glad I came.'

Her eyes spoke of love's renewal. She took his hand and led him through the gates of the Naval College, stoned immaculate on the side of the Thames. Entering a warm room, every eye turned towards the girl in the black dress but already Fergus's thoughts had started to stray towards football. As they ordered drinks and the poetry evening began, he texted Lance for news.

'Two goals down already,' he received a predictable reply.

Looking at his muse in her paradoxical dress as she rose to the stage to recite some of her own poetry, Fergus was more certain than ever that he had made the right choice. Seeing every man's eyes upon her as she spoke, he felt elated that it was his bed she would be sleeping in tonight. He would be the only one in the room to know the joy of stripping off that dress, touching the white and freckled flesh that lay beneath, and then going inside a body deep as the tunnels and corridors of this historic college and its grand maritime architecture. He would be the only one who would know of her secret turns and tunnels, the places he could touch to make her sigh like the sounds of the river beyond the whispers of poetry so much softer than the heated voices in the home of his mistress.

Then the phone buzzed. 'You're not going to believe this. We were two down, but we've just scored twice. The comeback's on. This has the makings of a classic and the whole stadium's rocking like Mendonca's days.' Suddenly the lure of Katy's poetry seemed less than moments before. He still hungered for her at the end of the night, but felt a greater distance from present surroundings as they mingled amongst the chattering middle-class crowd. And moments later the phone buzzed again. '3-2.'

Then four goals to two, before a fifth sealed the spirit of boyhood dreams, and late night scraps in Shepherd's Bush. His team had scripted a classic encounter on the first night of winter's chill and he had missed the greatest fucking spectacle of the season so far. He'd picked poetry—echoes of Heaney and Auden and Carol Ann Duffy—over the guys on the terraces screaming their lungs out as the referee added on six minutes of injury time.

'Not even we can throw away a 5-2 lead,' Lance texted.

But if there was any team in history that could fuck up forty minutes of great work in five, it was the one that Fergus had chosen to adopt as his own.

That was Charlton, the football club that sometimes felt like an incarnation of a rollercoaster ride at the funfairs of the Kentish coast—perhaps Ramsgate on a summer's night where everybody's drunk and you're up in the air, spinning around above the sea, and not certain you're strapped in the seat. You're loving the atmosphere, but just waiting for the inevitable fall.

And sure enough it came. 'Oh fuck it's 5-3.' Then, seconds later, Cardiff scored again. The rollercoaster dipped towards a dark sea as Fergus struggled to converse with Katy's crowd. But after an interlude of gnawing silence Lance texted confirmation of a 5-4 victory. Fergus bought another round of drink and left the College in a great mood until, going down the road, Katy began to ask about his frantic volley of texts in the midst of her poetry recitation. When he confessed what had happened she reacted as if he were a man emailing his mistress. 'I'm sleeping alone tonight,' she said. 'In the spare room.' 'Fine,' he acceded, as he watched the black dress and a second chance for a night of fantasy slip out of reach. 'Do whatever you like.'

Moving towards the bathroom she stripped in the hallway to show him what he was missing, took a shower, and left him to his dreams of football. They had never fully forgiven each other for the events of that night, and each resented the other's lack of attention for the rest of their relationship. And now she was in a place between farmlands and the sea, and he was alone in his garden looking out on a valley beyond an apple tree.

Maybe she was never in love with *him*. She was in love with whatever ideal form she wanted to change him into. Real love is when you accept somebody for who they are.

Unequivocally. Not Katy. She had things happen to her in the past. Shadows darkening her perception of the world. She'd tried to make him into a light amidst the shadows but he could have been any man, and not a red boy from the Irish border who'd once been a boxer.

He had his own shadows too. They were just as dark and deep. But it wasn't darkness that had come between them. Their separation was born out of red dye, the colour of apples before their stripping and baking.

Everything had gone wrong from the moment he stamped his colours to the mast. That was the moment the record player shook and the needle struck a hump in the groove. Cutting through the flesh of vinyl, the blade turned to fire, draining the lyrics, bleeding the disc to a pool of dark oils. There would be no more songs of blue eyes and baking, music of love coming down through the night air, from a garden with an apple tree above a valley. The poetry of their love had died, but at least the songs of the stadium would ring out every Saturday, certain as the dyes stamped upon his skin.

2. Before the battle

*W*hen you decide to get a tattoo, you're making a hell of a choice that you're going to harbour for a lifetime. That choice of image is a monumental prospect for the person you go to bed with and wake up beside every day, the lover who gets to look at you dressing in the half-light, or stepping fresh out of the shower. Back at the season's outset Fergus had made the great leap regardless of his lover's feelings, and set out on a journey that would lead him towards an appointment with a local ink-gun artist.

'This summer I'm going to get a Charlton tattoo,' he'd promised Lance on a hot spring afternoon at the final game of the previous season.

'Welcome to the tattooed men's club,' his friend laughed.

Unfortunately Katy hadn't welcomed the idea, or taken him seriously. 'People promise themselves crazy things in the heat of a moment.'

'This is more than a promise,' he argued. 'It's an intention.'

'I hate tattoos,' she protested. 'They're crass and look dirty.'

'Everybody's got them nowadays.'

'You don't have to be like everybody else.'

'One tattoo's not going to change the world or me.'

She hadn't agreed with his assertion. 'Tattoos are like a one night stand with somebody who's got an STD. Once you've got them, they're with you for a lifetime, no matter how much you regret the past.'

'Why would I regret it?' he'd asked but was offered no response.

She assumed he'd forget his promise but she didn't really know him. He had a clear goal in mind, and that was to stamp his skin in the Charlton identity, even the Charlton brand. Who owns the badge after all? Is it financiers who control the club on headed paper and spreadsheets, or the ordinary supporter investing their passion in that badge?

Fergus was determined to show that he belonged to the people on the terraces, that he was a part of their tribe and nobody else's. He was going to become a member of Charlton's family, concentrated mainly on the old Roman route out of London up, down, and across to the coast of Kent.

Lance had been a part of that family from the day he was born. His people had been immigrants, settling first on the Isle of Dogs in what was once West Ham and Millwall territory, before crossing the river.

For Fergus, it was different. Very bloody different. But he'd developed the same attachment, and all people stood equal on the terraces when the team came out to play every second Saturday of the season. Charlton belonged as much to him as to anyone else.

Katy mocked the very idea of a club being like a family. 'What? Weddings? Christenings? Christmas? Eid? Bar Mitzvahs?' She'd laugh sardonically. 'You don't even know each other.'

'But we all believe in the same thing.'
'Belief? Football as a replacement for religion?'
'It's so fucking easy to snipe from the sidelines.'
'Just get your tattoo and be done with it then.'
'I will,' he spoke into doors that slammed shut.

Fergus had mulled over possibilities for weeks, taking inspiration from Lance who wore the club crest on his arm with the words Addicted Forever scripted beneath. He'd lie in bed at night with Katy beside him and picture images from websites and other people's bodies. Then he'd take comfort in his lover's arms for a brief respite from their fighting. But when that was done, she'd turn her back and he'd return to dreaming of tattoos.

The summer passed quickly, and the season came around in a time of rain. He'd bought the house just a few months before, and the garden stood in a perpetual haze from wet days and warm evenings. Fences breathed smoke and spider webs in the night, as he counted down the hours to kick off.

Finally he awoke on the day of reckoning, a gorgeous sunny morning. He rose early and went for a run down to the Thames Barrier, where the river reflected a faultless blue sky. Afterwards, he hurried home and took a shower, seeing his body's reflection free of ink for the last time. He thought of Lance and the morning of stumbling onto a landmine, everything suddenly changed. Then he looked on Katy sleeping, with her freckled shoulders turned like leaves rusting in the sun. She'd been busy the night before, burning the midnight oil in her work as a fashion designer. She'd placed a proposal for a book and was waiting on answers from publishers and agents in a world that was far outside the borders of his obsession with football.

Looking at her, he knew that he was fortunate but she represented a different world, a different set of dreams. Though she'd grown up in Yorkshire, she was never of the plain dark earth he had known in the Irish borderlands.

Katy's family had money, a horse farm on the outskirts

of Huddersfield. She played hockey when he dreamed of being the next Barry McGuigan. The closest she'd ever been to Loftus Road was Notting Hill or Portobello. Men thumping each other's brains out held zero appeal for her. She couldn't imagine what it was like to be so deprived of any other escape routes. But she pretended. Radical chic, Lance defined her outlook.

Best then to leave her sleeping as he left the house, and sunlight shifted from her skin to the leaded windows of Charlton House. Partially he felt a traitor, having communicated with the tattoo studio in secret.

Like going on dating sites, when you're in a relationship.

'Perfect sunny day,' he texted Lance on his walk to the ground.

'Don't speak too soon,' his friend predicted, as Fergus stopped on a bench outside of Charlton House to weigh up his decision one last time, imagining the counterweight of a devil and an angel in his conscience.

'She'll understand eventually,' the devil insisted.

'What's more important,' the angelic voice whispered. 'Football, or the woman you're determined to spend the rest of your life with?'

'Is it Charlton, or just because it's a tattoo,' Fergus wondered. 'Would she hate tattoos less if I came home with her name across my chest?'

Probably, she'd hate tattoos regardless of their message.

Trapped between two worlds, he watched The Valley sucking in bodies for the day's battle. Steel and grass pitched in Floyd Road, down the steep gradient of Church Lane staggered in faded Georgian glory. Grand houses broken up into bedsits. Sprays of roses, and voices of men in love.

The mood bristled in optimism and laughter. Children formed a laughing frontline in new shirts red as double deckers on the roads beyond. Fathers flashed season tickets, and smiles sharp as pikes. Hungry for football, they'd spent a summer of Saturdays starved in shopping centres or at the seaside, riding rollercoasters of a different sort. Today's rollercoaster would take them to places of myth and legend, blood and spittle, craters of stud marks in the mud, *Back to the Valley* banners, and great days long ago.

Hull City were coming to town, a team not far from Katy's country. Nicknamed The Tigers, they played in black and amber stripes; colours that started to appear in Charlton's roads as the day progressed. Road of history, leading to the day's battlefield in football's simmering civil conflict. North versus South, Thames versus Humber, war of the working classes.

Before the day was done, southerners would hurl abuse across the terraces at the enemy's stockade. 'Jimmy Savile, he's one o' yer own.'

'Charlton's a shithole,' they'd sing back. 'We wanna go home.'

Fergus watched the people of his tribe gathering, shaking hands, making jokes in the sunshine. Then, all of a sudden, the day darkened. The sun slipped behind clouds. Blue sky turned black as a referee's jersey. Lightning flashed, swift and decisive as a whistle for offside. Supporters scattered, pelted in giant raindrops, seeking out shelter further downhill. Fergus rose to follow, taking this as a cue for his ambitions.

The devil emerged victorious in his conscience. 'I'm doing it.'

Fresh lightning seared the darkened sky, scalping furls of cloud above the tower blocks at his back, facing down on the Thames. Thunder shook the suburbs with the echoing force of a landmine blast, turning the rain to a harder shrapnel of hail skipping off the paving stones.

'In this weather,' he surmised, 'they might call the game off.'

Heavy rain could rip away a summer's worth of work in a few hours. The hard toil of getting the turf ready for another season's abuse. In parts of last winter, the pitch resembled a battlefield on the Somme. That was a consequence of lower division football, no money to pay for the luxury of undersoil heating. Once you fall from football's top table, there's a gaping hole that can suck you right to the bottom. But when you make your choice to follow a football team, you take the good with the bad.

He'd follow Charlton to the fourth division if he had to, so long as the club kept this same identity and awareness of its history's gravitational pull. From the minute he'd come here, he'd attuned to the gravity of this place.

Yes, it was time to get that tattoo and stamp his colours to the mast.

Drenched to the bone, he stopped at a studio in Charlton Heights. First he hesitated, reluctant to go against Katy's wishes. But what good would it do to postpone or abandon his appointment? He had to stand up for who he was and what he believed in. He'd come to the place where he'd reveal his true colours to the world. There was no turning back.

This was for Sam Bartram whose statue stood outside the stadium. This was for Jimmy Seed the former manager whose name graced the away supporters' stand. For Chris Powell, the present manager, and the team he'd built up from mediocrity into champions. Above all this was for Fergus Sharkey, many years after he dreamed of being champion of the world.

'*Dark River Dye*,' he read from a sign above the entrance.

The name made him think of the Thames. Blackened waters in the night, London's biggest cemetery, heart of the city, and leech of its flesh.

Gradually he galvanised courage to step inside. Pushing open the door, he entered a psychedelic cavern. Hieroglyphics of the modern age adorned the walls. Bettty Boop had her tits out smoking a cigarette. Dragons breathed flame. Tigers lurked in shadow. Dancers slinked against poles. Bulldogs scowled at foreign alphabets. A blue devil sported Millwall colours.

At his back, lightning flashed across the sky. Every glossy card upon the wall caught reflections of the blade, and Fergus thought suddenly of needles. 'Maybe I'm not such a brave buck after all.'

Katy's warnings came back into his mind. If he did this, she might well turn her back on him for good, might never bake for him again, or let him touch the valley of autumn freckles on the slopes of her shoulders.

She would never bring a tattooed man to see her family at the horse farm in Huddersfield, with its landscaped gardens and swimming pool.

Perhaps too, this was no place for a boy from Ireland's border country. Across the water, tattoos had always been the other side's terrain. Ulster loyalists decorated themselves densely as the pages of Marvel comic books. But instead of Spiderman and Captain America, you got Colonel Death from the UVF in the form of a skeleton rising up from the Somme's trenches.

'What am I doing here?' Fergus thought aloud, as other images flashed through his mind, hooded men, machine guns, and blood-red fists. 'Tattoos are for sailors, soldiers, and Premier League footballers.'

He turned to go, back out into the rain, without war paint for today's battle. Then through the blaze of colour a fresh sense stirred. Suddenly he had a desire to carry on towards the back of the studio, and complete his symbolic journey.

3. Colours to the mast

Dark African coffee suffused the studio in exotic flavours. The fragrance filled Fergus's mind with a dizzying curiosity, making him wonder if this was what the artist offered to stem the pain of needles. Perhaps a potion of intoxication for the fear that gripped the guts of customers as they gave their bodies over to the surgery of Marvel comic imagery.

He had come here with expectations of smouldering dyes and burning flesh. But this was something else, different, out of place. Warm and reassuring. Suddenly, he developed a thirst for deeper knowledge.

'The smell's coming from the back of the studio,' he realised.

Crossing continents of Chinese and Arabic lettering, he forged a path towards the back room. He guessed this was the artist's lair and he imagined a tough fucker with no fear of needles.

Colonel Death tattooed on his forearm, and perhaps a

Saint George's flag. Saint George, the Christian crusader who murdered a Middle Eastern dragon with a lance, and then gave the beast a Sign of the Cross.

Saint George's Cross, flag of England, emblem of football supporters.

'Might as well face the music,' Fergus edged towards a curtain.

He noticed the vibration of machines and a person's humming. Following the sound and scents of coffee, he stepped through a curtain. Sure enough he could see a percolator and he could see an artist.

He could see a human canvas too, naked from the waist upwards. Catching a flash of silver in the pink bubble of a woman's nipple, Fergus gritted his teeth, electrified by the shivering of needles. Girl, in her twenties, having her bosom decorated in a fresh blaze of Japanese kanji lettering.

The pathetic habit of nowadays—as Katy described it—adopting images and words without meaning, just for the sake of being the same as everyone else, or trying to wear the uniform of difference.

Transfixed for several seconds the girl's shriek brought Fergus back to his senses and manners. 'What are you pervin' at mister?'

'Sorry,' he backed away, brushing the image out of his mind as the artist continued working on the last curls of oriental calligraphy.

Everybody had their own motivation for getting a tattoo, he supposed. Originating in the Polynesian islands, Captain Cook's sailors had carried stories and images of this ancient practice back into the west.

Once upon a time meaning ran deep. These days you could pick up any one of a thousand standard cliché designs from a high street store, and have it stained in your flesh, easy as getting a burger in McDonald's.

'Be with you in a moment sir,' a more sympathetic voice spoke through the curtain as his eyes shifted again to

Betty Boop's slinky figure balanced precariously close to the devil in a Millwall jersey.

What the hell was he doing in Charlton anyway? But then, everything about this studio had so far defied Fergus's expectations. He'd always imagined a tattoo artist to be like a heavy metal roadie, a WWF wrestler, or a Hells Angels biker—a scary guy with gruff voice and grizzly appearance, overdosed on body markings. But the woman speaking through the curtain was very different to that, from the brief glimpse he'd caught. For a start, her being female had surprised him. The choice of colours too, in her dress. Amber and black, shades of a tiger, same as Hull City whose supporters had arrived in town under a wave of thunder and hailstones.

Through the window, Fergus stalked the day's enemy like a soldier in the safety of a trench, waiting for his turn in the theatre of battle. Gritting his teeth, he remembered the pierced nipple and the artist's careful efforts.

What would Katy make of that, he wondered, if he came home with a piercing instead of a tattoo? Best not to dare experiment, he figured.

'I'm ready for you now,' the tattoo artist's call finally came minutes later, and he swopped places with the kanji girl behind the curtain. 'So, you're the guy who wants the football tattoo?'

'That's me, the Charlton man.'

'Well, I like to give my customers what they want, and unlike a football match, you're always guaranteed a good result in Dy's dark river studio.'

'That's your name,' he supposed, as she clicked on a laptop, and brought a Charlton badge up on screen, humming as she worked.

'Shortened form of Dyana,' she studied the design for several seconds, turning a single sword into a matching pair in her green eyes. '*Dark River Dye* sounds more poetic, maybe more sexy.'

On the word *sexy* she lifted her eyes away from the

screen, and towards his. Those green irises in a face the colour of caramel seemed out of place as she leaned closer, beckoning him towards the high couch.

'So how long's it going to take?'

'Just over an hour,' Dyana rolled up the sleeve of his Charlton jersey, and traced out the musculature of his left bicep with fingernails that tickled. 'Don't worry, we'll have you done and dusted in time for kick off.'

'And stitched up if there's any blood spilled.'

She laughed out a deep rolling lyric. 'There isn't going to be no blood spilled, honey. You're talking to the Vidal Sassoon of tattooing.'

Then she turned around, and assembled the tools of her trade on a shelf, moving them gradually towards a trolley at the side of his station. Out of the corner of his eye, he caught coils and needles, and thimbles full of pigment. He could see his own reflection in her green eyes too, and a gingery face burning extra red from fear.

'There's no need to be so tense,' she ran a cloth down his bicep. 'I've been doing this for seven years, though only had the studio for two. I've never done a club badge, but it's more straightforward than some requests.'

Fergus tried to keep his mind off the cumbersome devices being wheeled slowly, terminally into position. One was electromagnetic, she explained, used for shading, and the other a rotary machine for colouring.

'Do you like football?' he made conversation to pass the time.

'Yeah,' she answered. 'Does that surprise you?'

'No, I run a girls' football team in the College where I work,' Fergus explained. 'I'm used to being around women who love the beautiful game.'

Just unfortunate that his girlfriend hated football, with a passion!

'I support England when they're playing,' Dyana began to attach the introductory needles to her equipment. 'And I like Tottenham, even though most of my friends always followed Chelsea or Arsenal.'

'Arsenal used to be based this side o' the river on Charlton turf.'

She spoke over the buzz of her needles drowning out the constant rain. 'Why do men make football sound so much like gang warfare?'

'Because we're divided into different tribes I suppose.'

Dyana paused the needle a few centimetres from his bicep. 'Gang members come here sometimes to get their colours done. So funny, seeing them scared and weak in a woman's presence. I feel like their mummy.'

'Maybe I'm in need of a mother now too,' he made her laugh.

'Don't worry,' she edged the ink-gun closer to his flesh. 'They say it's not the needle that's the first impression. It's the injection of fear.'

Seconds later he felt such an injection. Like the first time you get into a car, turn a key in the ignition, and your body becomes one with a machine. Momentarily he thought of roads and journeys. Joyride, death ride, a drive down the road that ended his boxing career, and brought him to England.

He'd been young and stupid like those boys in gangs he'd seen out on the streets in the 2011 riots, the first summer he'd arrived in London.

'Easy tiger,' Dyana said as he jolted back, crunching his teeth together.

'You're right,' he admitted, 'about that first injection of fear.'

'That's the buzz, part of what makes people addicted.'

'Addicted is a good word,' he told her. 'Charlton's nickname is *The Addicks*. It comes from the South East London pronunciation of haddock. In the old days after games, the players used to get free fish and chips.'

That's why Lance had the words *'Addicted Forever'* incorporated into the tattoo he got before heading out to Afghanistan. Fergus wasn't so brave as to desire an extra half hour for finely stencilled lettering.

'Won't keep you here as long as a gang member,' Dyana rounded off the silhouette of his circle before moving on to start the sword at the centre. 'I've coloured in just about every part of a man's skin at this stage. There's only one body part I draw a line under, and that's the bit downstairs.'

Fergus crunched his teeth again, imagining Katy's reaction to that.

'I've known customers who've had it, and artists who've done it.'

Again she stopped talking, this time for a couple of minutes, as she placed all her concentration into the completion of the Charlton sword. He could see its outline sketched bare and reflected in her green eyes.

'Yeah, there's a lot of things can go wrong,' Dyana edged towards the sword's short sharp conclusion. 'Nerve damage, scarring, and bodily functions permanently screwed up, both in the bathroom and the bedroom. That's a region of the body I refuse to touch under any circumstances.'

She laughed, suddenly realising what she had said, and how it sounded. Looking away from where she had started to blend her dyes and change the needles, for the purpose of colouring in the tattoo's basic outline, Fergus blushed too, then tried to ease the embarrassment.

'I reckon the way you're scaring me, you're some kind o' secret agent, a Millwall or Palace supporter planted in Charlton's turf!'

Again she laughed, dabbling in thimbles. This was where she moved from stencilling to shading, introducing stronger scents of ink into the equation of coffee and perfume. This was a new machine too, purring softly, instead of buzzing, creating a hush filled by the rain's steely beat, a sleepy soundtrack for the shivery feel of colour flooding his skin's dermal layer.

'Soon finished,' Dyana whispered, as she dipped

between needles, shifting shades of red and black. 'You'll be a proper Charlton man when all this is done, inked in membership like those boys from the gangs.'

Fergus could feel dye sinking into his flesh, as colours filled the badge, and suffused the layers of his skin so deeply it might even darken his bones. The outer circle of deep black converged into a lighter red centre, and then the sharp outline of a sword adopted from London's city crest.

This dagger didn't belong to London though. It was part of a relationship triangle between Fergus, Dyana, and Charlton Athletic. Usually when people pass through your life they leave only a shadow of memory, but this woman was scripting her signature on his skin.

Despite that, their paths might never again cross, such was life in London.

'Almost over,' she whispered, with maternal tenderness.

Breathing in her perfume, he could feel metals solidifying on his flesh. He was becoming a Charlton loyalist. He'd go to his grave with these tribal markings on his skin like a Maori warrior. Whether they buried him in England or Ireland, these were the colours he had chosen as his own. Charlton had become *his* team, even though as a boy growing up in Ireland he could never have imagined steering this course in his lifetime.

But he was one of the London Irish now, and proud of belonging to such a tribe, builders of this city, as the needle buzzed to a gradual halt.

'There, all ready for kick-off,' Dyana's work was complete.

'Thanks,' Fergus surveyed her artistry, and then looked into her eyes. 'Maybe I'm starting to understand why people get addicted.'

'Happy to be your dealer any time,' she held his gaze in a silence of several seconds. Then she turned towards the thunderous weather outside. 'We better pad this up good and proper. There's a shower coming down would piss my work into a puddle in thirty seconds.'

'It's a great day's work. You're a very talented woman.'

She laughed. 'Somebody's got to have talent in Charlton.'

'You sure you're not a secret agent for Palace or Millwall?'

'What kind of agent gives away secrets to strangers?'

'Do you give away many of your secrets?'

Christ, he was flirting now.

'Just predictions on match days.'

'What's your prediction for today then?'

Again she laughed, edging towards the window as he made his exit. 'You're going to get wet, very wet on the walk to The Valley.'

Seconds later, he was back out in the rain, drenched once more just as he had started to dry off. Going down the road towards the stadium, he was sure that he could feel Dyana's green eyes following him.

Haunted by their presence, his forearm tingled. Red dye mingled with his ginger blood. Traces of her needle itched his flesh, as he made his way towards a game where the Jimmy Savile songs had started as he got inside.

'So you got the tattoo?' Lance eyed his bandages.

'Yeah,' he peeled back the padding for a glimpse of Dyana's artistry. 'I'm the same as you, a Charlton man.'

'You can never be the same as me,' his friend teased, as the stadium filled and the spectators shook off the damp like dogs coming out of the sea. 'You'll always be a convert while I'm the real deal.'

'I've as much pride in this badge as any man.'

Sure enough that pride flared seconds later as the players emerged into the afternoon's unceasing rain. The home crowd rose to their feet, applauding their heroes fresh from a midweek victory against Leicester City, one of the favourites for promotion to the Premier League.

The match announcer spoke and the club anthems blared across the PA system. Fergus thought of Dyana again, as he looked down on the figures in amber and black moving through the mists, warming up for battle. Then the game started with a passion, but faded into a slog in abysmal conditions, passing slow as the tattoo drying beneath his bandages.

Finishing without any goals, Hull City set the stall for Charlton's season. Afterwards, he braved a long walk up the road in wind and rain, passing Dyana's studio with its electrics off and shutters down. When he finally got home and announced what he had done, Katy greeted him with silence and then said she loved him less for going against her wishes.

That night in their bed, she turned her back and a slow coldness set in. He feared it was only a matter of time until the relationship finished.

'It's just a tattoo,' he protested, but even he didn't believe his words.

4. Shooting for snakes

*T*he relationship with Katy decayed after getting his tattoo. She despised its red and black dyes with rivalry usually reserved for football. Rangers and Celtic, Liverpool and United, Charlton's unrequited feelings for Palace.

Through the cold winter of 2012, they fought all the time. Then she got an offer to complete a book. A publisher gave her a healthy advance. She could put her career as a fashion designer on hold, and write full time. Seeking peace, she moved to the coastal town of Ramsgate that like the fading Georgian glory of Charlton Church Lane had once seen better days. The golden age of English seaside holidays had long since taken flight.

Lance though had greater fears about something else.

'Crystal Palace,' he grumbled, on a walk to Woolwich.

In the closing weeks of the football season, Charlton supporters had been granted the illusion of a happy ending to their nine month odyssey. Following a bitter winter, results suddenly improved. Dark moods lifted. Steams melted, evaporated, retreated to the river. Skies changed, soft blue, fluffed in cloud. Strikers found a spring in their step. Shots struck the target. Headers drifted goalwards. Crossbars shook. Nets rippled.

Supporters rose from their seats, singing old songs. The tarantula of relegation had been slain for another year. You could imagine the beast impaled on a spear of lightning left over from Hull City's visit back on the first Saturday of the season when everything felt young new and pure. That was an afternoon more suited to fishing than football. A holy day in the middle of the summer holidays, a return for rituals and routines.

The afternoon Fergus Sharkey stamped his colours to the mast. Red, black, and white. Sword rising heavenwards in the very same image as that carried on the breasts of Charlton's tarantula slayers. Gladiators one and all, in South London's finest Colosseum, The Valley in Floyd Road.

But as crowds stood, sang, and mourned the passing of another season, something punctured the moment. Fresh noise, a rumbling in the basement of history. Tectonic plates pushing together, tremors before an earthquake comes, and vultures, bloody eagles, soaring overhead.

There's a badness, a kind of Charles Starkweather in Bruce Springsteen's badlands of *Nebraska* badness. You can hear a song drifting in the wind from a backwater of the Thames, far away in the distance.

The voice isn't Springsteen. There's nothing great and gravelly in this. More of a hiss, a ghost stirring in the rural outpost of Thornton Heath. 'Here's to you the famous red and blue, to CPFC we're always true.'

This is worse than staring down the barrel of Starkweather's Winchester 1906. You're sensing the awakening of a reptile on the far side of London, so far out of the city it's almost in leafy Surrey.

Thamnophis sirtalis infernalis—California Red-Sided gartersnake slithering and hissing out of South Norwood, down through Dulwich and Fulham, on a highway that leads all the fucking way to Wembley.

'How did Palace end up in this season's play off final?' Lance groaned again. 'Facing Watford at Wembley a couple of weeks from now.'

Charlton supporters of the 80s and 90s hated Palace. The affair between the two South London clubs had been a strange one. Back in the late eighties Charlton's owners decided to move away from The Valley. Overnight, Lance's boyhood team became tenants at Selhurst Park, the home ground of a rival football club, Crystal Fucking Palace.

'They screwed us right royally,' Lance grumbled. 'Our players weren't even allowed to change in the home dressing room.'

Horrible trek too, he added. Every week Charlton's supporters faced a Himalayan expedition to cross into cold territory. Finally, Palace put the rent up. Charlton fans left Selhurst with a bitter taste in their throats.

'They didn't even give us the dignity of hating us for a reason,' Lance clarified. 'Just treated us as some secondary caste.'

When Charlton's tenancy ended, their fans found it hard to forgive those who had sinned against them. The one most wronged always does. The other can get on with their lives, pretending nothing ever happened. Like Katy, dividing her time between horses in Huddersfield and reflective walks along Ramsgate's cliffs. Palace moved on, forgetting those who trespassed upon their turf, and casting them out on the shores of history.

'Everything about our time at Selhurst stank,' he continued. 'Even the toilets. We became the definition of second class citizenship.'

That's why it hurt so much to see Palace on the edge of admission to a first-class seat on the Premiership express. Lance named the figure as 120 million fucking pounds as they stopped by traffic lights.

They'd walked this road a hundred times together. Today felt different.

'Katy's found herself a new man,' Fergus confessed.

'Oh,' Lance said. 'Final whistle's blown then.'

'Maybe,' Fergus watched the red light change.

'You've got to let go,' his friend advised.

'Like Charlton fans and Palace?'

'That's different,' Lance argued.

'How's it so bloody different?'

'Romances end. Football's lifelong.'

The couple of miles between Charlton and Woolwich were non-spectacular. Aside from a few streets mapped out in semi-affluence, you're walking through a backwater. Pubs stand grim, boarded up. Parks loiter, locked from view behind brown brick walls. A few corner shops and fast food joints line the streets. Purveyors of goods for the poor, they offer fried chicken, calling cards, cigarettes, superstrength lager.

'If it wasn't for the Artillery Barracks at the top of the hill, you'd need an archaeological dig to find England as it used to be.'

Fergus knew the barracks Lance had spoken of. He passed it often on his circular run through Woolwich Common, out to here, and back again. Other times he ran in the opposite direction, down towards The Valley.

He'd pass *Dark River Dye* on the journey downhill, and remember the rainy afternoon of getting his tattoo of the club badge. Sometimes he'd catch shadows behind curtains, or a blaze of flash art through glass. Betty Boop or something new, the fashions of the age—vampires, warriors, and fifty shades of rough love. Worlds away from the simple insignia of Charlton colours.

Sometimes, passing by, he longed for a glimpse of Dyana decked in Hull City hues or the opposing team of any Saturday afternoon. Leicester City, royal blue and white. Middlesbrough and Forest, red as his own team jerseys. Watford, golden yellow. Derby County, white and black, spelling out echoes of Charlton's past, colours worn in 1947's solitary FA Cup victory.

'What if she appeared in Palace colours?' he wondered, silently.

Red and blue stripes, shades of a Bunsen Burner flame. There'd be something weird about touching a woman in the enemy's uniform.

The thought of it amused him, and quickened the pace of his walk, but Lance limped behind on account of Afghanistan. Out on patrol, daydreaming of Charlton's promotion charge, he'd stepped on a landmine. The blast turned his lower leg to crystals of bone scattered out across a foreign field.

Next thing he'd wakened in hospital, fighting to piece together his body's broken jigsaw. In those first weeks he'd wanted the Taliban to come instead of nurses, and shoot him like a fallen horse on Grand National Day. Wanted to go back in time too. Back to the terraces of The Valley, even back just a couple of minutes before the fuse slithered towards his foot.

Before the click, the hiss, the savage force of an explosion crushing him through a grinder beyond pain, towards numbness.

'If I could have gone back to any point,' he spoke through the splintered haze of memory, 'it would be the 25th of May 1998.'

'About a year before my joyride,' Fergus stoked his own shadows.

'The day we faced Sunderland for a place in the Premier League.'

'Remember listening to the game on the radio while the sun was shining,' the convert admitted. 'It's one of those matches that you never forget because there was something happening every second.'

'Was a great game,' Lance hobbled the borders of past and present. 'I was there at Wembley, wrapped in a red flag, standing loud and proud, on two legs working as perfectly as Mendonca's right boot.'

Clive Mendonca's name crackled out of Fergus's radio in the 23rd minute of the game as he latched onto a pass in the Wembley sunshine.

Swaying around, straightening up, as it dropped, the Charlton striker with an exotic name enacted a dummy. Seeing the keeper tricked, he shifted to the right. Supporters breathed deep. Fires of the imagination burned.

Small boys hoped. Grown men recalled days when they weren't grey. Every figure wearing red in Wembley Stadium took on the name Mendonca. Man, woman, child in the womb. Hearts hammered. Pulses raced. All blood as one. Mendonca shining bronze in the sunlight, the sculpting of an idol.

'I've never known time to go so slow as those seconds.'

For Fergus, listening to the radio, the execution passed in a blink. Mendonca, of West Indian heritage, made Wembley his own, his alone.

Unconcerned by the weight of expectation, unburdened by 77,000 pairs of eyes upon him, the striker ghosted between defenders. Gone, as if he'd never been, taking aim, low from the right towards the left corner.

Giving Charlton the lead, he caused the rising of a red tide.

If it sounded good across the Irish Sea, then it must have been a thousand times better in the flesh. Smothered in a poppy-red mist, north London rang out with the voices of a tribe from the south side of the river.

Somewhere in the mist, Lance remembered a woman screaming that she wanted Clive Mendonca's baby. 'Twins if he scores a second.'

Little did she know then what pains of labour she wished for!

Charlton's entire tribe started dreaming of the Premier League. Champions Arsenal returning to South London, and their manager Arsène Wenger standing on the sidelines of The Valley in his second season. If this victory could be attained, grown men would weep at the fleets of visiting buses lined up along Woolwich Road, emblazoned in the names of football's giants. Manchester United, Liverpool, and Arsenal.

Best of all, Crystal Palace relegated and going in the opposite direction, the snakes of Selhurst sliding into Division Two, as Charlton stood on the verge of rising up the league ladder. Vengeance, sweet vengeance. Blood vengeance, like a sermon from the book of Deuteronomy.

Triumphant stories of returning from the wilderness; reaching the Promised Land and slaying the snakes in your midst.

'To understand our football club, to know what your tattoo actually means Fergus, you have to realise what happened that afternoon,' emotion laced Lance's voice. 'You're not really a family, a club, a circle of friends, a tribe, or a band o' brothers until you go through some great trauma.'

After all of Charlton's suffering, that day defined a generation.

'If I could go back, I'd love to have been there with you too.'

Mendonca had given Charlton a lead they held until half time.

'Time went so slowly,' Lance surmised, 'and the break between the two halves was the longest o' my life, longest time has ever been, aside from the minutes after the landmine blast.'

When he wakened up in the hospital he wanted to be dead. He couldn't bear the thought of disability, of even being like one of those Paralympic athletes. He'd no desire to start all over again, finding his balance, and learning to walk. For days, in a sweaty, sticky, stinking hospital bed, he cursed the doctors and wanted the ground to open up again.

Click, and then explode, and finish him off properly.

'It was Charlton kept me going through those dark, confusing times, and the hope of going home to see days like Mendonca's again in the future.'

His team was 45 minutes from the Premier League, and games against Chelsea, Leeds and Arsenal. 45 minutes from walking up the famous steps at Wembley as winners of something major for the first time since 1947.

Just 1 minute, sixty times one second, multiplied by 45, and that was the difference between going home happy, and leaving the stadium in tears.

But then, six minutes later, along came a lanky striker spearing into the path of a corner kick, powering a low header past two defenders, and goalkeeper Saša Ilić. Niall Quinn, a great horse of a man who always ploughed in crucial goals, especially when he wore the jersey of his country. Suddenly it was a goal apiece. The other half of Wembley had awakened. Sunderland, the favourites, had come back into the game.

'Can I make a terrible confession?' Fergus interjected.

'What?' Lance stepped out of the past and back to the present.

'You have to remember that in those days I supported Liverpool.'

'Bloody convert,' Lance teased. 'Not fit to wear the badge!'

'I know,' Fergus admitted, 'And because Niall Quinn is Irish, me and probably the whole of Ireland supported Sunderland that afternoon.'

'Well your whole country must have been happy as on Saint Paddy's Day for Quinn was playing a blinder,' Lance upped his pace. 'But everything Sunderland threw at us, we came back with more.'

'Yeah, finished four goals each,' Fergus recalled, 'and the poor woman in the crowd was destined to have triplets by that stage.'

With the teams level, penalties ensued. Over in Ireland, Fergus waited and listened as the name of Clive Mendonca again came to the fore, scoring Charlton's first penalty to set the tone for the rest.

Next came steady Steve Brown, a defender, then Keith Jones, Irishman Mark Kinsella, Mark Bowen, John Robinson, and Eddie Newton, for the seventh, with a northern hemisphere rugby score of 7-6 at this stage.

The game's tempo had reached a point beyond addiction for players, supporters, and neutrals alike. They'd long since passed the peak of emotion, and slipped into automatic gear, clutching at cramp, and chugging along, low on petrol as Sunderland's Michael Gray stepped up to shoot.

Niall Quinn had scored their last. Alan Curbishley, Charlton's manager, buried his head in hands, on the bench, barely able to look. Fergus had listened and Lance watched as Michael Gray started to run towards the penalty spot, as worn out as every other man on the stud-beaten turf.

If time goes faster as you get older and the interval had been slow as child's time, those few seconds of the Sunderland player's movement towards the ball passed like days in the mind of a newborn. Or perhaps it was deeper still—time for the child waiting to be born, or time through the lens of a foetus in its early stages, or time going back to the very moments of conception.

Finally, Michael Gray reached the penalty spot's chalky pressure point, as entire legions of Charlton supporters cursed his chances.

The voice of atheists, just minutes before, rose to the heavens.

Deep down every one would feel sorry for the guy if he missed but as he went to strike that ball, they'd have done anything to stop him scoring—water boarding, white noise, even a lighted match to the nipples. But there was no need, because he was dead on his legs.

There always has to be one guy who takes the weight, and falls.

'Score and you're remembered as a kind of Jesus walking on the water,' Fergus thought back to all the guys he'd ever seen in this brutal, telling situation. 'Miss and you'll carry the cross forever.'

25th May 1998 wasn't destined to be the shooter's day.

'He shot straight into the path of Saša Ilić,' Lance fisted the air.

The goalkeeper scooped up the ball, then got lost in a scrum of players. Cue for the party to start on the terraces, every man from Curbishley to *Clive* in the womb, and women too for this was a family club.

'We stayed in Wembley for hours afterwards in the evening sunshine, and then on the Tuesday night in the rain, we all joined the victory parade.'

'Was that from Wembley too?'

'No, we had our party not far from here, just past the barracks and the parade ground. When we get there I'll show you the spot.'

'Okay,' said Fergus. 'It might take my mind off what's gnawing at me. He's a foreign guy, she says.'

'Who? Mendonca? He was born in Sunderland.'

'No, the guy that Katy's taken up with.'

'Forget Katy. Let's talk football.'

5. Empire's Cigarette End

*C*rystal Palace. The name reverberated off Woolwich's brown brick walls, evoking images of decay. Hated word, hated place for Charlton's fan base, especially those of long standing. Snakes sucking blood from the corpse of a club that young Lance loved.

Palace had conspired in the dark days of Charlton being held back from a return to The Valley, profiting on misfortune and mismanagement. Gates closed, the ground stood smothered in weeds and brambles. Rats rose out of the Thames and took up residence in the long grass.

'Cats got fat on the feast,' Fergus supposed, 'in a way that's different from fat cats in football nowadays.'

Lance wasn't listening, pushing on with the wheels of his story. Gypsies carted their horses down from Abbey Wood, and allowed the ragged beasts to graze unattended. 'Like you'd see in South Bermondsey, or Albania.'

Nobody noticed the cats and horses from a distance. Up in the ivory towers of local politics, they drew the blinds on the stadium by the riverside. Nobody cared except supporters, readying for a fight against authority.

'We battled for to win back The Valley from ruin.'

Meanwhile the snakes over in Selhurst kept sucking blood.

Lance, as a boy, had feared the slow death of his football club. Though they'd roots on the Isle of Dogs, members of his family, three generations, had followed Charlton since before the Second World War. Like most citizens of London, Lance came from immigrant stock.

'We owned a greyhound track over on the Isle of Dogs.'

Fergus knew the place well. He'd often gone across the river with Katy to Canary Wharf's sparkling boutiques and bars. But it hadn't always been a place of style and skyscrapers. The River Thames bounded this former marshland on three sides in the shape of a horseshoe and gave it the feel of an island, running from the old Docklands to the Limehouse Basin.

'The whole story of London's told in those few miles,' Lance insisted. 'You've got agriculture, you've got urbanisation, you've got shipping, you've got the rise of the unions, you've got international trade, you've got wealth, you've got poverty, you've decline, and you've regeneration.' He paused then, staring straight ahead like he was using the skyscrapers as a prism. 'But underneath it all you got crime, bad crime, beautiful crime, and the legends that give this place its edge and make it so different to Greenwich.'

Lance stood melancholic on the borders of two worlds that no longer existed. Woolwich's military grandeur had been reduced to one barracks, like the last man standing guard over the cigarette butt of the British Empire. The old Isle of Dogs had long since been buried under steel and glass.

'My family came from there,' Lance historicized.

'Shouldn't you be a Millwall or West Ham man?'

'They moved over the river at the start of the century,' he clarified. 'Lived on this side, but kept their business interests on the other.'

That business existed in a time long ago though. Echoes of the greyhound track and his family's glory days survived only in stories buried under far more than tonnes of concrete on the former docks.

'Football was at the heart of it, you know.'

Fergus felt a spark of curiosity. 'How so?'

'In that era of the Krays and Richardsons, you'd football's first gangs,' he moved away from the Charlton and Palace divide, out towards the sharper edges of a rivalry along the Thames, Millwall and West Ham. 'My family was somewhere in the middle, on the edges, without any of the Krays' celebrity, or the Richardsons' hard as nails proper gang warfare.'

Lance had been brought up on legends, tales of gunfights and pliers, codes of secrecy, and a silence about who shot who, and where the bodies had been buried without the grace of last rites.

'You'd some psychopathic bastards you wouldn't trust to offer you a cigarette, and others no more dangerous than Del Boy Trotter.'

'Suppose football offered an escape from that lifestyle?'

Like Barcelona in the days of Franco when the terraces of the Nou Camp provided a space for the Catalans to speak their language.

'Yeah the social part's just as important as the winning,' Lance agreed. 'Especially if you're a Charlton supporter.'

Down through the decades, nights at the races intersected with cold afternoons at The Valley in Lance's family lineage. He'd heard legends of other places too. Highbury, The Old Den, the pleasure of promotion at West Ham's Upton Park, and a foggy day at Stamford Bridge where the players left the pitch and keeper Sam Bartram stayed there unawares.

Charlton fighting for the league championship under

the management of Jimmy Seed. London's top team, with only Arsenal anywhere close. Palace, Millwall, and West Ham lay dormant in the lower divisions.

'In 1939 we came third behind Everton and Wolves,' Lance sighed, 'while Palace played Torquay United and Clapton Orient.'

'You told me before if it hadn't been for the Second World War, Charlton might have been England's top team in the early forties.'

'Yeah, but at least that great team built by Jimmy Seed came back again after the war to win the 1947 FA Cup final.'

Though things weren't so great in the years that followed, his family had stayed true to Charlton, as the fifties and sixties brought little pleasure aside from seeing both Palace and Millwall drop into Division Four.

'Times weren't good, but we knew the team was our own.'

'What does that mean?' Fergus grew curious.

'Same as across the water at the greyhound track,' he explained. 'People back then survived, thrived by their sense of community. Once you take that community, that trust away, there's nothing left.'

Charlton had its own myths and legends in London's gangster era.

'Forget Ronnie and Reggie Kray,' Lance laughed. 'Or Charlie and Eddie Richardson, even Mad Frankie Fraser and Jack 'The Hat' McVitie.'

The best stories of London's fifties and sixties took place further down the river, away from the Richardson family's scrap yards and the Kray's protection rackets, with the biggest scrapyard of all far out on the horizon, in the wilderness of South Norwood. Selhurst hadn't yet cast its shadow on the history of Charlton. His family escaped the pressure of the greyhound track every Saturday, to watch their team in action. The team that was in their blood, and had been for decades, ever since they crossed the river and found a place they could adopt as their own and consider *home.*

Lance's father and grandfather had watched the likes of John Hewie, South African born Scotsman who'd played in nine different positions, and Johnny Summers scoring five goals against Huddersfield, Christmas 1957.

Then in the 60s Keith Peacock, first substitute used in the English Football League. Before that if you got injured, your team went down to as many lumps as the opposition kicked out of you.

Derek Hales, gruff and grizzly, got kicked aplenty, but was able to give as good as he got, lighting up the seventies with his scraps and scrapes.

But come the eighties, attention shifted away from the pitch.

'Tough times for the greyhound track too,' Lance narrated the circumstances of a country trapped in recession, strikes, and conflict across the water. 'Everything was changing. Felt like we were losing the land, even country around us. And then the same happened to Charlton.'

The club, on the edge of administration, took flight to Selhurst.

'That's where the hatred comes from,' Lance freely admitted. 'We'd no reason to even care about the existence of Palace before that. Then one afternoon, at the start of the new season, we got leaflets telling us that we'd have to play our home games for the rest of the year, out in a hostile territory that was hard to reach, on somebody else's turf.'

'As bad as getting dumped by text message,' Fergus reckoned, as had happened to him with news of Katy's new man a few weeks before.

'No way,' Lance argued immediately. 'You're not tied to one woman, but your club's your family. I know you shifted teams, but that's different because you weren't born here. It was never in your blood.'

45

'Suppose not, but I was passionate about Liverpool.'

As a boy he'd chosen one of only two choices that most Irish kids of his generation had been aware of. Others could have Manchester United.

He preferred Liverpool because they were the first team he'd read of. He'd watched their games on black & white TV, dreaming of growing up to see his heroes in the flesh. Slept in pyjamas with their crest upon his breast, and followed their adventures across Europe and back to England.

Magical nights, sitting up late, catching highlights, as in that mercurial evening for Charlton supporters too when John Barnes, alongside Peter Beardsley, cut Crystal Palace to pieces in a nine-goal defeat.

But, in the end, he turned his back on Liverpool.

It hadn't been so easy for Charlton fans to do the same.

'Palace treated us no better than migrants,' Lance grumbled as they walked. 'Like those camped out on the coast of France in Calais, or even worse, the bastards who brought them into that mess in the first place.'

'Come on, couldn't have been that bad.'

Migrants, blockaded in the port of Calais, had been in the news for months. Every day, they fought running battles to break through the frontline.

'Rodeo on the roadsides,' the papers proclaimed, alongside pictures of brown guys, skinny as bullocks, fighting to mount long-distance trucks.

Newspaper headlines whetted hysteria. They shared tales from a place they christened *The Jungle*, a makeshift camp for migrants, huddled together like hungry bluebottles on the bloodied brow of Europe.

'Poor bastards out there through the cold winter,' Fergus said. 'They're no different to the rest of us, looking for a decent life.'

But there was nothing decent about *The Jungle's* rumbling discontent. Barricaded into cardboard slums, these poor bastards had nothing left but hope of escape from the refuse, indignity, and gangs policing them.

'Filthy as Victorian London,' the papers sermonised.

Without money and documentation, stateless people struggled in conditions basic as past centuries—unwanted by the continent they'd invaded. Katy supported them, signing petitions and the like. She felt sorry for the mothers and children, she said, fleeing the world's energy wars, dictatorships, and the legacy of international borders scribbled in haste—by men.

'What would *we* do,' she had often posed the question on nights with Fergus, watching news stories from the safe distance of a TV screen, 'if we'd been history's losers begging them for a place in their lands?'

'As the Irish have done for centuries,' he'd tell her.

Thousands of Fergus's people had crossed the seas for a fresh start in other places, just as he had done. That gave him some sympathy with people less well off, fighting for a future. Lance though didn't share his sense of sympathy. When the subject of migrants arose in conversation, the former soldier's opinions hardened. Like he was acting out a part in a western, a Clint Eastwood character chasing bandits across the Mexican border.

'We can't open our doors to all of them,' he insisted. 'Every leak starts with a trickle, and grows to a flood if it's ignored. And considering where they come from, who knows what they're carrying in their suitcases?'

'I doubt they have suitcases,' Fergus reckoned.

'I didn't mean it literally,' Lance protested. 'I'm talking about values, and beliefs, practices out of place in this country, this century even.'

'You can't believe everything you read in the papers.'

'I'm not talking about what I've read in the papers.'

'What are you talking about then?'

'Stuff I've seen with my own eyes.'

Fergus's thoughts shifted from migrants to soldiers. He imagined the anger and frustration of young men hunkered inside a bunker, far from home, holding machine guns, dreaming of girls, and football. Outside, the sound of Afghan men playing buzkashi, a kind of polo with the body of a dead goat, and the blaze of grass deep enough to hide a thousand IEDs.

Finally Fergus picked up the courage to seek answers to his friend's hostility, as they came towards the army barracks at the top of the hill.

'Do you hate migrants because of what you saw in the war?'

'I don't hate them,' he snapped. 'Just don't want them here.'

'Okay then, is that because of your time in the war?'

He shook his head. 'No, this goes further back than that.'

'Back to what, to where?'

'To the closure of my family's greyhound track,' Lance explained. 'Because of fucking immigrants, Vivaldi, and one of the henchmen in the family business.'

'Was Vivaldi one of the gangsters who worked at the track?'

'No, I'm talking about the music composer guy.'

'What's he got to do with the Isle of Dogs?'

Though he hadn't anything like Katy's knowledge of music and culture, Fergus couldn't imagine Vivaldi ever having been on the island. So far as he knew the guy died a couple of hundred years ago. Yet Lance talked about him as if he too had been a regular at the greyhound track, and nights at those races populated by gangsters, watching dogs break out of the traps and run for gold beneath the floodlights.

'He's the one brought down the whole fucking show.'

'I'm confused,' Fergus admitted. 'I thought you said there was never much over there until the Industrial Revolution.'

'Sit down on the wall and I'll tell you the whole story.'

'Okay,' he agreed since he wasn't in a hurry.

He might learn some new fact about music that he could pass on to Katy, since she'd grown very fond of composers and migrants in recent times. The name of her new man after all was Wagner, if he was telling the truth, for so much of his life seemed cast in mystery and suspicion.

But thoughts on that could come later, as Lance prepared to shift the story away from Selhurst and Afghanistan, two places that he hated more than anywhere else in the world. It was time to take a trip to the races on an island that once belonged to him and his people.

6. The Family Trade

Taking a seat on a wall outside the Royal Artillery Barracks, Fergus turned his attention upon Canary Wharf and the Isle of Dogs arrayed in architectural dissonance in the distance. That was the land, the island on the Thames, once populated by Lance's Irish ancestors. Lost homeland perhaps. Lance had more in common with migrants than he admitted.

'My people came to London in the middle 1800s, the same year as the greyhound Master McGrath's first victory on English soil. They found work in the new docks being built, and made their home over there.'

'These were the days before the dog track,' Fergus assumed.

'Sport wasn't for the working classes in those days,' Lance nodded. 'If you wanted to gamble, you went down to the old Chinatown.'

'They had a Chinatown on the Isle of Dogs?'

'London's first,' Lance elaborated. 'Created by Chinese

sailors who shipped goods in and out of Limehouse, and settled there.'

Mapping out a path across the skyline once more, he said that it was a very different place from today's Chinatown. The island's Chinatown played host to the city's opium dens and illegal gambling halls.

'Money laundering too. When you talked about going to a Chinese laundrette in the old days, you weren't going there with a bag o' washing, but you knew if you didn't go back on time, you'd end up in the wash.'

'So how did your family get into the business then?' Fergus was growing curious to know how immigrants from the 19th century could break into the Chinese monopoly of crime on the island.

'My great-great grandfather found work on the docks in the 1870s,' Lance embarked on the road of answers. 'He started out labouring for a timber merchant on Millwall dock, where Canary Wharf now stands.'

'Christ!' Fergus seized the opportunity for revenge. 'I'm growing more certain by the minute that you've got traces o' blue in your blood.'

'Must have been hard work in hard times,' Lance ignored the remark. 'Back then the island was poor, with little in the way of entertainment.'

His great great grandfather had established a boxing club and ran competitions between the men from different companies along the docks.

'Legend has it that in the middle of the eighteen seventies, my ancestors arranged the first ever fight between Millwall and West Ham.'

'But organised football wasn't running back then!'

'Boxing,' Lance named the sport that had once been Fergus's first. 'Morton's Jam Factory on Millwall Dock was the place that spawned a team of the same name, while West Ham came from the Thames Ironworks Company. About ten years before they ever kicked a ball, men from these two companies used to fight each other in my family's gym.'

'Hope it was cleaner than their modern scraps.'

'They didn't hate each other in those days,' Lance explained. 'Wasn't until the dockworkers' strike of the 1920s that the animosity began.'

'So are these the men you have to thank for the origins of the family business?' Fergus probed further.

'No, Jack the Ripper's the man we have to thank.'

'Jesus Christ almighty! Your family knew Jack the Ripper?'

'Nobody knew Jack the Ripper,' Lance corrected him.

'So what's he got to do with your story then?'

'The East End in the 1880s was a dangerous and crowded place, full of prostitutes and new migrants to London,' he explained. 'Over a thousand hookers worked the Whitechapel Road.'

'But what's that got to do with the boxing club?'

'A dozen women got killed in the late 1880s,' Lance elaborated, 'and that's the ones they know about.' He pointed across towards the Thames. 'There's probably many more in the biggest graveyard this old city's got.'

Lance paused, pointing out towards Whitechapel's modern incarnation squeezed between cranes and skyscrapers on the horizon with Liverpool Street rising up behind it in a series of commercial glass mountains.

'Was a dangerous, crazy place where the rule o' law got lost. They had so many people with such different customs and languages that nobody knew what the fuck was going on, least of all the police.'

Again he paused, to drink in a river of dark and secret worlds.

'The Irish were there, Jews too, and Russians,' he started up again. 'They got scared by all that was happening on the streets around them. They wanted and needed protection, somebody who could watch over their girls, and not help themselves to the goods along the way.'

'So they enlisted the help of your family's boxing club?'

'Yeah, thanks to Jack the Ripper and his victims, my family's protection business started, and grew from there. We got a reputation for being tough, especially for the way we dealt with anyone who messed around our clients.'

Association Football had started by then. Largely it remained a toff's game, but Morton's had given birth to Millwall Rovers in 1885, and Woolwich's gun factories to Dial Square who evolved into Arsenal F.C. Another team would blast from the furnaces in a claret and blue haze a decade later to become West Ham United.

Despite this new game, boxing remained the preferred sport of boys from the island, as the club stayed open in synch with the protection business. Come the early 1900s both club and business thrived.

'Then a new misfortune caused fresh opportunities,' Lance continued. 'This time it wasn't Jack the Ripper, and wasn't even protection.'

'I'm guessing you're talking about the First World War.'

'Yeah, and my family focused their efforts on the workers in the munitions factories,' Lance provided answers. 'We moved the business south o' the river to Woolwich for a time, and we fed the war effort on all the illegal booze and cigarettes needed on the home front.'

'I bet they didn't give your family medals for that though.'

'Several fought and died in the war,' Lance corrected him, 'and some came back as cripples, just like me. Course the technology wasn't so good then that they could rebuild a man's leg from scratch.'

'Sorry, I didn't know you'd family fought in the war.'

'They didn't make a big deal of it. It was supposed to be the war to end all wars, but it ended up as the one nobody's ever forgotten.'

'Certainly wasn't a war to end all wars either,' Fergus glanced down at his friend's permanent tattoo of battles in Afghanistan.

'At least it gave my family another opportunity,' Lance's

eyes misted over once again like the tea-bag fogs of Victorian London.

'I'm supposing it was men coming back from the war.'

Young men made old. Recruited half a decade before in the villages and football stadiums of England. Games, fucking games. Recruitment campaigns. Players and supporters piled into the trenches of the Somme. Heart of Midlothian seven men dead. Bradford City, nine dead. One named Harry Potter, spellbound in the lyric of *Dulce et decorum est pro patria mori*.

'They needed entertainment so we provided it.'

'And that was the birth of the greyhound track?'

'Yeah,' Lance answered. 'Times were tough and this was nothing fancy, no Master McGrath or the Waterloo Cup. Just a place for men to drink and gamble, and forget their hardship for a night.'

By then his family had moved across the river to Charlton, using the Thames as a line of demarcation between work and play. Times were good between the wars, Lance explained. Business boomed upon the island. His grandfather, as a young man, watched Charlton Athletic booming too, soaring to the heights of English football as the 1930s fizzled out.

'Then came the Second World War,' Lance groaned, in the pain of a small man looking up at the vast tapestry of history. 'If it hadn't been for Hitler, we'd have been bloody champions of the league.'

'A second dark figure in your family history.'

But where Jack the Ripper had given birth to opportunity for Irish immigrants with a boxing club, Adolf Hitler burned their hopes to the ground.

'Times were tough then. Ordinary people suffered, as the docks burned and the Thames blazed.' His voice angered in the heat of recollections carried down through family history. 'At night in the early forties the whole island was lit up like a horseshoe on fire. They sent the kids off to the country, and adults down into air raid shelters. Then one night half the track went up in flames. Twenty years o' work wiped out.'

'Half of London must have been rubble by the end.'

'Half of fucking Europe,' his friend reminded him, as a new flood of immigrants arrived on England's shores in the wake of war. 'Everything changed after 1945. The Chinese cleared out of Limehouse into the secrecy of Soho. New gangs appeared, new ways of making a dishonest living.'

Out of scrap metal and the streets of Camberwell, the Richardson gang emerged in the decades after the war. When the smoke of the Blitz cleared, the Irish came with picks and shovels to put the shattered city back together. In the midst of this Lance's people rebuilt the greyhound track.

'Bigger and better than what Hitler's pilots destroyed.'

They even gave the track a new name and marketed it as a historic venue, drawing crowds to the Isle of Dogs at a time when it was a wilderness, wasted and wounded by war, tossed back a couple of hundred years.

'*King Edward Greyhound Track,*' he spoke the name with pride. 'Because the island's been associated with dogs going back to the days of King Edward. Even Henry the Eighth kept his hunting dogs there.'

By the late sixties, the dog track was full five nights a week, quiet on Fridays as the customers took their winnings to town, or stayed in on account of their losses. And when you have gambling, there's room for money lending too, and they got into that game along the way as well. At that point though London's crime scene had turned hardcore. The Krays and Richardsons had begun a running feud that others navigated like a set of landmines.

'To survive against the other gangsters, my family had to bring in henchmen from the toughest parts of Glasgow and Belfast because we knew they'd no secret loyalties to anybody else,' Lance continued. 'In the days before your place went up in flames, these guys were hungry for action, just itching to get across the water for a fight.'

These were the people on the fringes of the track, men who offered protection and kept the police distracted. Just as you don't build a mansion without labourers, you don't run a Mafia without henchmen.

'Strange word,' Fergus thought. '*Henchman.*'

From Middle English, a combination of horse and man. Originally a term for a groom or a servant in the royal household, over time it changed usage and became a derogatory word for a lackey.

The henchmen in the gangster world, according to Lance, were the guys who got their hands dirty, the shadowy figures who pulled teeth out with pliers in the bath as the bosses watched. These were men of mythology, Centaurs doing the work of a ploughhorse and a jackal at the same time.

They were part of an island conspiracy too, where everybody exaggerated tales of their own turf, so as to mythologize these men as cast-iron bastards that other gangsters never wanted to cross.

'When somebody needed bumped off or treated to a beating,' Lance said, 'you left all the blood on the hands of the henchmen. Remember the police were always trying to put away the top men, especially after the war. They'd have found a way to send you down, just for giving somebody a nosebleed so the henchmen's job was to keep the heat off.'

'I'm guessing you're getting ever closer to Vivaldi.'

'Yes, as we reach the eighties and nineties.'

By then times had started to change upon the island. Even before the diggers and dozers arrived to build Canary Wharf in the late eighties, the scent of coming transformation had spiked the dog track.

'Nights at the races brought the first signs.'

It wasn't just the dust carrying in off the development site, and the spine of skyscrapers starting to rise above Millwall Dock. This change was subtle, starting with a repopulation of the old streets and estates. People from all corners of the Empire, especially Bangladesh and Pakistan, had started to make their way into the island's post-war tower blocks.

Crowds thinned and changed at the track. Champion dogs with exotic names gave way to the second hand racers playing out lower league battles. The old crew fled down the river, heading for Kent and Essex.

These were men who'd spent a lifetime earning reputations. They didn't want to get old in a place where nobody observed the traditional customs anymore. Not just the newcomers but their own kids too.

'They wanted it all without the work. They didn't know what it took, and how long, to build up a life and a business that gives you the flash cars, the honour, the right to call in favours, and expect nobody to take liberties.'

Everybody in the decades after war accepted that life could be hard. But by the eighties, expectations were changing.

'The island had been awash with drugs since the days of Chinamen and their opium dens,' he paused, sipped, and went into overdrive again. 'And if the swinging sixties had a patron saint then his name was Charlie.'

'Cocaine,' Fergus presumed, and Lance nodded.

'But the new drugs coming in during the eighties were the product of a different world, more races, fewer borders, and a greater hunger to get high. Everybody was fucked out of their faces, and getting very greedy.'

A new breed of gangster had emerged, a whole century after Jack the Ripper's mutilated corpses in the Thames gave birth to a protection business. Suave white boys and swaggering brown boys made more money in a month than a year of races down at the dog track.

'We tried to recruit this new generation at the start, and train them our way,' Lance started out on the closing chapter of family secrets. 'But it was hopeless. They'd already mapped out their own directions.'

The dog track was on the verge of going bust by the

time Canary Wharf's first completed tower rose above the bones of Millwall Dock.

'They'd have colonised the whole fucking island if they could,' Lance said. 'Moved out the natives, and built a British Manhattan. They gave everything shiny new names, plastered on leaflets pushed through your door asking you to sell your home, so it could be turned into flats.'

'So I guess the gangster days just died out?'

'They would have come to a natural end,' Lance's eyes dipped. 'Business was bad, gone to the dogs I suppose you could say. My father had already left that life behind, earning an honest living in a bookmaker's shop in Woolwich, and following Charlton. But my uncle was still involved and interested in selling up, to move into the car business.'

'So you wouldn't have been heir to the Empire then?'

'Nah,' Lance admitted. 'That would have been my cousin Timmy.'

'So why didn't he take over the business when it was struggling?'

'He was young then and too much of a hothead,' Lance admitted. 'He'd hair the colour o' yours, a red man even though he was West Ham.'

'And what about your uncles?'

'They were doing most of the work down at the track,' Lance said, 'but it was my grandfather's name on the deeds to the King Edward. He was like the Queen, wanting to hang around forever and give work to the henchmen. But then Vivaldi came along and fucked the whole show.'

There was nothing glorious about the way that henchmen lived. Images from TV and magazines proferred celebrity upon the Krays, but very few gangsters ever made any money to retire on. Spending time in and out of prison, they'd a poor existence for all their exertions.

'One of our henchmen lived in a tower block swamped with new tenants from across the world. Same as what's happening now in Greenwich and Woolwich, the rich were taking over the riverside, and the poor being pushed further back, out into the margins.' Lance paused then to clear his throat, growing emotional at the storytelling. 'This guy had been around so long we actually didn't know him by any nickname other than *The Henchman*. His wife had died young from cancer, just a couple of years before, and he tore into the drink with a vengeance.'

'I've been doing that myself since Katy left.'

The Henchman would get drunk every night, battling to keep bare scalps and mastectomies out of his dreams. Seeing your wife dying again, every night in your sleep, must do terrible things to a man's mind.

'Lack of sleep and noise harassment does the same,' Lance supposed. 'About a year after his wife died, a Pakistani woman moved into the flat next door, a young bird who started out as an escort, and then gradually worked her way downwards into the world of prostitution.'

'Like the women up around Plumstead Common,' Fergus supposed.

'In the beginning she'd been a looker,' Lance said. 'She'd go out in short dresses, high heels, and a blonde wig, like a brown Marilyn Monroe.'

'Maybe the old henchman should have knocked on her door.'

'The days of the Brown Marilyn didn't last long,' Lance sent Fergus swirling back to echoes of his own former lover.

He tried to forget Katy. 'What's Vivaldi got to do with them?'

'Noise,' Lance whispered into the city's incessant rattle and hum. 'The tower block had been badly designed, and the walls paper thin.'

During The Henchman's trial, a year or so down the blocks, all the lurid details would come pouring out into Woolwich Crown Court.

'What lurid details?' Fergus leaned.

'As he was lying in bed at night, trying to sleep, and fighting to forget his wife's dying flesh, he could hear the hooker's clients through the walls.'

Away from the sparkling towers of Canary Wharf, nobody hired American and Argentine architects for social housing off the main drag.

'The music was driving him crazy,' Lance carried on.

'And she was playing Vivaldi, I'm guessing?'

Lance nodded. Antonio Vivaldi's music had haunted, taunted and terrorised the furious Henchman through many months of sleepless nights.

'He used to tell the boys down in the pub that some night he'd go in there and give that cunt *the proper Vivaldi* if she didn't shut up.'

'So why didn't anybody try to help the poor guy?'

'Everybody thought it was just talk,' Lance admitted. 'On the island, *Vivaldi* became a codeword for rough sex, wild sex, any sex.'

But by the time the Brown Marilyn's stereo reached full blast and the Henchman cracked, the joke exited the stage of the island's colloquialisms. Nobody would ever dare speak lightly of the composer again.

Nobody would ever ask that famous question with a nudge and a wink. 'Did you get the full Vivaldi Saturday night?'

The name of Vivaldi grew tainted, like that of Richard Wagner after the Nazis adopted his music and his political leanings as their own.

'One night, he finally cracked. The Brown Marilyn was playing Vivaldi loudly as she was getting dolled up to go out on a Saturday night.'

Lance stood up suddenly, animated by his memories.

'He went around there full of rage, banging on her door.'

Fergus felt his own heart hammering too.

'She answered, back again in the blonde wig and red dress, but out of her head on smack, a long way from being anybody's movie star. He asked her to turn the music down and she laughed at him.'

He pushed her up against the wall. She went to defend herself with keys she grabbed from her pocket. He crushed the keys in her fist, and then the fist in her breast, as he pushed her out of the doorway back into the flat.

'She'd sold off almost everything by this stage to feed her habit.'

He pushed her down on the settee, the only solid form left in the room. She fought back, hissing and yelling for help in her own tongue.

'Nobody came though, as they'd heard it all before.'

Rough sex they probably guessed, or a nasty client.

Disowned by her own people, they left her shrinking under the weight of a man twice her size, unveiling the full savagery of his anger.

Nobody had ever taken the drunken veteran seriously in his words. '*I'd do hard time and gonorrhoea for teaching that bad whore a lesson.*'

By the end he'd beaten her senseless from a rage that had been building up through all those sessions of late-night Vivaldi, pumping a dark music into her naked body before throwing down a score of change, as if to compensate, maybe even thank her for his release.

'Any man who strikes a woman's a coward.'

'Yeah,' Lance agreed. 'But he did a lot more than strike her. Very soon the news got out to the community that had shunned her before. Suddenly she was one of their own, brutally attacked by the other side.'

'So I'm supposing the Henchman got arrested?'

'No,' Lance shook his blonde locks. 'These new kids on the block had the same ideas about justice as the men from the boxing club in the times of Jack the Ripper.' Lance's voice saddened. 'A couple of days later an Asian gang came to the track with about seven cars of six guys each, armed in cricket bats and wheel braces, looking blood for blood.'

By then the Henchman had cleared out, off to the other end of the city.

'So they came back in the dead of night,' Lance's voice grew sadder, without any sense of surprise. 'It was Christmas Eve and the place was all locked up, and the family over in Charlton for Midnight Mass.'

'So what happened? Anybody get hurt at the track?'

'There was nothing of King Edward left by the time they'd finished,' Lance sighed. 'What Hitler hadn't managed, they achieved. His bombs left a shell that we could resurrect. The Asian fire left nothing. We heard the news when we came out of Mass. My cousin Timmy rushed across and found a pile of ashes, not even anything left of the decorations. Family business and all that history gone in one night like it never existed.'

Fergus could sense his friend's pain at the memory of that fire.

'Maybe that's why I don't like migrants. It's just too personal.'

'Come on they're not all bad,' Fergus tried to lighten the mood. 'You've met the girls on my football team. They're mostly second generation.'

'Yeah, I suppose,' Lance's mood changed as his mind shifted direction. 'Victoria's got as much talent as some of the Charlton men.'

'She's good enough to play for England one day.'

'And will you support her when she's wearing the Three Lions?'

'Of course. I'll tell the whole of Ireland that I discovered her.'

'Yeah, but you don't support our men's team when they're playing,' Lance growled, then laughed. 'Typical fucking foreigner.'

7. Children of a changing world

Less than a week before, on the morning after the Championship's play off semi final between Palace and Brighton, Fergus had taken his school team, as South London's U-19 champions, to a tournament at Manchester City's stadium. His mind should have been on that, but a certain image constipated his thoughts.

'Shit,' the word blazed in his skull.

Before the game somebody used the away dressing room as a toilet. Finding faeces smeared over their changing space, the angry Eagles defeated the Seagulls by two goals to none. Only the Hornets from Hertfordshire now stood in the way of Palace's grand 120 million pound sting. The snakes of Selhurst stood on the verge of rising up the ladder to the Premier League, and the grand payday that comes with TV visits to the finest grounds in England. That for every Charlton fan including Fergus had been cause to get drunk, and he'd suffered next morning.

On the train ride north, his head felt heavy as a pig's

bladder ball from bygone days—maybe the sort they used in 1914's Christmas truce. On that afternoon, against orders, two sets of working class guys stopped shooting each other across rat-infested trenches on the borders of France and Belgium. As the guns fell silent Tommy and Fritz climbed over the razor wire, swopped cigarettes, chocolate, songs, and stories of home.

Then they played football deep into the dark on the frayed map of *No Man's Land*, before migrating back to their opposing trenches. But there'd been no migration for Charlton fans onto the Palace side, as he drank with Lance in a pub by the riverside. Everybody to a man cheered on Brighton & Hove Albion in their blue and white stripes.

'Never again,' Fergus repeated the drinker's mantra.

Passing through Bletchley, the hangover was a code he couldn't break. Reaching Staffordshire and seeing the Britannia Stadium rising up above smoky potteries, the furnaces stoked his guts. A game of Victorian Subbuteo was taking shape inside his head—rough, ragged, and lawless.

'Drinking's got an awful lot in common with football,' he thought. 'Every bad game's going to be your last, but y'always go back for more.'

'Are y'alright sir?' his team spoke in chorus.

He'd strain his neck to nod, trying to disguise his suffering, but it was hard to block out the thump of Subbuteo, and the news lying beneath.

Dipping his head to the paper, Fergus read more on the play offs. 'Palace Number 1 in town, on a night of Number 2s.'

Seeing the headlines and match report, Fergus felt a thorn cut through an otherwise decent ending to the season. Wilfried Zaha, twenty years old, had struck two goals to push Palace to the Premier League's frontier.

This wasn't how 2012/13 was supposed to end; a season that had started off with the realisation of a promise from a few months before. He could never have imagined where that walk down the road in the midst of a storm would lead in the months that followed. He'd expected Katy to get over the tattoo sooner or later, and accept it as a fact of life.

'Something was lost and we couldn't get it back,' he mused.

An emotional thorn had slipped through the stitching and punctured the pig's bladder, as he thought again of Victorian Subbuteo. Outside, fields of elms and beeches slowly gave way to the dark stone façade of Stockport.

Soon the train was out of there too, and heading towards Manchester. Brief flashes of red brick terraces brought Coronation Street to mind, and then changed again to traces of industry as they reached their destination.

He gathered up his team of teenage girls, and led them out of the station. 'Welcome ladies to the heart of football.'

'No way,' protests began automatically. 'London's the heart o' football. Who's got Wembley? Who's got the most clubs?'

'Maybe he has a point,' interjected Victoria, his team captain, star striker, and at eighteen, the most mature of the teenagers making their way out of Piccadilly Station. 'Manchester United are champions, and Wigan beat Man City in last Saturday's Cup final. Wigan's north, ain't they?'

'Yeah, Wigan's north,' Fergus agreed, 'but I'm thinking more of the game's origins. 'If it wasn't for working class folk up here, football might still be a game for Nobby Clarkes instead of Nobby Stiles.'

'Were those guys Charlton players?'

'No, but Nobby Stiles played with the Charltons.'

'Huh?' That confused them even more.

'Defensive midfielder for England and Manchester United in the 1960s,' Fergus explained, as he glanced up at the blackened lettering and faded relief panels of a fire station on the London Road, remembering the smudged pages of 1980s football magazines. 'That was before any of today's endless TV coverage and millions of pounds attached to the game.'

The old days of English football were much like this fire station, fashioned out of dark and harsh northern clay, different to the sparkling towers that greeted visitors on arrival in the country's capital.

He wanted to tell them that there was life in Manchester before Wayne Rooney. Still, he supposed, those old days seemed ancient for girls born at the turn of the century. They probably cared little about football's past.

'Sometimes I reckon,' he tried to raise a laugh, 'you ladies think the world was black and white before colour TV came along.'

'Wasn't it?' asked Victoria, and he stopped dead in his tracks in the doorway of a pub—until the others laughed and he realised she was joking. 'But hey, we know there's football north of Arsenal.' Her sloe-black eyes sparkled bright with a proposition. 'Bet we can name ten teams.'

'Go ahead,' Fergus coaxed his girls into action.

Suddenly Manchester's London Road rang out with a combination of accents—native, immigrant, and second generation. 'Accrington Stanley, Bury, Huddersfield, Sheffield Wednesday, Crewe Alexandra we saw from the train, and Stockport County,' they dipped in and out of England's geographical and divisional spaces. 'Middlesbrough, Hartlepool, and Halifax.'

'And the team with same name as Mrs. Beckham and me,' the captain spoke. 'Northwich Victoria who once beat Charlton in the FA Cup.'

'I'm impressed. You know more than I gave you credit for.'

'Course,' spoke the huskiest of the voices amongst his crew. 'You're surprised we know anything more than iPhones and boy bands.'

'Why do you say that?' Fergus tested the sudden insolence.

Rebellious and headstrong, Chelsea Wilson was always more likely to win a fight than any beauty or popularity contest. 'It's your nature—you might be a manager but you're still a man.'

'Yeah, why don't we get wo-managers?'

'Dunno,' Fergus joked, 'but there's plenty o' woe in management.'

This though, he began to explain, was the land where football, if not born, was refashioned in the image of the working classes—something the establishment, to this day, had never forgiven. Manchester, as they walked towards Oxford Road, carried echoes of the game's origins.

'Modern England's origins too,' he suggested.

Here the Industrial Revolution was born, with the development of railways, mills, warehouses, and the canals that gave shape to cities—a pattern repeated from Trent to Tyne, and Lagan to Liffey.

'People have been playing football in these isles for centuries,' Fergus explained. 'It was only in the 1800s the rules were formalised in England. Before then it was lawless.'

'Like Chelsea when she's in one of her Suarez moods,' a girl at the back piped out another reference to the Premier League. 'Or when she's seen somebody she fancies on the other side, and is trying to show off.'

'Fuck you,' Chelsea growled, 'with my middle finger.'

'No need for that,' interjected Fergus. 'Stick to the football.'

The girls cackled like goblins. 'You embarrassed sir?'

'Long ago,' he returned to his story of England's game, 'there was a partition in football between north and south. Up here, it was a game for working men, and working women too, either side of The Great War.' Again he paused, as their hotel's clock tower came into view. 'Down south, football was for guys from public schools, golf clubs, and universities. You know Blackheath, up above Greenwich?'

The girls nodded. 'Where rich folks live.'

'Nowhere near as rich as your average footballer,' Fergus laughed. 'Anyway, Blackheath FC was one of the league's first members but dropped out to play rugby, which was probably good for Charlton.' His story was gathering speed, as they reached the hotel. 'If southerners had their way, the game would have stayed amateur, and today we'd have Blackheath as rivals instead of Crystal Palace and Millwall.'

But the power base shifted northwards with the Football League's formation in 1888, and a single division of twelve teams. Half this number hailed from Lancashire, and the rest from the Midlands. Professional football was born, and the amateur spirit relegated to the sidelines.

'Wasn't until 1893 that a London team joined,' Fergus continued. 'Woolwich Arsenal, also born out of industry, not public schools.'

Maybe that was a good point at which to end his story, as the girls stopped listening in their stampede through the hotel doors.

'Sheesh, this must ah come right outa the movies,' the goalkeeper dived across a winding staircase. 'Like the one they had in Titanic.'

'Quiet,' Fergus warned. 'Don't wreck anything—you're not in the classroom, and you're not Brighton in an away dressing room.'

Gradually, staff swept into the picture to sort out their booking.

A boy with Bollywood looks approached in a Coronation Street accent. 'You're t' Ladies' football team, then?'

'No shit Sherlock,' Chelsea still had Brighton on the brain.

'Aye,' interjected Fergus, amused by the boy's greeting. 'Here for a tournament up at City's ground, for two nights.'

'Nine rooms booked. Eight double, one single.'

The girls overheard the conversation. 'So we're sharing?'

'That's right,' he answered. 'College isn't made of money.'

'Do we get to choose who we're sleeping beside?'

'Nope,' Fergus was insistent. 'It's the hotel's lottery.'

'It's not fair,' they protested. 'You get your own room.'

'Yeah, but there's nobody he can share with,' Victoria pacified her team mates' grumbling as they scrabbled for key cards.

One of the others spoke up in brave stupidity. 'Chelsea.'

Some laughed. Most didn't. Chelsea's eyes cut the girl to the bone, and brought to the surface a soft wounded side she normally didn't show. Swallowing hard, she was trying to contain a volcanic temper. 'Hey, you never know, one o' you frigid bitches might get lucky tonight!'

'That's enough,' Fergus shouted, as he led them up the stairs. 'You're sharing rooms and that's it. Besides, they say the hotel's as haunted as Greenwich, so you'll be glad o' company in the dead o' night.'

'Maybe you shouldn't be sleeping alone either, sir.'

'I'm Irish. Grew up around ghosts,' he closed the argument.

Getting inside his double room, Fergus unpacked his bags, looked out the window on a view of the bustling Oxford Road station where a group of Klezmer musicians had started to busk in the side alley. He listened a while and then showered the last traces of Subbuteo from his skull.

Lying down on the bed afterwards, he went back to the papers and the digestion of Crystal Palace's fortunes from the night before.

Outside he could still hear folk music from the buskers rising up through incessant rumbling of traffic. Soon after, he was disturbed by knocking. He rose, pulled on his trousers, and answered.

Victoria stood in the hallway. 'Can I have a word, sir?'
Tall and strong, her dark eyes towered over his.

'Can we change rooms?' she asked insistently.

'No,' he answered immediately. 'It'd be chaos.'

'Yeah, but we ought to have some choice.'

'Who are you with?' he probed, to make sense of this.
After a few seconds she spoke. 'Chelsea Wilson.'

'I see. That's what this is all about then.'

'You know how people tease and talk,' the teenager
protested. 'Being captain, I can't have the other girls saying
things, making jokes about it.'

'Being captain requires leadership,' Fergus insisted.
'When others are looking into the gutter, you've got to
focus on the stars.'

'Oscar Wilde—we studied him in English class.'

'Yeah and maybe in History class you'll learn how he
was treated. What society did to him seems crazy in this
day and age, but it was done because so few dared to stand
up and defend him.'

'Nobody's talking about sending Chelsea to prison.'

'But you're not allowing her to be herself,' Fergus
argued, 'because you're afraid to be yourself and be mates
with her for who she is.'

'She doesn't even know who she is.'

'Do any of us?' he asked, starting to realise it was best
not to be seen barefoot and bare-chested out in the
corridor with a student. 'Just go back to your room
Victoria and rise above the gossip.'

Returning inside, as she walked off, he crossed to the
window. Looking down again on Oxford Road with the
musicians packing up their instruments, he wondered if
he'd been too harsh. It was tough being a teenager. There
was a lot of pressure on these kids from their peer group.
The same desire to be cool in front of the crowd had once
shaped his random decision to steal a car, take it for a ride
to the coast, crash over cliffs, and go to prison.

But sometimes good results come from bad things.

'Maybe I missed out on being a boxing champion,' he mused, 'but I came to England, started again, and ended up coaching these girls.'

Then he drifted off to sleep, still cursing Crystal Palace. Next morning, bright and early, fresh music rose from the station. This time it was a fellow with a violin playing Irish folk, not Klezmer. For a while Fergus listened and then went downstairs to gather up his team for breakfast.

'Any ghosts sir?' some of the girls asked as they ate.

'No such thing as ghosts,' he told them a white lie.

Dreams of Katy had haunted him for most of the night.

Shaking her off, he assembled his team and caught a taxi bus up to Manchester City's ground, now known as The Etihad. Manchester's streets buzzed, wedded to moods of early summer. Flashes of canals turned to the whip of trams emblazoned in names of lower division football teams as they passed through Piccadilly onto the more stylish side of the city.

This part of Manchester resembled London—a place of commerce, weekend breaks, and five-star plate glass bubbles staring down on architectural glories of the past— as gateways to inner-city poverty. It was a side effect of City and United, the upper layers of a wedding cake celebrating the marriage of wealth to football. At the top, you find Middle Eastern dates soaked in the best brandy that money could buy. Then at the bottom, there's dark leather and a pig's bladder slashed from the heart of December days in Bolton, Burnley, Crewe and Accrington.

Suddenly, the thought was so strong he could smell the rising damp—factory chimneys steaming from coal-fired power stations—a world away from the modern science of Sunday matinees at Old Trafford.

There, the match ball was ' aerodynamic, synthetic, shiny, and corporate; designed for top corners, tabloid headlines, GIF files, and goals by the gifted—Luis Suarez, Stevie Gerrard, and Wilfried Zaha. The Nike T90 Seitiro was the Macbook of footballs fit for the best league in the world—cutting edge, eye-catching, and made for overseas markets.

'We're here, we're fucking here!' Chelsea exclaimed.

Racing towards the entrance gates, the girls grew excited. They'd arrived on the doorstep of a world they only knew from television. Premier League football. Architectural splendour. The chance of meeting superstars from every corner of the world, getting autographs and grabbing selfies, fashioning new profile pictures on their social media sites.

'I want to see the home dressing room and find Sergio Aguero,' Victoria stopped to glance up at a place now synonymous with victory, wealth, and daily headlines on Sky Sports News. 'If I get lucky I might even be able to get some hot goal scoring tips from him.'

The others teased their captain as she stood in a daze.

'Ain't his tips you're going to be trying to get off him.'

'Seriously,' Victoria protested, 'how can you think of anything but football when you're standing here at this ... this temple?'

'Far cry from the City of the eighties,' Fergus thought.

Manchester's gallant losers. Glorious stories of near triumph usually ending in defeat and playing second fiddle to their neighbours. But no more. The world order had changed as new owners brought some of the world's finest footballers to perform in City's soft blue shirts.

'If Charlton ever get owners as rich as this,' he told his team. 'I just hope they keep the things attracted me in the first place.'

'He's on the same planet as Victoria,' the girls giggled. 'She wants Aguero for his tips, and he's in love with Charlton Athletic.'

'But it's Palace going to be in the Premier League next year,' Chelsea deflated his grand notions of ever coming here to see his team in action. 'Beat Watford and *we* get to face City next season.'

Suddenly Fergus hated that thought with all the rage of a convert. Surely they couldn't. The Gods of Football would never be that cruel to send a gartersnake slithering through a back door into the Garden of Eden. But then again life's cruel. He'd realised that from his romance with Katy.

'Okay ladies,' he gathered his troops in the foyer of the stadium. 'Let's forget Palace and Aguero, and get this tournament won.'

Forget Katy too, if such a thing were possible.

8. Lamentation for London

*T*here are no first lines when your heart is torn, only echoes of the last, and the roads that have led you there. Katy Prunty thought of this as she stood on the shore trapped between the seaside town and the blaze of unsettled waters. She had reached a crossroads of the heart, with nowhere left to run. Sun sinking, the pale shadow of a moon rising, she had to reach a decision about what to do next.

Reflectively she gazed across the marina pebbled in pretty boats, now framed in majestic fire. As the boats slipped into shadow, the sky burned chilli red. Tonight, as always, this fragment of the Kentish coast looked spectacular in these last seconds of seabirds dazzling against a sunset.

'Van Gogh could have painted this,' Katy mused.

Turner too, except for the anachronism of planes dipping seawards.

Feeling echoes of journeys past, Katy willed herself

towards a window seat, sipping coffee, closing a book, on the descent for *home*.

Her favourite view. The London night, from a plane.

Leaving holidays behind, you feel sadness and exhilaration. Memories flood the tunnels of the mind and the backs of your eyes. Your ears pop, a consequence of tightening altitude and emotion. Facing sideways, you're dipping towards a scattered vocabulary of light and stars— gradually giving way to the dark comma of the Thames.

You're at peace, until the sharp intrusion of Canary Wharf's sparkling towers. Then you land and the clamour of London invades. Trucks, buses, forklifts shifting cases, and voices raised on mobile phones.

Thinking of that, she loved the peace of Ramsgate. This evening though, as the sun began to sink, there had been chaos on the beach. For days now, the papers had raged with the story of a missing Albanian migrant, prowling in the darkness as police scoured the largest seaside towns of Kent's northeastern coast—Ramsgate, Broadstairs, and Margate.

'Gypsy Roaming Loose,' the red-tops roared.

The dark stranger had crossed from Calais, a former fishing village in a corner of France that had once belonged to England, and now to chaos.

He'd been living in a camp, which the papers nicknamed *The Jungle,* but was forced to escape after resisting a protection racket organised by his countrymen. Those crooks had been taking money off people who'd arrived with nothing more than the clothes on their back.

Katy had read of their journey. Sold lies to begin with, they came from the hottest and darkest parts of Africa, walking thousands of miles through desert and wilderness to reach the Arab countries in the north.

Then they're traded like cattle, herded onto boats, and shipped across the Mediterranean, hoping they don't drown along the way.

If they survived the treacherous crossing that

swallowed thousands, they moved illegally and invisibly through the flesh markets of Europe.

By the time they reach Calais they're as brow-beaten as George Foreman fighting Muhammad Ali in the heat of Zaire. Rumble in the Jungle. That fight Fergus described as the best of all time. Dazed and battered, they're easy pickings for pimps, pushers, and peddlers of fake dreams.

The young Albanian hadn't wanted to be part of the exploitation. Risking his own life he went to the authorities who took his statement and then sent him back to his former masters. Fearing death, he had to escape.

Some other migrants helped. Outsiders too, in the form of a travelling theatre company, which outraged the tabloids. *Shakespeare for Migrants.* Volunteer actors performing in the camps of France, for the sake of dignity and humanity, treating the dispossessed as human beings.

Hidden in the back of the actors' van, he'd made it through customs. Onto a boat bound for Ramsgate. The chalky white cliffs of England. Channel of hope that stretched less than the mileage from Charlton to Dover.

Then, as he approached the shore, he dived overboard, escaping the clutches of the coastguard. For three nights he'd gone on the run. Hunted like the last pawn on a chessboard. He'd become the frightening face of the future, a liquid plague carrying itself across the virus-riddled sea.

Helicopters, waiting for checkmate, guarded all routes out of a town that had seen better days. Once it was a popular retreat for artists, including Vincent Van Gogh who stayed here in the summer of 1876.

From a room above the marina, he scribbled snapshots of the sea's changing shades and moods. Wrote letters too, whole volumes, to his brother Theo in France. Katy had read the collection in the sanctuary of Ramsgate Library, to which she often retreated in the afternoons. In his words she found a strange arousal, wishing she could have lived here more than a century before, when the world had a greater sense of solitude.

Van Gogh, unlike the Albanian, encountered a warm welcome in the seaside town on the brow of Thanet. Long ago, in the Bronze Age, tribes from Belgium had been the first to colonise these shores. Later the Celts portrayed this as a magical island of deities and the dead, getting its name from a combination of words for fire and heights, a place of smouldering poetry.

Then the Normans came, uninvited, and conquered the land with their soldiers, churches, castles, and linguistics. England, her country, had always been a sponge of the world's races and languages, and never as unwelcoming as this new age where celebrities tweeted demands for gunboats to blast the foreigners back to Calais.

'Such hysteria,' she thought. 'Such madness amidst beauty.'

Shortly before sunset, sirens sounded. The ground shook as helicopters edged into position, shaking the bones of the sleepy seaside town. It appeared that the police had found the Albanian visitor.

'Stop,' loudhailers ruptured her thoughts as she hurried towards a prime view of this rumble from *The Jungle*, a ringside seat by the dark sea. 'Come out of the water and give yourself up.'

The migrant was up to his ankles and then knees in the sea, until he could go no further and waded back towards a caravan of boats.

Amongst them, Katy could see the last of *The Little Ships*, part of Dunkirk's evacuation at the start of the Second World War. Now they stood with backs turned to Europe, penning in their visitor.

Exposed to the sharp glare, he was frail, frightened, and fairer-skinned than she'd imagined, wearing a dark red Albanian soccer jersey. Against the eagle on its breast, he clutched a package—an indecipherable object.

'Drop whatever you have and get down on the ground.'

Against police orders the migrant stood junkie-eyed,

transfixed—with a chopper above, and clusters of armed officers clambering over jetty walls. Out at sea, coastguards edged into focus, trapping him on all sides, leaving him with nowhere to go, unless he fancied a cold swim back to France.

'Put down your weapons,' another policeman barked, as Katy slipped into a signpost's shadows so as to become invisible in the commotion.

'Weapons?' she pondered. 'Has he a gun, or bomb?'

Maybe Lance's prediction's carried substance. Sooner or later he reckoned we're going to bring the legacy of wars to our own doorstep, if we leave these giant cat-flaps on the coast for mongrel visitors.

'We're telling you for the last time,' the police insisted.

Still the migrant cradled his bundle—looking up in search of stars drowned out by the might of a helicopter above. Stacked in formation with weapons lowered, the cops offered him one final avenue of surrender.

'Take it,' Katy shivered with goose bumps.

'Drop your weapons,' orders rasped afresh.

Briefly his grip on the bundle slackened and he seemed ready to scatter his belongings onto the shore, away from the eagle on his breast. Then at the last second he turned as the police cried 'Halt.'

Officers, giving chase, steadied themselves and readied to fire.

Their target stalled, trying to salvage shelter in boats tethered to the marina's edge. But the young man's mystery bundle slowed his movements, as he scrambled over the hardshelled shadows of fishing boats.

Surrounded by police, he was a matter of seconds from being shot.

A sting of weaponry drowned Katy's sudden cry, 'No.'

They had opened fire with the laser darts of an electroshock weapon. Struck from behind, the young man's legs buckled—sending him tumbling, face down, towards a boat that whacked the side of his head.

81

Dazed and wounded, he lay bleeding as the helicopter's lights encircled the silhouette of his belongings. At first there was a call not to touch them, fearing weapons or explosives, such was the hysteria of the age.

'Careful,' they roared, before seeing the contents spilled out.

The helicopter's lights had exposed them like an X-Ray. Instead of guns and bombs, they found traces of a pastime.

Laughter slackened the police lines. 'Brushes and paints.'

The Shakespearian stowaway was no more dangerous than an artist. Katy stood and watched as police lifted and bundled him into the back of a van, wondering what had happened to the England of history.

The England of foreign kings and queens, of coasts layered in different levels of invasion, and a society shaped by the intermarriage of each.

In the past she might have called Fergus. After all, he was an immigrant too. He'd come to this country and built a new life though he still loved Ireland. Alone together, they found a home in each other's hearts; experiencing a journey as much travelled as the Irish Sea.

'We're all immigrants when it comes to love,' she supposed.

People cross borders and boundaries, entering new territories—building lives afresh, moving from thoughts and words to the feel of flesh. Lovers had been immigrating to these islands for thousands of years.

First the Celts came. Then the Romans sailed down the untamed banks of the dark river *Tamasa*, and built the city of Londinium. Next, between Saxons and Normans, love went astray with the heartless Vikings. Toughened by the Danes, England changed from raided to raider.

Going out into the world, she absorbed new races in return—Africans, Indians, Huguenots, and ship loads of Irish fleeing famine. Fresh lives, fresh stories took shape on these shores. Then, as happens in stories of love, babies arrived, transported out of Dutch and German ghettoes on ships in the darkness; escaping pogroms, fires and breaking glass.

By the end of the same war, more had followed—Poles and Lithuanians, fresh from forests of genocide, landing in the ruins of London. Then the blacks, the Irish, and whole villages from Kashmir.

Looking out at the coast, hard as a tortoise's back, she felt angry now. The blood inside her skull boiled and stabbed her with a migraine. Maybe she was sick, afflicted with love, an infuriating malady. She'd given up Fergus for a writer's life on the coast, and found a new lover shortly after. And now she was having doubts. Perhaps that was the cause of her sickness, and nothing to do with the pain of migrants suffering within touching distance.

It was barely more than a few weeks since she had finished with Fergus. The end came suddenly on the evening of a sexual explosion. She'd been baking bread in the kitchen of her rented boathouse, as goblins cackled on a television in the background—wicked, malevolent, and mischievous laughter.

'Coffee bread,' she recalled the scene clearly.

Fergus slipped in behind, trying to resurrect the passion that had been fading since he got that damned tattoo. Kissing her neck, he released the chopstick from her hair, letting the bun fall loose about her shoulders.

'Let me finish this,' she continued to knead the dough as he searched out the flesh beneath her flour-dusted, butter-smeared apron. 'I want to reach thirteen braids, my highest number in one single loaf.'

'I'll take it to work, and share it with the other teachers.'

Glazing the dough, she wanted to scream 'NO.'

This was baked for him alone, as an act of her love, a letter to the heart that should take up residence in his stomach, and not be shared with others. When it comes to reading female minds, men can be so fucking dyslexic.

Gas hissed, stripping back layers, down to the yeasty fermentation of desire. Trapped between the worktop and Fergus's body, the goblins' laughter grew loud as the roar of a football stadium. She thought of The Valley on match days over the fence and down the hill from their garden.

Once long ago, passing through an estate, another choir of goblins, a cluster of goblins, a murder of goblins, a cacophony of goblins in the form of a teenage gang surrounded her as she walked home with a friend.

They dragged her down to the dark bowels of a warehouse, where she never thought she'd see the light of day again. Though she'd broken free before they harmed her, scars glistened on the tissue of her memory.

'Let's go outside,' she proposed, wanting to disperse past tensions that were always present, even in moments of love. Running free, the evening belonged to them alone, laughing like children, as they headed for the shore. But it felt as if the goblins had broken out of the TV, and given chase, clambering down towards the same shoreline.

'Have you ever made love in a boat?' he asked suddenly.

'No,' she admitted, as they edged towards the harbour.

'There's one right here. What's stopping us?'

'*Valkyries*,' Katy read the nameplate on a distinctive vessel.

This abandoned houseboat, steeped in the day's dying light, was a deep shade of blue, bordering on the melancholy of a Van Gogh painting. Like the barges at Battersea or Stratford, on the far side of the inner city Thames, this was a boat with personality, one you could look upon, and dream of living in—of cutting the rope, and setting sail to places on the far side of the world.

Entering *Valkyries*, they secreted their way down steps to a cabin.

There, they drew curtains and placed heavy oars against the door, for fear of owners turning up unexpectedly, catching them in the act.

'That makes it all the more exciting,' he suggested.

'Secrets under the eyes of the world,' she felt a strange arousal in imagining *Valkyries* made of glass, and their passion visible to the whole continent, across to France and beyond to the Mediterranean islands dazzling magical in the moonlight as a night of fertilisation on a coral reef.

Outside, roosting birds chattered as the red sun began to peel, turning the horizon to chilli fire. Inside, as the temperature rose, their bodies felt languorous, statuesque, weighed down in footwear and layers of clothes. Stripping off, the fear of getting caught subsided into naked laughter.

But as their bodies merged into one, she heard goblins laugh again, infecting her mind with visions of someone she'd met a few weeks before, whose voice was a GIF of walking barefoot through nettles.

Suddenly, in her imagination, it was as if she was in a boxing ring crushed between the bodies of two men fighting for the title belt of her heart. Lying with both in the same bed, each invisible to the other, even though they were making love to her at the same time.

'Concentrate, concentrate,' she fought fantasy but despite her resistance was caught between one man's flesh and another's image.

But then as desire reached a crescendo, one face filled her thoughts. Suddenly, the sun's chilli fire broke through the boat's outer layer, and filled her loins as she felt something other than Fergus's body inside hers. Another man's face in her mind, bringing her to a state of orgasm that stayed even after Fergus rolled off her body. Feeling guilty she dressed with her back turned to the sunset, the cries of roosting seabirds, and the rolling tongues of a sea darkened to coffee.

Fergus irritated her with a cliché question. 'If the mile high club's for planes, then what's the society for having sex in boats?'

'I've got to get back to my baking,' she rushed away

from the scene of her fantasy, for fear he'd be able to see through her even when dressed.

Whatever had happened, whatever had changed, whatever dark spirit of *Valkyries* had slipped inside her soul, she couldn't escape its numbing shadows. Back in the house, she treated her braided coffee loaves as a series of goodbye letters lifted gently from the stove. Wrapping them in silver foil, she placed the pebbles of her desire deep in Fergus's rucksack.

'Take them *home* to London,' she said, as they sipped nightcaps, and prepared for bed, in the closing hours of their weekend.

Shortly after, as she lay awake in the upstairs room—listening to sounds of the sea in the distance—Katy suffered inside, burning from the last traces of making love in a boat at sunset. There was a Portuguese word for the suffering she felt—*saudade*—a deep, melancholic longing for what's lost.

'At the start you wrote me love notes you'd lay beneath my pillow so they'd be there to greet me in the mornings. You swore you'd always tell me stories, always write for me, but you don't anymore.'

'I will again once the football season's over.'

'Sometimes I feel like I've lost you to a mistress!'

'Don't tell me you're jealous of Charlton?'

'Jealous of your season ticket,' she jagged her joke.

'Season's over soon,' he'd started to drift off.

'Jealous of Wolves too,' she whispered softly.

He'd had to leave next day because of a match against a team called Wolverhampton Wanderers, choosing football ahead of her once more.

'But Wolves are a big team,' he protested, as if their love was just a small thing in comparison. 'One of the first I ever saw on Match of the Day.'

'This is 2013,' she argued. 'You're not a boy anymore.'

She wanted to spar some more for the championship of their hearts, but Fergus fell asleep, exhausted and punch-drunk from their rumble, so she rose and wandered back down to the shore, outside an empty café.

There she sat, looking up at the indifferent sky, thinking of Fergus's lost letters, love in a boat, and the terrible nature of passion that never lasts.

Fighting hard to get it back, she feared the opportunity had passed. Football had stolen Fergus's attention, causing her eyes and heart to wander. Just a game in the beginning, the rules had changed along the way.

That was when she decided to finish one romance and start another.

9. Fair Game, Sparrow's Lane

Back from the elegance of The Etihad, the girls settled into routine. Saturday morning practice session. Sparrow's Lane. Charlton Athletic training grounds. No Sergio Aguero or Gulf oil money here. Just plain pitches framed in trees on the edge of South London.

Flashes of skin, tattoos, and shin pads. Studs tearing up the soft mud. Stylish boots, different colours, not like long ago. Shades of pink, blue, and bright orange set against the torn grass and punctured earth.

Traffic cones, bags of balls spilling out into a tirade of slow dribbles. Then passes angled neatly across the turf to set up strikes on goal.

'I want total passion,' Fergus demanded as they lined up for his whistle. 'We don't get to rent these grounds often. Make good use of them.'

This leafy edge of London had housed Charlton's youth system for decades, and also been home to the women's teams. Many famous players had left stud marks in this hallowed ground down through the years.

You had Rob Lee and Scott Parker who sounded like a couple of jazz musicians. Jon Fortune, who relegated the hated Crystal Palace in 2005. Jonjo Shelvey, Liverpool star, and Chris Solly the marauding right back who had stayed with Charlton his entire career. Then Katie Chapman, Eni Aluko, and girls like Victoria tramping around the pitch with her ankles still bandaged from the Manchester tournament.

'Come on, let's get going,' Fergus snapped them into action, running on the spot and loosening their muscles as he sorted out two sets of bibs, one red and the other blue. 'You're not going to be Ladies' champions again this season if you don't put in the effort.'

'Yes sir,' they cried out in their combination of accents.

They wanted the title and another shot at The Etihad.

'Get into teams,' he ordered as they finished their warm-up. 'Red and blue. Imagine one side's Charlton and the other's Millwall.'

'That's not fair,' a skinny girl with hairy legs and dreadlocks piped up. 'You're always going to be on Charlton's side, sir.'

'Okay, something neutral,' he struggled to identify sides.

'France and Belgium,' a spindly Somali girl suggested.

'Alright, France in blue, and Belgium in red,' he agreed.

Seconds later he tossed a coin to decide which shade should kick off. Victoria, captain of the Belgians, won the toss, and positioned her team. Since Manchester she'd grown in confidence, even if she hadn't found Aguero.

Soft drizzle had started to fall, blowing across the faces of trees and players towards the glass scalp of Avery Hill's Winter Gardens. There he had one of his first dates with Katy Prunty. Strange then, that this training ground was also where he received his fatal text about four weeks before.

That was a couple of days after his last visit to

Ramsgate.

On the penultimate Saturday of April, Fergus returned to London and watched Charlton beat Wolverhampton Wanderers 2-1 with a last minute goal, on a day of sunshine golden as the visitors' jerseys. There'd been some blockade on the way home, which he'd glimpsed on the train from London Bridge through New Cross, but he'd made the match in good time.

At the ground, he caught up with Lance and all the usual faces. He grabbed a bite to eat from the fish shop and bought his copy of *Voice of the Valley*, the club fanzine. Then he talked to the guy in the cap who manned the Supporters' Trust stall and renewed his membership for another year.

Glorious day, they agreed, and eagerly awaited the purchase of their tickets for next season. *Who knows—could be the year that promotion comes and we get back to the days of the Premier League?*

When that conversation was done, he'd moved on through the turnstiles and into the stadium where he took his seat in a row full of familiar faces. A man who used to get through the games with a sip of whisky from a secret flask, and now relied on electronic cigarettes instead. Then a woman they called *England's Oldest Football Supporter*, fan of Charlton for maybe fifty years or more. Others too they couldn't name, but they were as much a part of the weekly furniture as the seats and the soil.

'Bloody red-bibbed bitch,' the Somali girl's piercing cry broke through the bubble of Fergus's daydreams as somebody fouled her on the edge of the box. 'She thumped me hard enough to send me all the way back to Manchester.'

'Free kick,' he agreed, as referee.

Kick taken, the goalkeeper saved and booted the ball to the far end. Fergus returned to thoughts of Katy, a Sunday training session, right here on the morning after Charlton pushed Wolves into the relegation zone.

Suddenly his phone had buzzed from a fresh text message.

'Sorry Fergus,' it said, and he knew the signs weren't good.

The training ground was probably the last place where he had wanted to hear bad news. He decided to put the phone away, concentrate on the match, and forget about his lover. And he did, for a few minutes, then thought about her again, and struggled to forget. Eventually he succumbed.

'Going to the toilet,' he passed his whistle to an assistant.

Crossing the field, the phone scalded his palm in premonition of what she was likely to say. Great beads of sweat dropped down off his forehead, and onto the ground. Towering palms in the distance created the effect of a religious moment, as he entered a portacabin.

'Sorry Fergus,' the message read.

Christ, great, at least it was cordial in its genesis.

His eyes had moved on, burning as each word crossed them. 'I realised something when you left the boathouse on Saturday morning. Though our few days had been great, this can't go on.'

Maybe he should have stopped where the signs weren't good but he couldn't resist going on, even as his fingers grew numb from the grip.

'You've got Charlton, and I've got a book to write. The wolves have been at the door for a long time. But this is no longer just about me and you.'

Now he knew the matter was serious, and she was about to reveal something heavy. The words started out as a pebble rolling across his eyes, before gathering speed, striking him right in the balls.

'There's somebody else I've been thinking of lately, and I want to get to know him better. You've met him. You may remember when you came to Ramsgate after I first arrived, and we still had something.'

'Yes of course I remember everything,' he screamed out on the inside. 'Why are you talking as if I'm a stranger all of a sudden?'

'We haven't had anything for a long time, but I still need something.'

The pebble was turning to a stone, and then a rock rolling down a snowy hill, crushing his heart beneath an ever-gathering weight.

'I need to love and be loved. I want fresh-cut flowers, compliments when I'm having a bad day, coffee in bed, and Belgian chocolates.'

'So love comes down to chocolate in the end?' he'd voiced his anger.

'I didn't plan on this Fergus,' Katy continued. 'By now, he could scarcely breathe under the rock's weight. 'Somebody brought me wild flowers from the cliffs, and memories of something I had lost, which I didn't even realise was missing, until that moment.'

If cyberspace were an envelope, and the phone made of paper, he'd have ripped them both in half right there. 'I could have given you that.'

But Katy's words came from glass and ink, not flesh as she named the ultimate reason for their sudden separation. 'It's Wagner.'

Wagner had snatched Katy from under Fergus's nose with the stealth of a wolf. He was the handsome stranger who had brought her wild flowers, and perhaps entered her bedroom with coffee and Belgian chocolates.

Wagner, the young barista who rode a motorbike and had passed through so many places he couldn't name the actual city he came from. He'd spent time in Morocco, and then in Spain before making his way up through France, and into Brussels. Finally he crossed the English Channel to Ramsgate, where he said he'd come for surfing lessons.

Claimed he was going to move to the south of France afterwards and become a tutor of surfing, and Katy's eyes dazzled as he told that story.

Through all his smooth talk, he'd been hunting Katy, and finally won her on the morning after Wolverhampton wandered down to London.

Fergus had found it hard to contain his emotion for the rest of that morning, going through the painful routine of conducting a training session. The day before at five o'clock he was celebrating victory with a beer in the sunshine, alongside Lance, on the waterfront at Charlton.

'Less than twenty four hours later I was like Wolves,' he recalled the grief that remained embedded like a thorn in a dog's paw—even though four weeks and a football tournament had passed since then.

'Yes,' the present screamed out at him once more.

He had to concentrate on the here and now of Sparrow's Lane, where a cheer rose up from the goal at the far end of Charlton's training grounds. Belgium had struck the back of the net's lacy brassiere. Victoria had scored a goal fine as anything he'd expect from Scott Parker or Eni Aluko.

'Even the bandages can't stop her,' the girls laughed.

Victoria had taken a hell of a kicking up in Manchester as they made their way through the early stages of the tournament. By the final, her ankles had swollen to the size of eggplants.

Against a team from the North West, the southern girls found themselves bullied, outweighed, and on the edge of defeat—not helped by a referee who gave every decision against them. Goals disallowed, constant free kicks given to opponents, and then Chelsea sent off for lashing out against a defender who'd almost ripped the shirt off her back.

Fergus knew that life wasn't fair—losing Katy to Wagner. But you expect football to be different, for all things to be equal on the pitch.

It wasn't though, as even the most obvious of decisions went against his team. Once, when clean through on goal, Victoria had been scythed down in the goalmouth in a rugby tackle by an opposing defender.

'Penalty!' his girls had cried from one end to the other.

'No,' the referee insisted and booked Victoria for protesting.

That was when Fergus realised there was no straight way to win. Come half time, his girls lay down on the pitch despondent.

'Might as well go home now. We can't win this.'

'We have to,' he rallied his troops. 'For the spirit of the game.'

'How?' the Somali winger threw her bottle across the turf.

Feeling the minutes tick away he struggled for solutions.

'Wait,' he realised, as the referee gestured for them to rise again. 'Maybe I've an idea. One thing you can't fix is a penalty shoot-out.'

'Yes,' the girls entered into his conspiracy.

Playing out a scoreless draw, they brought the match to a shoot-out, awakening echoes of Charlton's Wembley heroics in 1998.

Just as on that sunny day, every player struck the back of the net to score until one girl on the opposing side thumped the ball over the bar. Victoria stepped up to take the last penalty, ankles so badly swollen she couldn't wear boots. She had to take the kick in her bare feet.

Her team mates gasped. 'Even Eni Aluko wouldn't attempt that!'

'Up she ran,' Fergus memorised the moment, 'and the other team's watching, waiting for her to fail, thinking they've kicked her into submission, and nobody's ever going to score a penalty without boots on.'

But they'd never seen a Charlton girl in action. She moved slow, putting every ounce of her strength and weight into the right side of her body, so as to accentuate the power of her shot at the very last moment.

He heard the crack of his captain's toes as she struck

the ball, so full of anger she'd have killed somebody if that was a punch.

'Go girl go,' he'd gritted his teeth in anticipation.

Then he watched the ball rise in slow motion, dipping in such a manner that the other team's goalkeeper would feel all the pain and suffering of being a fingertip away from stopping the shot. No words could describe seeing that ball bend into the corner and seal victory for the spirit of football.

Best of all, if the cheating referee had made her retake that penalty a hundred times, you knew she'd have scored with every attempt.

They'd won the tournament and this session of hiring Charlton Athletic's training ground was their reward. Even if everything wasn't fair in life, they'd managed to make everything fair in football for one afternoon.

Off the pitch though, the bad guy won so far as Fergus was concerned. He had met Wagner before, when Katy first arrived. They'd talked football, and the barista's favourite team, Arsenal. Wagner said that nothing mattered outside of the Premier League. Fergus disagreed. A century and a half of football history couldn't be undone in a couple of decades.

'No,' Wagner insisted. 'Football lives only in the present, not the past.' Then, in a rare moment, he gave away something of his own guarded story. 'I wanted to be a footballer once, but was born in the wrong place at the wrong time. I did play as a teenager and had an agent. Got screwed over in the end though because the whole system's rotten.'

'Imagine him at Charlton,' Katy said later that same afternoon. 'You'd get far more women in the crowd, don't you think? They'd pay to see him whip his top off every time he scored a goal.'

'You can't do that in England,' Fergus murdered her moment of fiction. 'You'd get booked for inciting the crowd.'

'If the referee stopped him, there'd be a riot,' she laughed.

He should have seen it then, and as they talked a couple of days later. 'What position did you play, in your football days?'

'Striker,' Wagner clarified. 'I was going to be Africa's Gary Lineker. As a boy, I dreamed of an African team winning the World Cup, any team. I was four years old when Cameroon lost 3-2 to England on penalties. The original Lineker scored both goals for England, and broke Africa's heart.'

'Such a sad and beautiful image,' Katy interjected.

'Look,' he showed her a gold pendant in the shape of Africa around his neck. 'I wear this across my own heart every day, every night to remember the place where I was born and left when I was a teenager.'

'Wow,' Katy sighed, glowing in his presence, almost purring.

'So where are you actually from?' Fergus severed the intimacy.

'My father was North African and my mother Kenyan.'

'Same roots as Barack Obama,' Katy's eyes dazzled again.

'We travelled around a great deal though,' he put Africa to his lips as he spoke. 'My father was a music teacher and went wherever the work was.'

'Is that where your name came from?'

'Yes,' he turned to face Katy's eyes. 'All the boys in my family were named for male composers, and the girls for females.'

'Wow,' she voiced her admiration once more, leaning in close to Africa in a blaze of afternoon sunshine. 'That's hardcore. I like it.'

'I don't know any female composers,' Fergus felt out of his depth.

'Amy Beach, Clara Schumann, Nadia and Lili Boulanger.'

'Precisely,' Wagner's eyes danced to her knowledge.

'I read a lot, and love classical music when I write.'

'What're you reading now?' Wagner pounced.

'Vincent Van Gogh's letters,' she began a monologue that excluded both men but left the way open for more conversations after Fergus left.

On the way home, he'd feared some seed of contact forming between them. But Wagner seemed too young and casual for Katy, and she was determined to get her book written and edited.

She'd have little spare time for sitting on the shore getting charmed with tales of Africa and Europe by a guy who looked as if he could have stepped right off the cover of a sports' paperback. He knew the sort, arrayed in bookshops and airports in a gallery of rippling muscles—six packs and Speedos or jeans that leave nothing to the imagination.

But that wasn't Katy's sort of guy, he reckoned at first.

Then Wagner's name crept into conversation more and more. She'd struggle with the editing of her book, and go to Wagner's coffeeshop to sketch out her ideas as she sat facing the marina's motley gallery in the dusk.

'He calls me Sketchbook Girl,' she boasted one night.

Maybe she called him Motorbike Boy, Surfer Boy, or Striker Boy.

'He taking me for a ride,' she said another time. 'We're going round the coast up to Margate, and then on to Whitstable.'

Later that same evening, the texts stopped shortly after supper at the seaside. Fergus told himself it was nothing. You'd have no free hands to text when you're riding bareback down the coast in the moonlight.

Or maybe there was a stopover in a pub along the way, off the beaten track, in one of those quaint Kentish villages, where you lose a sense of time, and then it's late, almost midnight, well past last orders. Maybe they'd have to wander the streets, and find a hotel, a couple of rooms, a couple's room for the night. That's a beautiful time in any romance—the wandering and wondering stage. Then, one night, somewhere along the road of their moonlight drives, they must have moved beyond wandering.

'Yay,' a shout rose up from the field, as Belgium scored again.

Maybe this was to be his life now, as Katy had hers. He'd carry on training his team and watching Charlton at weekends. They could ride motorbikes from Ramsgate to hell and back, for all he cared.

When they entered his thoughts he spoke one word. 'Vomit.'

Across the field, half a dozen girls in Belgian bibs cried out. 'Yes.'

Victoria's header smacked the underside of the crossbar and rippled the net's fringe, after a Beckham style cross from the mercurial Chelsea. Fergus clapped. The girls celebrated. He rolled up his sleeves and blew the whistle for the restart. Fresh stud marks formed. The game continued.

10. Playing Away From Home

Maybe if Fergus hadn't got that tacky badge, everything would be different. If he'd paid closer attention to her stories he'd have known she hated tattoos, since the ringleader of the gang that tried to attack her in the past had been a tattooed boy. But Fergus had never given her motives a second thought. He was busy imagining endings she never wanted, and thinking of the fucking football season.

Katy rose out of bed. The next stage in her daily ritual was going downstairs, and preparing coffee in the machine. As she did so, she thought of the man who had started to drift in and out of her life in recent weeks.

Wagner's art was the creation of coffee. Since arriving at his café on the marina, he'd shaken up this sleepy town with Mocha Java smoothies, hot caramel Frappuccino, and potions involving liquorice, sex, and iced mint.

He drew you in, and lured you back for more, getting under your skin. Brought you to the point of addiction.

Aphrodisiac, insulin for a tired soul. More than simply good looks and coffee. His voice too contained flavours of the exotic. Above all, he paid close attention to her stories whereas Fergus had been too busy with his two football teams.

'Men don't listen,' she thought. 'And that's all it takes.'

Preparing the coffee, she turned on the TV in the background. On the morning news, they were still talking about the death of Margaret Thatcher, several weeks after the funeral. For a few minutes, Katy listened as the media painted the former Prime Minister in eulogies of pastel blue.

Background images of Saint Paul's Cathedral brought London to mind. But for the first time in as long as she could remember, she had no desire to go back to the city she'd adopted as her own.

In truth, she missed Fergus but not his mistress.

Things had been better once upon a time, in a world before football.

'You'll grow to love the game,' he had assured her.

Sometimes she accompanied him to matches—usually at The Valley, his second home, down the slope from their house. Going there, admittedly she sensed what was special about following a football team. You were part of something, a tribe perhaps, a shared religion, or an extension of the eleven men wearing your team's colours down on the pitch.

But it was also cold, windy, and, for the most part, infuriatingly passive. At least in the beginning, football was a backdrop to seduction.

Fergus had fallen in love with his local team and dragged her into the affair. They'd gone to half a dozen games in their first season together. Sheffield United, and then Hartlepool, with a monkey for a mascot, stood out in her mind as they travelled the opening roads of romance. They'd kissed on the terraces, and outside the stadium beside the statue of Sam Bartram, goalkeeper of bygone days. But by the new season, when they'd moved in together, football was more of a chore than a scene of seduction.

'Do you really want me to go today?' she'd ask.

'Of course,' he'd have her coat ready before she agreed.

In the August sunshine, she'd followed him to a midweek game against Leicester, a team in blue with foxes on their shirts. Then they'd gone for a weekend break to Nottingham, watching Charlton lose against Forest.

Enough football for one year. But he had insisted on more. By late September, she'd finally sickened of the game as he dragged her to see yet another match. A month or so had passed since Fergus came home with a tattoo, and the latest game was one where the ink of history ran deep.

Police horses lined the streets on a Friday night as Crystal Palace arrived in Charlton. From what she could gather, there'd been a history between the two clubs. Once upon a time, they'd been together in a relationship—sharing the same stadium in the 1980s, Selhurst Park, the home of Palace. As always, when such affairs end, those who feel most wronged can't let go. They can become obsessive to the point of blindness.

'Palace are toffs,' Lance insisted in a pub before the game. 'Opposite of Millwall who are chavs, fucking pikeys. Millwall invented the South Bermondsey breakfast to get them going in the morning.'

'What's a South Bermondsey breakfast?' she asked.

'Shotgunning,' Lance explained. 'Involves a hammer, a nail, and a can of super-strength lager. You pierce a hole in the can, tear off the ring pull, and then suck in the beer that's shooting out at high pressure.'

'Gets you drunk super fast,' Fergus added as they finished their pints, and he kissed her on the cheek with beer on his breath.

'Classy,' Katy thought, as the image stayed in her mind and they made their way towards the stadium under a setting autumn sun.

'Good crowd tonight,' Lance enacted a moment of mental arithmetic. 'Upwards of twenty thousand, like back in our Premier days.'

Mostly home fans drifting lazily through the streets. Wearing red. Badges that reminded her of Fergus's tattoo. She could see a giant version on the East Stand, where they'd take their seats for the game.

Police on horses stalked the slow parade of away supporters to the southern end of the ground, snaking along the road in a purple haze.

'You're only here for the Palace,' they taunted the home fans.

'You're only here for the holiday,' Charlton fans roared back.

'Tame compared to some London rivalries,' Lance enunciated. 'West Ham and Millwall's hardcore, going back over a hundred years.'

In 1926 the Trade Union Congress called a General Strike on behalf of coal miners. Working men from Thames to Tees went out on strike.

'There's a legend that a group of Millwall dockers crossed the picket line and broke the strike,' Lance explained, 'while the men from Thames Ironworks, birthplace of West Ham, stayed true to the cause. Even if not perfectly true, the tale's taken on Hollywood proportions. West Ham play the part o' good guys in every battle, and Millwall the scabs.'

His family had come from the island where the rivalry started. They'd owned a greyhound track and seen it all collapse because of a gangster's attack on a vulnerable woman in her own home. But in Lance's stories, these brutes took on the role of legend with morals not that far from football. She'd thought of that as they made their way to the ground and he carried on with tales of the time a hooligan crew from Leeds turned up on the Isle of Dogs for a rumble a hundred years after Millwall had crossed the

Thames.

Getting closer to the east side, the colours were thickening, deepening and congealing to a red dye, more homely, more welcoming than the opposition fans bound for the southern end of the stadium. You'd no real sense of danger here, handbags at twenty paces compared to West Ham and Millwall, or gangsters on the Isle of Dogs sorting out the Leeds fans.

'Bring it on,' Lance fisted the air. 'Let battle commence.'

In the sunshine, his hair shone golden and Fergus's gingery as Vincent Van Gogh's. Bright shades of hope followed them through the gates to where TV cameras faced out pitchside across a perfect green baize.

'Is this a library?' the away supporters sang with gusto and Katy wished it was a place of books as both teams came down the tunnel.

Then Charlton's club anthem of *Valley Floyd Road* drowned out the rival chanting until the game kicked off, with both sides cautious and cagey, picking up tension from the crowd. A whistle sounded and the game started, played out in gathering darkness framed in floodlights.

The visiting fans chanted 'eagles, eagles', and sang songs about red and blue, though they played in yellow, which she couldn't understand. Palace seemed faster and fitter, flowing forward in the opening minutes as Katy's eyes wandered to the men's physique and choice of shoe colours. The number 16, a boy called Zaha, moved with a dancer's learned grace.

'Boot him out of it, and stick in yer studs if needed,' a great barrel of a man roared from the seats behind, showering everyone in beery spittle.

'We hate you more than Brighton,' Charlton supporters projected their voices the full length of the pitch from the North Stand.

Unlike West Ham and Millwall this confused Katy as to whether it was Brighton hated Crystal Palace, or vice versa, or both these London sides hated the south coast town, as a place (?) or as a football team (?)

'Get the ball in the box,' Lance barked out instructions. 'Don't let these bastards boss us in our own backyard.'

Palace hadn't won at The Valley since 1968, mirroring Charlton's lack of success over Millwall, home or away, in the past two decades. This was a crucial battle for ownership over bragging rights in workplaces and cyberspace over the months ahead. Lance prayed, as his team's attackers preyed in enemy terrain, retreating empty handed every time.

Then, a cry of suffering—a short sharp stab of pain as if a shard of the floodlights or an edge of the Charlton dagger had plunged into the home crowd's hearts. Waves of noise ascended from the Palace end towards a starless sky, mirroring the shades of red and blue celebration. The visitors had scored, engulfing cyberspace, and the solid terrain of the ground in which there was suddenly nowhere to hide for the red army on the turf or in the stands. Lance's face burned in shame and anger. Fergus, she noticed, could never feel the same for he could not tattoo conversion out of his system. Fifty minutes on the scoreboard and Palace had the lead.

'Bastard,' Lance cursed the young man who'd scored.

'Crackin' goal though,' the convert offered more grace.

'Easy when your defenders seem to be on holiday.'

'Really?' Katy dared to crack a joke in the midst of Lance's anger, as the away supporters released flares in the Jimmy Seed Stand to celebrate. 'Does that mean the season's over so soon after it started?'

Everyone around her swore and grumbled, cursing back the clock, as she willed it forwards to a whistle bringing the battle to a close.

'It's just a game,' she wanted to tell the fans, as they grunted their way to a defeat they took as personally as a favoured pet's death.

Palace had won, with a stellar performance from Zaha their No 16. They'd leapfrogged Charlton in the table, erasing everything since 1968.

Afterwards they headed back to the pub, as police escorted the away supporters out of the southern end and down the road to the train station. Lance cursed the result for the entire length of their walk.

'At least,' she observed, 'the night was warm, for once.'

They should play football in the summer. March to October seemed the ideal time for a league to take place. That way, involuntary spectators, or those masochists who chose their suffering freely, wouldn't have to endure two hour spells of torture on afternoons hacked off the edge of an iceberg.

She was glad to have found an escape to the English coast, where even the wind coming in off the Channel was made pleasant by the scenery. Here on the islet there was a warm, safe glow. She could feel it now as the tides retreated, tugging at her heart and rumbling stomach.

But it hadn't just been football that caused the slow decay of her romance with Fergus. Meeting Wagner played more than its part. It was an afternoon after a morning of struggling against writer's block, when she had gone into a café facing out on the layers of the sea.

Stepping through the doorway she was greeted by a familiar series of sounds—custom, conversation, background music. Then, after the wave of noise, came layers of fragrance—roast beans, hot coffee, fresh baked bread. But then sound again as she scanned the menu and the voice came upon her suddenly. Coffee became flesh. 'Can I help you madam?'

She stirred. 'A flat white please, with no sugar.'

'Yeah, you seem sweet enough already.'

His dark lashes fluttered as he spoke, glittering as cormorants in water. *You can't say that to a customer*, she wanted to tell him. This is England, where you're not allowed to flirt, even for fun. They'd only met five minutes ago, and already this man made of coffee was breaking the rules.

'No,' she corrected herself. 'He's as much of a boy.'

Compared to her, perhaps he was. His features suggested youth—thin cheeks, sparkling eyes, and a grin full of arrogant mischief. Slim too, behind his uniform. At first she tried to ignore temptation by scanning pictures.

'Here you are,' he snapped her away from images of coffee beans grown in faraway places. 'One perfect flat white, madam.'

'You're confident,' she struck back at his flirtation.

Shrugging his shoulders, he wiped his smooth hands on a towel. 'Where I come from, we get a taste for good coffee from an early age. Back there, we grew our own on farms with miles and miles of coffee trees.'

Coffee trees echoed on the tip of Katy's tongue.

'Yes. You seem surprised by that.'

'What makes you think I'm surprised?'

'The light in your eyes that turned so blue.'

Could he see through her, and sense the warm glow she suddenly felt?

The lyric of his voice was a hot trickle of coffee on her fingertips. His words, like a shot of caffeine, awakened something in her she'd long forgotten or abandoned—a deeper curiosity to know this random stranger.

'I never thought of coffee growing on trees, that's all.'

'Some day you should go there, and take a walk through the farms, and see the sweat that goes into creating one cup of red berries that wakes you up in the morning and keeps you going for the day.'

'I'm already there,' she thought.

She was walking into daydreams deep in the shadow of Africa's mountains, imagining coffee trees as tobacco brown with white blossom. Breathing in fragrances of flowering plants and sun-scorched soil, feeling tingles of heat from the cup in her fingers, she wanted to reach out and touch the polished wood standing before her, here and in her dreams.

Then, seeing another customer advance towards the

counter, she took leave of coffee trees, and stepped back into reality. She already had a lover, waiting for her at home, on the other side of a train ride, and this man was no more than a random stranger with an enchanting voice.

Probably he played out this role with every woman who walked through these doors, conquering their hearts to dilute his boredom.

'Thanks,' she said, when he finally passed her change.

'Have a good day,' declared the young barista, with the parting shot of eyes that set fire to her subconscious, 'and there's a library down on Guildford Lawn if you don't believe me about the coffee trees.'

'Maybe you can teach me some time.' Jesus Christ, Mohammed, Buddha, and Virgin Mary—the words came out so reckless and unplanned.

'When the day's work is done?'

Not answering, she found the safety of a seat. There she sipped her coffee, looking out on the marina, as *he* teased fresh targets at the counter. Even from a distance as she tried to concentrate on the boats, his voice was awakening dissonance in a town normally so routine, the only thing that struck the senses sharply was dead seaweed on the shore. She was in a relationship with Fergus, and not on the lookout for another romance.

That afternoon, she left Wagner a tip and went out without saying goodbye, tracing a path to Guildford Lawn. Suddenly narrow streets blazed in colour. Fifteen degrees of glorious sunshine shimmered on the calligraphy of shops, pubs, and houses, but she could sense nothing except the sting of the barista's voice. His words had become an aphrodisiac, and a GIF file embedded in her cerebral cortex, torturous as swimming nude in a sea of nettles. Why was this happening? Strolling the seafront, she wanted to shake the barista's voice out of her mind, and return to a sense of calm.

But at the same time she wanted to take that GIF file, and use it as the cure to rub against the sudden ache deep down in her being. She would rub it there until it stang more, and then the sting went away.

On the path across Guildford Lawn, she had brushed against thoughts of being in the library after dark, listening to his stories of coffee trees—swimming against shots of histamine through her thighs.

She could feel blisters forming, the sting spreading— creeping upwards to where it became a terrible itch, for which she craved the cool massage of a dock leaf, a dandelion, ice cream, ice cubes, anything that would stop the swirling intoxication of her senses.

Approaching the library, she told herself that she must forget this fire. But she found traces of flames there too. A small plaque depicted a tale from one of Ramsgate's darkest days. On Friday thirteenth August 2004, a suspected arson attack reduced the town's library to a blazing shell.

'Forget fire,' she fought to control her desires.

Inside the library she found another volume of Van Gogh's letters. Choosing one from April 1876 she began to read of an afternoon visit to an inlet of the sea down the shore from Ramsgate. Hearing Vincent's descriptions of the place, she wanted to walk there too. But already the visit in her head was not with Fergus. The more she tried to think of water, the greater the force of fire in her skull.

Her mind drifted back to an image of a library burning, and the pattern by which flame devours a book. Inks melt and pages bend, one by one, pushing inwards on the spine until there's nothing left but a pool of ash. Imagine the horror of hundreds of books, thousands of texts, consumed in flames, devoured and destroyed in a matter of minutes.

Suddenly her brain hurt so much she could no longer see the words written by her favourite artist on a late April day a century before she came into the world. Wanting to escape these images of burning books, she ran outside— seeking safety on Ramsgate's shore, where she'd be free from fire. But then, out of the distant shape of surfers, something else burned her eyes.

Standing at full height with waves covering the bottom half of his body, Wagner appeared. He caught her eye, dropped down off his board, and slid his body towards the shore. Seconds later he was within reach, dripping inks from the ocean into the sand. Letting her eyes stray, she was submitting to the flames, sinking deeper into a haze of desire.

That night when she went home, she found herself in a fever—a malady, a frantic desire to keep busy, and so she began baking a cake; to be given as a simple gesture of their friendship, and nothing more.

Wagner's voice had sparked the return of something she didn't know was missing—romance; the fragrance of love letters for her attention alone, and the satisfaction of bundling her emotions into one perfect cake.

That was the final whistle in her romance with Fergus.

11. Cool Customer

On Saturday morning after another training session, Fergus reached a decision regarding the tattoo studio that had given birth to his badge. He'd go there and see Dyana to satisfy his curiosity of how she was getting on. Besides, he wanted some female company and if Katy could enjoy a taste of the exotic then he could drink from the very same cup.

'*Dark River Dye,*' he read the name above the door.

Standing there, a sense of trepidation returned. Shoot-out kind of trepidation, the nerves of a girl with no boots taking a last minute penalty. Through the window he could see the artist with her back turned, preparing her tools in the morning light. She flooded his mind in memories of a rainy day, Hull City, Betty Boop, and the shivery feel of tattoo needles. He was on the edge of being either Clive Mendonca or Michael Gray.

Suddenly, she turned and her eyes caught his through the glass. He froze unexpectedly, like a faulty rabbit on a dog track. Dreadlocks whipped the sides of her face. She'd changed hairstyles. Everything else remained the same—even the Millwall devil with his eyes upon Betty's breasts.

'Hi,' he said, as he entered the studio.

'What can I do for you?' she asked, without a flicker of recognition at first. Then she smiled. 'Wait, I remember you now, the guy who got a Charlton tattoo, who was so much afraid of needles at the start.'

'And you're the girl who follows Tottenham.'

She laughed. 'Nobody's called me a girl for a long time, nearly as long as since Tottenham last won the FA Cup, beating Nottingham Forest.'

'You know your football,' Fergus edged closer.

'For a woman?' she met his gaze with hers.

He wasn't going to venture down that road. 'For an artist.'

'So what can I do for you?' she asked nervously, and then carried on speaking before he had a chance to answer. 'Ah, now I remember. Your session was on a rainy day, thunder and lightning.' She pulled a dreadlock across her lips. 'I remember faces and tattoos, not names.'

'Fergus,' he rekindled the memories behind her green eyes.

'So Fergus, Charlton Man, are you after a second tattoo?'

'No,' he shook his head. 'Once was enough for me.'

'That bad?' she furrowed her brow.

'Just have no reason for a second, not yet anyhow.'

'You've not come for a removal?' Dyana raised her eyes to the ceiling. 'Changed teams or heard rumours you're merging with Palace?'

Again he shook his head. 'No, it's nothing that dramatic.'

'What then?' her pupils blazed. 'I'm intrigued.'

He liked the sound of that word. Standing before him, Dyana assumed the living form of *intrigue*, originally from French, meaning to plot or deceive. Maybe he was engaging in trickery too, using her to forget Katy.

'I want to ask you out,' Fergus proposed suddenly, forcefully.

'Sorry?' she seemed surprised, shielded behind machines.

He hadn't known that brown people could blush.

'I want to ask you out,' he repeated.

'This is London,' she composed herself. 'You don't just walk into a stranger's studio and say that. It's not how things are done.'

'Why?' he probed. 'Isn't that more natural than speed dating or signing up to a website like *Guardian Soulmates*? Would you rather we created profiles where we list out our hobbies, and search the dictionary for original adjectives to find that there's very few left? And then when that's done, we get pictures from five years ago and create pseudonyms.'

That's what Katy's friends did. Always jumping from lover to lover, because they could never settle on any one person. In their twenties, they'd enjoyed a glorious time. Come the thirties, they struggled.

'Aren't some women like wine?' Dyana asked. 'Better with age?'

Her face had shifted back to its original shade. She wasn't going to make this an easy conquest, if she allowed it to become that at all.

'You could be Miss Inky Fingers,' he suggested.

'Miss Inky Fingers, I like that,' she pulled a dreadlock back across her lips. 'And what would your profile be, Mister Charlton Man?'

'Why don't we discuss that over a drink in The Dictionary?'

'What'll we sip, a cocktail of words?' she wondered, and then loosened, stepping forward from the protective shield of machines.

'Yeah, I'm sure they can whip you up a cocktail.'

He'd sparked interest. 'Where is this Dictionary?'

'Down in Woolwich,' Fergus mapped the direction.

'Why there?' she wondered. 'And why now?'

'I live close by,' he answered the opening question first. 'And it's getting towards the end of the season. I've been thinking about you again.'

'I thought about you too sometimes,' she admitted. 'It's hard not to think of Charlton on match days when the whole streets turn red.'

'Do you wear the other team's colours every week?' he readied to ask, but before the words came out another customer had entered.

'Take my card Fergus,' Dyana spoke quickly. 'It's got my number.'

'I'll call and arrange a time,' he promised, 'to continue the intrigue.'

Stepping outside, Fergus felt a fierce consciousness of the day's colours. This wasn't black and amber in the rain, a wet tiger moving through a steaming forest. Instead, a blue canopy covered Charlton's scruffy streets.

He decided to take a walk down the emptiness of Floyd Road, humming a Paul McCartney song. Mull of Kintyre, the shadow you can see from Ireland's north coast. Once upon a time, the roads of Ireland had been all he'd ever thought of travelling. When you're a child you don't imagine you're going to spend your life away from the land of your birth.

Emigration is for other people, long gone, faces in photograph albums whose lives away from Ireland never seem quite real. But the road of life never turns out exactly as we plan. He'd stolen a car and gone on a joyride.

Then—a crash upon the beach, and the cold sea of moonshine impassive. Thrown forward, expecting death, he knew the joyride had come to an end. The girl beside him, dead—though he didn't know at first.

'Forget that road,' Fergus ordered his mind.

This was his new home, his new station, and he had to make the most of it. He'd walk down to The Valley and get his ticket for the next football season, even if this one wasn't quite finished. Officially, it wouldn't end until the final whistle of the play off between Palace and Watford on Bank Holiday Monday just over a week away. Promotion to the Premier League offered a generous reward to the winners—120 million quid.

Charlton would remain in the second tier, the forgotten lower divisions of English football, as the gap increased between rich and poor. Some day they'd go the American sports' way, and close the borders to all but the rich.

Moving along the sweep of Floyd Road, he thought of this as he edged towards the stadium. At the North Wall he stood beneath a giant replica of the club badge, identical to the tattoo Dyana had inked upon his arm and into his blood. Katy used to accuse men of wasting their lives, their thoughts, and their emotions upon football. Standing here, in the shadow of The Valley, he begged to differ. This had become the one form of constancy in his life, the thing that kept him going week to week.

Approaching the ticket desk, he was more than a consumer, more than a customer. He was putting the seal on another year's connection to this football club he'd adopted as his own, nine months of the calendar, forty six games a season in sunshine and in hail, victory and defeat.

'I want to renew,' he nailed his colours to the mast for another year.

This was his club and nothing could ever take that away from him. After all, it had earned him a date with the hottest ink-gun artist in town.

12. Dictionary Date

*F*rom teaching young people, Fergus had learned that you have to move fast in London. It's not a place that operates to the same rhythm as Ireland or the seaside to which Katy had retreated. Formula One speed. Premier League pace. This was a place with Etihads on every corner. Only a space for winners, guys sharp as Sergio Aguero.

'Like a fucking jungle,' his basketball class told him.

Fergus took the sports classes in a Foundation College that was first set up to help disadvantaged kids take a first step into employment. These days it had moved towards degrees because that's where the money was, and like everything else in London, education was all about money now.

In London's jungle, a man needed to pounce quickly. Aside from Katy, he'd never dated anybody in this city and wasn't sure he knew the rules. Maybe in some ways that helped him with *Miss Inky Fingers*.

'Chasing a hot bird like that, you're going to have

serious competition,' Lance played the part of counsellor in the bars of Greenwich. 'She's probably got her pick of guys, and if not then you have to ask why not?'

'So you think she's going to like this Dictionary?'

'Doesn't matter if it's the Dictionary or the Dog N' Bone,' his friend carried on with the lessons of somebody homegrown in London seduction. 'You have to know how to strike before the ink's dry.'

That was the part Fergus had never been good at. When it came to women, he was more of a Chris Powell than an Aguero. The steady guy at the back who might not score often but when he does it's spectacular.

'Don't try too hard,' Lance warned. 'And don't look nervous, or the last of the gangsters are going to think you're an undercover cop, and they don't like that sort coming into their pub. Like my cousin Timmy used to say, you'll never find a Blind Beggar anywhere on the south side of the river.'

That name earned notoriety in March 1966, a couple of months before England hosted the World Cup. Ronnie Kray walked into The Blind Beggar pub on Mile End Road and shot George Cornell from the Richardson Gang straight through the skull. Afterwards the killer turned around and walked out, calm as you like, certain nobody would grass. You never ratted on one of your own breed. But the cops refused to play by the rules of the old school. Nipper Read, Chief Super of the Met's Murder Squad, found a barmaid who'd give evidence against the gangsters, and bring down the Krays.

'Something changed that day,' Lance said.

'The life o' the guy who died,' Fergus joked.

'More than that. The way business got done.'

Plenty of business had been conducted in The Dictionary down through the years from police activity to deals brokered with bent politicians. According to Lance, the place earned its name because it was always where gangsters went to have words with each other. Located on the waterfront at Woolwich, this century-old pub offered a prime meridian between the various gangs on each side of the river, back in the old days.

Looking at it from the outside, it seemed no hub of gangster activity.

'Don't judge a book by its cover,' Lance had warned him the night before. 'Those old guys you'll see lined up on barstools were probably henchmen and gangsters once upon a time. You'd get some great stories about the old ways outa them for a price of a pint. If they've Millwall tattoos they might have served with the Richardson crew.'

'Maybe they went to Dyana for a blue devil,' Fergus thought as he made his way to up to the entrance down a narrow sidestreet between the grand architecture of the old Town Hall and the river.

Then there it stood—The Dictionary—on a watery shelf. Historically an old man's boozer, a spit and sawdust pub, Fergus detected creeping gentrification in the décor, the clientele, and the food on offer.

Sure, some of the last remaining old men on stools had West Ham or Millwall tattoos alongside Saint George's crosses and English bulldogs. Maybe they remained gangsters in their own minds but London's crime business had long since changed beyond recognition. The focus had shifted from scrapyards and slot machines to corporate and cyber crime.

'Meet you there at seven,' he'd texted Dyana.

She'd agreed, though the appointment had been made faster than she'd expected. She had something to do, though didn't specify what it was.

Moving towards the bar he could see a sign advertising a live showing of the play off final between Crystal Palace and Watford, as a foxy young barmaid served pints of ale in personalised tankards to the men on stools.

The girl's name was Jiss, according to the demands of those barrel-bellied men. 'Go Jiss, give us another couple o' pints.'

Jiss was no more than in her high teens, dark headed and tattooed in several places, as most of working class London seemed to be. Fergus studied the blaze of kanji on her backbones, as she pulled the pint that he ordered, took his money, and said *fanks* in the Cockney vernacular.

One evening, Katy had traced out the story of the working class London accent, and how it was spreading outwards into the rest of the country, becoming a subliminal badge of pride.

'Vomit,' he forced his mind to forget his former lover.

Waiting on Dyana, he needed to think of something else to pass the time—perhaps Lance's story of what happened in the aftermath of Vivaldi. He'd gone on the run for weeks after his attack on The Brown Marilyn.

Then he resurfaced in the midst of an ongoing feud between the Asians and the owners of the greyhound track savagely burned to the ground. Lance's cousin Timmy had sent his men out on a freezing New Year's Eve to intercept a drugs shipment from Amsterdam to the coast of Essex. Nobody got hurt but the Asian boys had to watch as Timmy's henchmen emptied twenty grand's worth of ecstasy tablets into the Thames Estuary.

'Things were going to get very dirty,' Lance said, 'unless they found the man who had spilled the first blood in this feud. By good luck he turned up again this side o' the river, drinking himself stupid one afternoon.'

Bitterly cold January day, knocking back tequilas at the bar.

'Timmy found him and knew something had to be done.'

Normally in such situations a henchman might expect to end up as fish food in the Thames, Lance explained, but the burning of the greyhound track changed the equation. The crazy thing was that Timmy knew the Asian boys. They'd grown up together, chased girls together, raced cars, got drunk, and even worked on deals to one another's mutual benefit. Take any one of them out of the crowd alone over a beer or a joint, everything would all be okay. But with the woman and then the drugs, this had got too big and too hostile. He had to speak to the group and ask them to name their price. When he found the Henchman, babbling and saliverating at the bar, he called them.

'Blood for blood,' they laid out the terms directly.

Those were tense times on the island and in the country as a whole. Britain, and its working classes, had just started coming to terms with the changes to the ethnic fabric of their society.

The Henchman could have started a race war on the island, just because of a stereo and a smacked-up whore next door.

The punishment had to be enough to meet the crime, so that the feud came to an end there and then, with each side satisfied.

Timmy agreed, and drove the Henchman to an old timber yard along Millwall docks, where his family first started out in business.

According to Lance, Timmy drove like a man who knew he was dying and cruising the streets of his life before he never sees them again.

'All the time in the back seat the old Henchman kept blubbering.'

'What did your cousin do to him?' Fergus asked.

Lance had feigned a toff's accent as he described what happened next. 'The judge said that it was the most barbaric case he had ever seen on the British mainland, a method of torture imported from Ireland.'

'Kneecapping,' Fergus gritted his teeth.

Lance glanced down at his own leg as he answered. 'Yeah, a double kneecapping through the front rather than the back so as to inflict the most possible damage, leaving the fucker on crutches for the rest of his life.'

Fergus made a guess. 'The guy turned informer?'

That was what brought down the once-invincible Krays in the end. Happens to most gangsters sooner or later, everywhere in the world.

'Fucker turned canary but it was the police sought out Vivaldi's Henchman, and not vice versa,' Lance lamented. 'The times they were a changin'. The network of secrets was long gone.'

He stopped talking then, pausing for a few seconds before continuing, like this terrain of his family history remained a hard one to cross. Maybe just as hard as remembering Afghanistan when he stumbled upon a landmine, knowing that everything was going to change afterwards.

Finally he composed his emotions, and then his voice.

'This wasn't the island of the old days. It was a steel fortress made for bankers and yuppies. Timmy, always the hothead in the family, had carried out the kneecapping right under the gaze of CCTV cameras.'

'Without a mask I'm guessing.'

'Yeah,' Lance admitted.

'So what happened Timmy?'

'He went down for five years and that was truly the end of the family business. By the time he got out, all had changed on the island.'

Fergus had looked down on his tattoo, with a thought he didn't voice. 'Those who live by the sword really do fall on the blade in the end.'

'At least things turned out well for the old Henchman,' Lance growled. 'Spent the rest of his days under witness protection.'

'Hopefully soundproofed,' Fergus joked.

But it was no laughing matter for Lance. 'Timmy should ha' just pushed him drunk into the city's biggest graveyard.'

'What did Timmy do when he got out?' Fergus changed tack.

'Got into cars and headed out to the coast of Essex,' Lance explained. 'These days he runs a legit business, and I hardly ever see him. After I came back from Afghanistan he wanted me to go work for him. But it was too far from Charlton, and I'd miss my views across to the old island.'

Fergus was remembering this, when a woman's footsteps signalled a surprise arrival. He caught the sound of respectably mid-sized heels clicking on tiles, and then the sight of a woman's toned calves crisscrossed in leather straps with golden buckles. Heads turned, away from Jiss.

The young barmaid's eyes burned. Arms and shoulders tightened, fingers pausing their act of pumping out London bitter.

'Who's the 'ot black bird?' a man with Millwall tattoos mumbled.

'Dyana,' Fergus whispered, as she walked into the bar.

Sometimes even men in different jerseys have the same tastes.

13. New Cross Rose

$\mathcal{S}$oon as Dyana entered *The Dictionary* she seemed in a strange mood, different to the woman who'd hummed as she inked images of Japanese calligraphy onto a human canvas. Prickly. A rose dressed in red, armoured in thorns. She had bright red lipstick too, almost purple. That gave her face a heavy appearance to match the weight in her green eyes and the bags beneath them, from a lack of sleep.

'What do you want to drink?' Fergus edged towards her.

She didn't care. 'Anything. Bitter or sweet, doesn't matter.'

'Vodka and lemon,' he proposed, and she nodded.

Miss Inky Fingers didn't match the Charlton Man's expectations. Crossing to the bar, he watched her in the mirror as she took her seat. Waiting on Jiss he read the advert for the Crystal Palace game again.

Maybe he'd ask Dyana if their supporters had started

turning up for tattoos to mark the event. He imagined them in the days before the match—ordering one that said *Championship Play Off Winners 2013*.

Then he pictured the embarrassment a defeat would bring.

'They deserve that,' he thought. 'A tattoo for their arrogance.'

Finally he caught the attention of Jiss who served him. Then he brought the drinks back to the table where Dyana sat with head dipped towards the light of a mobile phone, beneath pictures of olden day Woolwich.

Some of the pictures featured a place known as the Dusthole, an area of slum housing where many Irish had lived. Another was of a birdseller's store on the High Street. Frozen in the sepia haze of time, a couple of men stood guard over grilled capsules for poultry and cages of songbirds waiting on a new home. They all seemed sad, and Dyana the very same.

'Don't you like the place?' Fergus pierced her silence.

She wet her lips. 'Same as any other pub.'

'This used to be a haunt for gangsters,' he fought to spark her interest. 'My friend Lance has some great stories.'

'Maybe now's not the best time to tell them.'

What did she want? What did she expect? He couldn't figure this out as she sat gripping her vodka glass tightly in a set of red talons, seeming like a wounded bird from one of the pictures on the walls above her.

Feeling discomfort, his mind drifted again to Charlton's season just passed and the Wolves that came between him and Katy. Then suddenly Dyana spoke as his thoughts veered towards Selhurst, and a crawling king snake making its way north west to Wembley.

'Growing up in New Cross we had boy gangsters, not old men.'

He leaned in cautiously towards the scent of lemon. 'Okay.'

'They make sure you know they're boys too.' He detected a hint of sarcasm in her voice. 'We had the Ghetto Boys from the estates where I grew up and the Peckham Boys further out. Bad boys, my mother said.'

'You've the Woolwich Boys around here,' he mapped the local turf. 'Then Cherry Boys in Charlton and T-Block over in Thamesmead.'

'They should call themselves the mortuary boys,' she suggested. 'Maybe the casualty boys, A & E boys, coz that's where they end up.'

Wanting to snap her out of this grave seriousness, Fergus wished he could direct the conversation to those imaginary Crystal Palace tattoos. But she was far gone, deep in thoughts of London's ultra-violent youth.

Why was she behaving this way, he wondered—making time drag in a place where you were conscious of history's frightening speed. The end of gangster days, and a time when Woolwich fed from the feast of Empire.

Up at the counter men with Millwall tattoos talked of olden days as Jiss, the young barmaid, fuelled their memories with fresh bitter. Some of them might have been here on the night that Lance's cousin Timmy found Vivaldi's Henchman drunk and escorted him to the docks for a kneecapping. But Fergus hadn't come here tonight for legends such as that. He'd arranged this date to know Dyana better, and see where things went from there.

'You've been worried all night. What's wrong?'

'Let's go outside for a walk,' she finally proposed.

'Sure,' he washed down his pint and rose up.

'Fanks,' Jiss called out from the bar as they left.

Outside the night felt cool and moist in the freshness of spring. Trees in full bloom climbed the side streets away from a broad central square with a giant television screen, around which groups of people clustered.

'This place has been reborn since the 2011 riots,' Fergus looked out across streets resurrected since those fires two years before.

'Yeah,' Dyana dipped her green eyes to the ground.

Her heart ought to have been full of spring's gladness, Fergus thought. Yet she seemed far away from her surroundings, focusing on grey concrete, and not the signs of rebirth on the streets of Woolwich.

'So what's wrong?' he resumed his investigation.

'I was at a funeral today,' she spoke suddenly.

'Oh,' he wanted to reach out but sensed thorns again. 'Sorry, you could have said and we'd have postponed the meeting.'

'I needed to get out for fresh air,' she answered. 'It was hot and griefy inside the Gospel Church, down on the New Cross Road.'

He asked the hard question. 'Was it a friend of yours?'

'Yes,' she gazed straight ahead, drifting towards the riverside.

Dyana's voice bristled with emotion as she started a slow description of the service. Small and plain Church dominated by a shiny black coffin resting peacefully at the altar. Inside, sounds of sobbing and an immense wave of song shaking the bones of the building and the hearts of the congregation. Outside, a carriage dark as the coffin drawn by a couple of white horses standing perfectly still against the endless rush of traffic.

'The New Cross Road never stops,' she spoke sadly. 'All through the service, you could hear the cruel sound of life moving on.'

He knew the road. Not far from Millwall's ground, and Goldsmiths University specialising in Arts and Social Sciences. Crossroads of cultures, home to all the races of the world, a Noah's Ark in the middle of London. Student pubs, hair salons, bedsits, and bakeries. He could imagine Dyana's chocolate flesh set against the fragrance of patties and fish pepper soup.

'Been there a few times for a drink with Lance.'

'Some people went to a pub after the cremation.'

'Never been to a cremation. Only funerals.'

'He wanted his ashes scattered over the Thames,' Dyana sniffled as she spoke in a moment of thorns drawing back and petals opening out. 'There's me thinking, what the hell was the point in doing all that ink work.'

'So this guy was one of your customers then?'

Again her guard came up. 'Sort of.'

'Somebody from the gangs?'

'Never,' she answered sharply, as they approached the Royal Arsenal Gatehouse perched like a tower above the river. 'He hated seeing *our* communities tear themselves apart.'

Fergus could tell that she cared for the deceased man. He felt a sting of jealousy. Perhaps they'd been close friends, or even lovers.

'So what was the story with this guy then?'

She stayed silent, gazing out across their immediate surroundings. Maybe he'd pushed too far, too soon.

'We all wear masks in our lives,' Dyana spoke as cryptically as Katy. 'From gang members to gospel preachers we all put on a show, and most of the time we don't even know the real people behind their masks.'

He could see a tear forming in the corner of her eye, transformed to a vesicle of orange when she turned her head towards a streetlamp.

'This boy, behind the mask, was called Demetrius.'

Fergus tried to put a face to the figure. Black guy, tattooed.

'We grew up on the same estate,' Dyana bared some more of her petals. 'He was a little boy when I was a teenage girl dating his cousin.'

'So he's younger than you then?' Fergus felt relieved.

'Yeah, by about seven or eight years,' she answered, and then moved back to her own narrative. 'He grew up to be a musician not quite as famous as guys like Dizzee Rascal, and Danny Weed, but good all the same.'

'The girls on my football team talk about those guys.'

They had reached the riverside, and a series of

apartments advertised without irony as *'village living in the heart of London'*. There were no dustholes in 21st century Woolwich. Once upon a time it was the poor they pushed towards the river, out of sight, away from the industrial heartland. Nowadays it was the rental-rich, and the radical chic.

'Demetrius was never going to own anything like this, or even want to,' Dyana pointed towards penthouses with panoramic views.

Fergus gazed up at the barricaded towers. 'You'd have to be a Premier League footballer, or a merchant banker to afford these babies!'

Dyana turned her head away from the wealth along the waterside. 'Demetrius was happiest in the estate where he grew up. Even if he was no saint, his music was about helping others and promoting causes.'

'What causes?' Fergus sniffed for answers.

'Anything that allowed him to fight authority,' she laughed.

'You make it sound so...' He wrestled for a word. 'Intriguing.'

'Demetrius was an intriguing kind of guy in his lifetime.'

Fergus sensed a deeper story in the way she dipped her head, and caused the dreadlocks to fall; forming a beaded doorway across her face.

'He'd been doing stuff connected to those migrants in Calais,' she paused below the sparkling lights of penthouse balconies. 'He was working on a new album, playing with the ideas of the camps as a jungle, drawing on characters from Rudyard Kipling's Jungle book.'

'There's one that rolls back the years!'

'He was going to take a small boy and trace his path out of a Himalayan village to England, dreaming of Peter Pan and Paddington Bear, characters he knows from stories his mother told him in Nepal.'

'Not what you'd normally expect from grime music!'

'He'd a thing about the breakdown of expectation,' Dyana pointed out. 'Growing up in the estates, seeing people die, left him that way.'

'And so the kid's dream dies too in the camp at Calais?'

'I don't know,' she admitted. 'He never got finished.'

Fergus imagined a child, somewhere in a song, trapped behind razor wire waiting for the dead artist to come and write the ending he'd expected.

'How did he die?' he broached a taxing question.

'Gunned down in the street in Deptford,' she explained, 'while he was on his way home from a radio interview in Brockley.'

'Jesus!' Fergus exclaimed, stopping dead in his tracks.

'Funny you should say that,' Dyana whispered into the night.

'Why's that funny?' Fergus searched her doleful eyes.

'You'll see when I show you the story,' she whispered. 'I keep a press cutting in my handbag as if it's a part of him, like his ashes.'

Maybe there was something more between them than simply a childhood friendship and the fact of his being a customer in her studio. Perhaps in that place of ink and addiction, it was more than her needles had brushed against his flesh and filled him with an injection of sensation.

'I'd like to see his picture,' Fergus proposed suddenly.

'You will,' she answered. 'It's in the article.'

'That might complete the puzzle,' he reckoned.

But something else had caught Dyana's attention.

'Look where I'm standing,' the Tottenham girl laughed.

They'd stepped close to the spot where football's most famous migrants came into being, in a square beneath the last remaining arch of an armaments workshop. A small sculpture and plaque with a potted history marked the location of Arsenal's birth amidst the furnaces and factories that had fed an Empire from Korea to the Crimea.

'Twenty years later they crossed the river to Highbury,' Fergus told his New Cross Rose. 'Moving on to bigger things, they forgot their roots.'

'Demetrius never did,' Dyana brought the musician back into focus. 'Let's go inside the pub and I'll show you his story.'

14. Holy Evening

Above their table, board games rested on a shelf.

'Scrabble,' Dyana said. 'That's funny.'

'Yes, after coming from The Dictionary.'

'Maybe we can play some other time,' she dipped her head and took a first sip from the cocktail he'd just bought her.

'You're not in the mood for it tonight?'

'Brain's too tired for Scrabble,' she answered.

'Snakes and ladders?' he reached for the shelf.

She caught his elbow. 'No games tonight.'

Fergus again sensed the presence of a wounded heart. Bruised heart. Like a fire gone cold after the energy of the church service.

'So what's in this article you told me about?'

He took a cold sip of his pint and waited for her to respond.

'The story of Demetrius,' she reached towards her handbag.

Fergus watched the slow movement of her red nails across the clasp, remembering their ticklish touch on the day of his tattoo. He shivered, as she burrowed through a compendium of objects in her bag.

Finally she produced a page from a newspaper, folded neat as origami.

'You might recognise his stage name,' she opened the news cutting, slow and gentle as the unfolding of a paper crane.

Then she shivered as her eyes surveyed the face of a young man.

'It's from a record cover. On the edge of Woolwich.'

'The old skate park by the Thames,' Fergus recognised.

Leaning in, he caught sight of an ordinary young man looking out across a river that bent in two directions towards a twin landscape of barriers. One side had silver shells, holding back the tides. The other had towers, the territory of T-Block. Follow the river in their direction, and you find the marina from Stanley Kubrick's *Clockwork Orange*.

'Is it saying he's caught between different gangs?'

She shook her head. 'He's not saying anything at all.'

Sure enough, the kid had a silent aura. Nothing to say, nothing to do. Dyana traced out a line with her talons towards a ferry terminal. She paused, drinking in the view of her young friend with braided hair.

He looked peaceful and reflective, but angry at the same time.

'The song's about his generation,' she touched the boy's face. 'They're waiting for a ferry that never comes as chances pass them by.'

'Can I read what it says underneath?' Fergus probed.

'Sure,' their fingers touched as she passed him the cutting.

Now, he could see a second picture in the middle of the article. Everything appeared orderly and regular at first. Then an image screamed from the centre of the page, smudged and tear-stained. Suddenly, he could see why she'd been so sorrowful back in The Dictionary.

-YOUNG MAN LYING DEAD ON A HIGH STREET-

Market stalls stood nearby. Shoppers looked on, as smokers peeped from pub doorways. Double decker buses moved in a red blur in the background. Life carried on in London, despite the immediacy of death.

Fergus read the headline, so slowly aloud that each word in the sentence carried its weight like a curtain hook.

'Jesus Christ Dead In the Cross.'

'That was his stage name, his way of sticking two fingers up at authority,' Dyana interjected, 'but he's always Demetrius to me.'

'Think I've heard the name before,' Fergus laughed.

She touched his arm again. 'Don't make a joke of this.'

He moved his eyes across the press cutting. The subheading stood out in bold black print, half the size of the main headline.

'Young musician gunned down on the streets of London.'

He'd been walking back from a radio interview in a place called Brockley, childhood home of Charlton striker Bradley Wright-Phillips.

'Day of the Wolverhampton Wanderers game,' Fergus realised.

London's April sunshine had been golden as the shirts of Charlton's visitors. He'd been on his way home from Ramsgate. Hold ups on the New Cross Road, observed on a train from London Bridge.

'Strolling through the spring sunshine he approached Deptford, with its market in full swing, the last relic of a tradition going back centuries.'

Once home to dockyards and abattoirs, Deptford had seen better days.

'Here, in May 1593, the playwright Christopher Marlowe died.'

Like the young musician who took on the name of Jesus Christ, Christopher Marlowe had been an irreverent figure of his time.

Agents of government had been implicated in his death, which still remained a mystery. Four centuries and a score later, fresh mystery shrouded Deptford's markets. 'The controversial musician angered many within his own community and the wider world with his contentious choice of name.'

'Controversial and contentious,' Dyana whispered disdain. 'It's like they're already telling you he's done something to deserve this.'

Fergus kept reading. 'He had just crossed into Deptford's main drag when a hooded gunman stepped out from behind a butcher's stall, and opened fire. Somebody walked out of the shadows, in broad daylight, pulled a trigger and caused the death of an urban artist, 420 years after Christopher Marlowe fell in these same streets.'

Three shots, the reporter said. One straight through the heart.

'The assassin knew what he was doing,' Fergus assumed.

'Yes,' Dyana's soft voice raged.

'Somebody told me that the word assassin comes from Arabic,' Fergus lifted his eyes from the page. 'From a group of killers known as hash-eaters.'

'Whoever shot Demetrius wasn't stoned. This was clinical. There's even rumours of a getaway car waiting for the gunman in Greenwich.'

'Just as they were escaping I'd have been at the game.'

'Wolverhampton Wanderers,' Dyana recalled. 'I know because it was just before the match that I got a phone call from a friend. She said there was rumours that Demetrius had been shot. They blamed gangs at the start.'

'How do you know it wasn't gangs?' Fergus asked.

'This was professional,' Dyana insisted. 'Not Boys.'

She paused, as he handed her back the press cutting.

She folded it gently. Then slipped it back into her bag like a precious banknote.

'When I heard the news, the pain pierced me right through, like a needle going into both nipples at the same time and heading for the heart.'

Fergus grimaced, recalling the flash of a pierced nipple.

'Right there, my whole body felt the pain of a thousand piercings,' she touched her chest as she spoke. 'Everywhere imaginable.'

Fergus wanted to reach out and caress her pain, in every single part. 'Have they any idea who might have murdered him, and why?'

'Maybe, like Marlowe, somebody wanted him dead.'

'Why would anybody want a musician dead?'

'He was astute. He could speak two languages.'

'What languages?' Fergus wanted to know.

'Street talk and smart talk,' she surprised him.

Then she explained that he could go from Dizzee Rascal to Derek Walcott in the same breath. Proud of his roots, he'd quote literature in his songs. He wanted to be the voice of a new generation, kids of all colours fighting for some stake in this society. He'd been educated, and completed a Media degree in the University of Westminster, first in his family to do that.

He'd even appeared at a debate in the Houses of Parliament, discussing lack of black and ethnic minority participation in politics.

'Sounds like a decent kid,' Fergus sensed her admiration.

'He was, and he was proud of where he came from.'

'That's important. I'm proud of Ireland too.'

Dyana smiled and paused then, to have another sip of her drink.

'He stayed at home in the streets where he grew up, while everyone else who makes it big catches the first train out o' there. Everybody successful forgets their roots. But Demetrius stayed in a high rise looking out towards

Deptford Creek, and died on his own turf.'

'Sounds like somebody I'd like to have introduced to my girls.'

Dyana raised her voice in sudden surprise. 'Your girls?'

'My football team,' he explained and she laughed.

'I'm going to find out exactly who killed him,' her fingers tightened on the stem of the cocktail glass, close to empty. Darkness gathered on the square as the young professionals dined, alfresco style, unaware of gangs, guns and grime. 'I'm going to that radio station tomorrow, and I'm going to listen to every word of his last interview for any clues.'

'If I can help in any way let me know.'

'You can get me another vodka and lemon.'

She sounded thirsty for escape from her grief.

'Okay,' he made her a promise. 'We'll make this evening by the river in Woolwich as good as any night in a cocktail bar in London's West End.'

'You can't see the sky so clear in the West End.'

'Beautiful sky,' he observed as he rose from his seat.

'And attentive guy to share it with,' she whispered.

Returning with fresh drinks, he had Dyana's full attention at last. Conversations shifted between cocktails, tattoos and the scenery.

'Woolwich Common at sunset,' she said, 'has beautiful skies.'

His place for running. Black and bleak in the depths of winter, but glorious and green in summer. Mixture of scorched heath, and fine parkland, owned by the British Army. The old military buildings had long since been vacated and bought up by Irish property speculators. When Ireland's property crash came, these passed into the hands of their government.

So now the Irish owned a small part of England's military history, transforming the old academy into a series of costly apartments. Grand places, self-contained, with sweeping views of the Common.

'So where exactly do you live then?'

'Across the road from the hospital.'

'In the posh new flats I guess.'

'I couldn't afford one o' those on a tattoo artist's wages,' she laughed. 'I'm in a Council property across from the hospital.'

He sipped his pint. 'I think I know those houses.'

Right or wrong, he had a stereotype deep in his mind. Grim social tenements far from the grand Academy. Grime, crime, and poverty. People not taking pride in their homes. Living off the system.

'I've a little two bedroom flat. My piece of the world.'

Except it's not. It belongs to the government, the welfare state.

'I've a house just down the road in Charlton.'

A house he bought. House he struggled to pay for, since Katy's departure. House he'd have to get a tenant into very soon, to keep paying the mortgage. House he wasn't just given, because some people got lucky in a lottery and others didn't. He'd listen to his girls in the football team talking about how if you have a baby, *they* give you a house, *they* give you benefits, *they* give you anything you fucking ask for.

'I grew up in New Cross, like Demetrius, but I love my house in Woolwich,' she carried on. 'I wouldn't swap it for the whole world.'

Fergus belied his feelings. 'The Common's great for a run.'

'Maybe you can call in some time,' she suggested.

The thought of that warmed the chill in his skull.

'Yeah that'd be good. Best before the run though.'

She fixed her green gaze upon him. 'Why before?'

'You clearly don't live with a man whose sweat glands seem to be located somewhere in his socks whenever he runs.'

'I don't live with any man right now.'

'And I don't live with any woman.'

141

'God,' she said suddenly. 'This is starting to sound like *Miss Inky Fingers* and *Mister Charlton Man* skirting around the turf on a first date.'

'Whoever said it was a first date?'

'I'm making it a third,' she answered. 'Third time of meeting, and you know what people say about that. It's then or never.'

The speed at which Dyana had accelerated this had taken him by surprise. A couple of minutes ago, he'd been dealing with the knowledge of her abode. Thinking of her as a chocolate princess in the Academy's castle. Then feeling the chocolate fade into stereotypes of the world she occupied. Now she had resurrected his hunger to know her, in the flesh, once again.

'Fergus, I don't want to sleep on my own tonight.'

15. Dream Catcher

---

*L*eaving the bar, Fergus felt like the guy who'd just won a game of Scrabble with the longest word possible. But maybe, he was a guy who'd cheated. Gone to the toilets, and looked in the dictionary. Passing the square that claimed to be the birthplace of Arsenal, he was acting one way, and feeling another.

He'd kissed her on the cheek as they rose out of their seats. Her skin came smooth to his lips, and she had a strong body fragranced in perfume. He wasn't sure where the night would lead beyond the Plumstead Road, but already she made him feel soft on the inside, hard on the outside.

'Chocolate princess born again,' he reimagined her, wondering if it was treacherous for a Charlton man to sleep with a woman in a Spurs shirt.

Then, coming towards the traffic lights, she stalled.

'Fergus, there's something else you need to know.'

She lingered on the roadside as the lights flickered from

red to green, and he ventured to cross. Pulling back, he sensed seriousness.

With eyes that cut sharp as the sword in his tattoo, she struggled to detonate the words on her lips. 'The reason I've got a Council flat is because I have a child Fergus, a little girl. Her name's Poppy.'

'I see,' Fergus felt the Spurs jersey in his imagination incinerate. Suddenly all her mysteries made perfect, painful sense.

'She's staying with neighbours tonight,' Dyana carried on speaking into the echo of his thoughts. 'But she's here all the time in my heart.' Then she paused as they edged towards the Common. 'If you're just after a good time Fergus, maybe this isn't right for either of us.'

Again chocolate melted on the back streets of Woolwich. He wasn't sure how to answer, so he took her hand and walked on.

'Hun, you've gone quiet,' the rhythm of Dyana's voice matched the mood of these streets leading towards a bleak rectilinear truth.

Tower blocks rose like Beefeaters in the night, guarding sentry lines of Coronation Street sandstone terraces. Woolwich's glory days as a royal dockyard seemed as long gone as Arsenal Football Club.

The Thames, this far out, felt physical and mortal too, a receptacle of infection, sewage, shopping trolleys, used tea bags with the flavour screwed out of them, and rubbish barges stacked high with human waste.

'It's grim, fucking grim,' Fergus thought.

Breeding grounds for poverty, alienation, and sickness like a swamp, giving rise to a plague of mosquitoes sucking the blood out of an entire country. The streets stank of subsistence and welfare.

'Almost at the Common, baby,' Dyana mapped their route.

Fergus needed time to gather his thoughts as they approached lights upon the bleak space but time raced at the speed of a greyhound.

Dyana kept on talking like Cinderella fighting the clock at midnight. 'I don't want Poppy to be the same as me. All through childhood, men would come and go at the top o' the stairs. They broke my mama's heart until it stopped pumping one day, and she dropped dead in the street.'

'I'm sorry,' he imagined the grieving of a child.

'Anyway, we're almost here,' she pointed towards a particular block of flats. 'Welcome to my castle on the edge of London.'

Thinking of melting chocolate once again, Fergus followed her into a lift shaft that was like a leftover from a 1930s *film noir* set.

Dyana pressed a button with her fingertips and the capsule cranked upwards, stopping at the fifth bump.

When they escaped out into the corridor, every door looked the very same, as if they'd stepped through an iron curtain into a communist state.

Loud music blasted from one doorway. Behind another, a mother screamed at her screeching kids in a mix of Urdu and English swear words. Images of Vivaldi's Henchman coursed through his skull.

'Such places would drive anybody mad,' he figured.

This was noisy, claustrophobic, and habitable only by lack of choice. He'd always been taught that a house should have a soul and be a home. This place had no soul, character, history or shared human feeling.

'Just an assortment of random strangers,' he presumed.

'This is me,' Dyana's voice lanced his thoughts as they approached one of the identical doors differentiated only by numbers. 'My little flat!'

Fergus half expected to see a scattering of cockroaches as she turned the key. Filthy, cannibalistic creatures winged their way out of the shadows in his mind hurdling obstacles of dirty saucepans and glue traps. Lovers of darkness, strong enough to survive a nuclear bomb.

Dyana sighed and flicked a switch. 'Home again.'

Light flooded the room, as they stepped inside.

'So silent without Poppy here,' she added.

Silent, yes, and soundproofed, without a cockroach in sight.

'It's pretty,' Fergus labelled his first impressions.

Dyana had sharp ears. 'You sound surprised.'

Fergus had to divert questioning away from negative expectations. 'Just not in the habit of coming back from pubs, and going into a new place.'

'Take a seat,' she led him towards her living room. 'Make yourself at home. I'm going to the bathroom for a freshen up.'

Sitting alone, Fergus drank in the ambience, the soul of Dyana's apartment. Pleasant fragrances rose from fresh flowers on the table, and scented tea lights in the windows. Dolls and teddy bears decorated the spine of a deep burgundy sofa. Across the way, CDs and children's books lined the shelves of a wooden press.

'She's turning her daughter to a proper little reader,' he scanned the titles—everything from nursery rhymes and classics to Peppa Pig.

Some old ones too of characters he remembered from his own childhood. Andy Pandy. Donald Duck. Mowgli from the Jungle Book.

Dyana returned. 'So what do you think of my home?'

'Like I said, I'm not used to this. I'd no expectations.'

Her eyes cut through him. 'I'll pour us a drink.'

She crossed the room to a locked cabinet where she kept a couple of bottles. The choice, she admitted, was more limited than a West End cocktail bar. 'Mostly gifts from customers at Christmas,' she pointed to whisky, vodka, and a solitary bottle of Irish Cream. 'I'm not used to this either.'

Seeing Dyana pour the drinks and then cross into the kitchen for ice cubes, Fergus still wanted to see her in that Tottenham shirt. But sitting here, surveying her baby girl's reading list, he felt foreign. It was for the best that they slept together once, and then he closed the door on this world.

That was generally what single men did with single mothers, the way of the world whether in England, Ireland, or Africa. The important thing was to make sure that little girls don't get hurt. If he left in the morning before Poppy returned to her reading, there would be no harm done.

'I get a feeling that you're going to leave me,' Dyana predicted a lonely fate as she handed him a drink, and sat down beside him on the sofa. 'Is that what you're going to do after this night Fergus?'

As he leaned in close she pulled away, awaiting an answer. She'd probably been in this situation before on this very same settee. That's why she had to be careful. Dyana couldn't afford waste men coming and going at the top of the stairs. She needed a steady man in her daughter's life who'd tell bedtime stories and bathtime stories—not lies.

Again she tested him. 'Are you thinking of running?'

He answered tactfully, truthfully even. 'I'm still here.'

This time when he reached out, Dyana's toes rose to meet his fingertips. 'Will you stay the whole night?' she asked.

'As long as I'm wanted,' he assured her.

'Liar,' she suggested playfully, using her foot as a weapon.

'No, it's London that's the liar,' he wanted to argue.

When this city looks in the mirror, it sees only reflections of theatres, towers of commerce, West End shows, grand buildings, manicured parks, a world of high windows, Premier League teams, and designer stores.

None of Tottenham or Woolwich's crude realities exist in such a fiction. These tower blocks and their occupants got swept under the public carpet like the dead cockroaches he hadn't found a single trace of so far. There was no space for chocolate princesses in England's royal fairytales. They just got screwed and abandoned in the end.

Trying not to dwell on his own haste for departure, Fergus moved Dyana's foot closer to his groin and leaned his mouth into hers.

This time she tasted of a different Irish Cream, a sweet liqueur bedded into a serenade of punchy malt. Breaking through the layers, he moved from the taste of lipstick to feel of teeth and then her tongue.

'Isn't it time to change into that Tottenham shirt?'

'Maybe we'll save that for next season,' she was playing games too. 'You might even get to see the full kit.'

'On the night you play Watford,' he roused laughter from Dyana's lips with a joke Katy would never have understood.

'Or take away your pain if it's Palace.'

This was a warm up, a friendly testing of the waters. Playfully, she rose off the sofa, took his hand and led him into a small room with a double sized bed at one end, facing out on a balcony loaded in leafy plants.

He noticed the window open and suggested they close it, but Dyana said she wanted to keep it open, joking that things might soon get very hot in the night ahead, as she pulled him towards the double bed.

Above the pillows, the hoop of a Dream Catcher trailed down the walls to where its feathers rippled gently in the breeze against a headboard.

'That protects me and Poppy,' she said, 'from bad spirits.'

Then she put her mouth to his, to suck away badness and catch his dreams as his body fell against hers, warm and leathery as a wetsuit.

Though she wasn't dressed in Spurs colours, he stripped off her kit. Then searched her body for a sighting of tattoos, going downstairs, venturing into places her needles never touched on the bodies of others. Finally he found the solitary image of a rose blazing blue upon her breast.

He made a joke that he'd expected her to have inked the Tottenham badge on her own skin, the crest of a cockeral. On hearing these words she doubled over, curling beneath him, bringing her knees to his abdomen.

'Is this an Irish thing?' she asked, as they floated away from a sense of flesh towards a sudden rumble of laughter. 'Do you usually get into a woman's bed and expect to find a cock beneath her clothes?'

Laughing, their lovemaking continued.

'I haven't had anything human inside me for a long time.' She knew what she wanted, using Fergus's body to please her own, fearing that she might have no more chance of this tomorrow. She wanted as much pleasure, she said, as it was possible for one night to offer, and savoured every second of their rumble. 'When you're scared a man's going to leave you, there's no point playing around, wasting the time you've got left.'

'Never said I was going to leave you,' he protested as the rumble finished and they lay back sweating, panting, and shivering in the breeze creeping through the open window, fingering their upper bodies.

'You don't have to say it honey. I see it.'

'And what if I stayed?' he pressed against her naked body where the tattoo's colours glistened like fresh ink through the sweat on her skin.

'I guess that if you stayed, your life would be a sacrifice,' she admitted. 'I've had to give up as much for Poppy as my mother did for me.'

'Did you ink your own tattoo?' he tried to lighten the mood.

'No, I got this old blue rose done a long time ago, back in New Cross when I wasn't even a tattoo artist,' she spoke heavily after an interlude of silence. 'A few days after my mother's funeral.'

'What's it meant to symbolise?' he asked.

'Beauty and sadness at the same time.'

'Why sadness?' he pushed for answers.

'You're asking questions that are putting a swelling in my breast,' she turned her bosom from his palm. 'If you ask me to show you the lump and then run, it's going to hurt even more.'

Before he could answer, she had risen from the bed to pull curtains across the balcony. Sharing her flesh with the city might have been bearable, but sharing her naked soul seemed a step too far. Getting back into bed, she slipped under the sheets, readying to bare the lump.

'When I was a child, we had to leave home in West Africa,' she narrated the tale of her journey to England's green and pleasant land. 'My father got murdered in the civil war, and the village elders wanted my mother to marry another man. She refused, and we had to get out of there and start a new life elsewhere.' Fergus reached out to touch her hair, hearing the crackle of tears against a pillowcase. 'My mother sold our little house in my home country, and we paid some people to get us to London.'

He detected the echo of a child's hopes in her voice.

'Take your time,' he put a hand on her shoulder.

'We had visions of landing in a paradise where all the people would be kind and help us get back the quality of life we had before,' she enunciated, and then laughed at her own childish innocence. 'We travelled hundreds o' miles in a cattle lorry from Liberia to Cameroon, hidden in a compartment beneath the animals.' She paused, retching the words out of somewhere painful. 'Can you imagine the smell? It was like having a sickness on your breath that you can't take away from your nose.'

Slowly she inked the path of their journey across the flesh of Africa. When they reached Cameroon's vast land mass in the west, they boarded fresh trucks for the north, herded on by men who carried whips. Those men, and their trucks, breaking down every fifty miles or so, ferried them through new countries called Chad and Niger, all the way up to Morocco.

'You're going through the Sahara,' she explained. 'It's

dry as a bone. It's the Hell that Bible stories talk about. You go through days that leave you terrified of heat for a lifetime. If the weather's cold you can wrap up in layers, but there's no escape from burning skin.'

'Take your time,' Fergus wrapped his arms around her body.

Dyana's heart pounded in the landmass of her bosom as she remembered. 'It's not possible just to travel in the cool of night. We had to keep going even in the day, when forty degrees feels like a hundred. But we faced all sorts of complications, no cover from the sun, almost no water to drink, police checkpoints where they beat the adults and asked for money, and then the villages you pass through and stop in for a few hours. Everybody robs you with angry eyes, and you're afraid for your life. We'd become nothing more than sand people gambling on an escape.'

He was sure that she was crying, even if he couldn't see her face.

'After we got out of the desert, I can't remember much,' she admitted. 'The men in trucks dumped us in an Arab country where everybody and everything looked different, and we waited there for days on a boat. Then we got to Europe, first Amsterdam, and eventually London.'

'Why'd you stop in Amsterdam?' Fergus wondered.

'We'd extra debts to pay, picked up from the journey.'

He could imagine the debts, the last stages of a flesh market.

'My mother had to earn the cost of the crossing from North Africa. Our little house wasn't enough,' she groaned. 'They'd have expected the same from me if I'd just been a couple of years older, I suppose.'

The pain of her voice had swollen to a lump, as Fergus tried to reach in to the shores she was now inhabiting, but with no success.

'At least Amsterdam was only for six months and then we came to England where we eventually became legal after a long time fighting. I got the chance to go to school, and we ended up in New Cross.'

'You made it,' he said. 'The worst was over then.'

'It wasn't,' she spoke insistently. 'When times got tough, my mother went back there to the same world as Amsterdam. Though she never said that was where she was going, I knew. She pretended to work in a factory. A factory of third world flesh bought by first world customers to fund my second class honours degree.' She was angrier now and her breast lay bare, with the tumour of pain fully showing. 'Then about three months before she died, I fell pregnant just as I'd earned my degree. I knew we couldn't afford a pregnancy, not after all of my mother's sacrifices.'

The lump had risen out of her bosom and into her throat now.

'What about the baby's father?' Fergus probed cautiously.

'He was the boy your mother tells you to stay away from, the one who does drugs and is going to end up face down in the gutter. But when you're in Art School, guys like that seem cool. He's dead now, for your information.'

'I wasn't trying to dig at anything hurtful.'

Her voice changed then. 'You keep asking me about Demetrius, like you think he was my lover or something. He wasn't. His cousin was a Ghetto Boy, the father of my baby, though she never met him. He's dead now too, from a syringe, not a gunshot. Because of that, Demetrius always looked out for me, and loaned me the money to open my own studio.'

'That's why you want to find out who killed him.'

'Yes, and because nobody else seems bothered,' she answered. 'He's just another statistic, and there's nothing worse than being a statistic.'

They lay back in silence, together, Tottenham girl and Charlton man. Soon as her head hit the pillow, she had fallen into a deep sleep, as if under anaesthetic after going through surgery to neutralise a tumour.

'Seems like I'm staying for the night,' he whispered into her dreams. 'But will I be here by the time Watford come to Spurs?'

16. Desperation Stations

Crossing bleak landscapes in the light of a cool dawn, Fergus left Dyana's flat. He thought of the Common changing through the seasons, and then the changed season of his own life. The woman he'd slept with had gone to collect her child and visit the radio station in Brockley where the boy Demetrius had given his last interview. She hoped to sift through the recording for clues that might lead her to his killers.

'If I can help,' he offered, 'please let me know.'

'No,' she insisted. 'I need to do this alone.'

While Dyana embarked upon detective work, he'd concentrate on football. Tomorrow morning he'd another training session with his girls. Afterwards he'd go home. Watch TV. Last weekend of the Premier League season. Nothing much to play for. Manchester United had already won the title, in Alex Ferguson's goodbye season.

'Up to anything exciting?' he texted Lance, as he got into the house.

'Yeah,' the reply sailed instantly across the few miles between them. 'Few of my army mates from the west country are up for the Yeovil game tomorrow. They'd a spare ticket so I'm going with them.'

Yeovil Town versus Brentford, League One play off final. The winners earned the right to play in the Championship next season. They'd face Charlton, and the losers of the second tier's final between Palace and Watford. Winners of that game would face Manchester United, without Alex Ferguson. Football moved on fast. Look at Wigan Athletic, FA Cup winners one weekend, and relegated three days later, from a 4-1 defeat at Arsenal.

Charlton would face Wigan next season too.

First time they'd face the FA Cup holders in a league game at The Valley since December 2006. Some of the best players in Europe appeared in SE7 that afternoon as Liverpool rolled into town.

Only eighteen months previously, the visitors had come back from 3-0 down at half time to beat AC Milan in the Champions League final, and then go on to win the FA Cup the year after with a victory over West Ham United.

That day, Charlton had been put to the sword by the team that Fergus had supported since childhood. He'd listened to the game on the radio.

Lance had been there in the flesh, on a bad day for the men with a sword in their badge. Liverpool won 3-0 and left Charlton on the edge of relegation. But the ground was full, and the fans expectant of survival.

Such days seemed long ago now, as Fergus made a cup of coffee, and switched on the computer, to detect football's latest news. By the time he'd reached Charlton, the Premier League circus had rolled out of town.

His first memories of English football, in the flesh, featured the country's lesser lights. Teams in the third tier. Names he'd known since childhood from the classified football results on Saturday afternoons. Hartlepool United, Tranmere Rovers, Oldham Athletic, and Rochdale.

Thinking of this, he switched between the BBC and his email account.

Shockwaves engulfed the moment. That feeling you get when you're expecting a rainy day, and you're glad because it gives you a chance to do things inside. But then you pull back the curtains, and see sunshine.

You're glad of that too, and at the same time you're not. You don't know what exactly you feel. Temptation? Resistance? Weakness?

'Desperation stations,' the cryptic title scalded his eyes like a flash bulb exploding into a gallery of half-forgotten images.

This was like his dreams in the years after the joyride, even after coming to London. He'd waken up seeing the face of the girl he had killed. But today's ghost still existed in the flesh, though hadn't been in touch for weeks. She'd warned him never to email again. He'd been tempted to say hello but resisted—using thoughts of vomit as a shield.

He should resist this temptation too. He should take this email and delete it immediately. Too much poison had passed between them. The only thing she could offer now was a spur to get on with the rest of his life. It was time to give up Katy and concentrate his energies elsewhere.

'Delete,' he flushed her cryptic vomit out of cyberspace.

He'd come full circle from fights over tattoos to a night spent with a tattooist. Despite this, he wasn't certain about Dyana. He'd slept fitfully, emotions constantly shifting like a pot of spaghetti. They'd started out hard and then softened as they boiled, but might cool and harden again.

He'd never hurt a woman physically. But he couldn't guarantee he'd keep the emotional side of the bargain. His confusion led him away from football websites towards a search for other information.

'Guys' attitudes to dating a single mother'-'Would you ever date a woman with a child?'-'Social attitudes to black single mothers'-'Advantages of dating a single mom' -'Disadvantages of dating a

single mom'—'*Meeting the significant other in her life*' -'*Never a nappy ending*—

His head became like an episode of the Jerry Springer show on 24/7 replay. Worse, he feared. A repository of Jerry Springer shows.

The facts were simple. Single mothers carried baggage, stigmata even. Regardless of wounds, he was becoming emotionally attached.

According to one site, it was all the fault of a chemical substance called oxytocin. This was a love chemical, a more cuddly feely androgynous version of testosterone. Once released, it's like a snake's poison that spreads through the whole body, down to the marrow.

'You'll never have her full attention,' argued another opinion writer. *'The child will always take first place in a mother's life.'*

Just a few months back, one of the most promising young women on his football team got pregnant. Walked away from the team, the game, the future. Once they're brought into the world, *they* become the woman's life.

He spent most of the day thinking of this and subsiding into thoughts of whether or not he should resurrect Katy's email from the thrash. Come the evening, Dyana rescued him with news of her venture to the radio station.

She had been given access to the digital recordings of the interview. Tomorrow, when Poppy was at Sunday school, she'd have a listen. Then she might get at the truth of the situation. In the meantime they'd just have to wait and pass their Saturday nights in very different ways. She'd read another story to her daughter from the pages of The Jungle Book.

'I'll go for a run across the Common,' he told her. 'Then get a good night's sleep for tomorrow's training up at Sparrow's Lane again.'

On the Common he found a funfair with lights ablaze like a cruise ship, acting as a marker while he ran through seas of darkness. Forgetting the deleted email and getting back to the house, he slept more soundly than he had done for a long time. Feeling energised, he set out for training.

He thought of Dyana too, engaged in her detective work.

She texted. 'Poppy's gone. It's time to listen.'

As she listened to the recordings, he drove to the training session. His girls had already assembled by the time he reached Sparrow's. Standing in her Arsenal jersey, Victoria commanded the field as usual.

'Away in Newcastle today,' she kissed the cannon on her club crest. 'We need a win to finish above Tottenham.'

Fergus wondered if Dyana would follow the games in between her attempts to uncover the mysteries of the young musician's death.

Or what would she find, if anything? If he'd known anything of the likelihood that he was to be shot, surely he'd have been more careful. He'd never have gone down that road towards Deptford out in the open.

'Hey sir, who's blue today, who's red?'

Chelsea's voice scissored his thoughts.

'Maybe I'm blue,' he wanted to say, but cast his feelings aside. 'Chelsea you captain the blues, and Victoria take the reds.'

Watching them start out on the game, under a canopy of trees, he thought back to the day Katy had dumped him by text message. She had been so cold, and yet he couldn't shake thoughts of her out of his mind.

What had she meant by that cryptic title? What was the station of desperation that she had reached with Wagner down on the coast of Kent? Was it literally a station? What was so desperate?

'Goal,' the blues cried out in chorus.

Chelsea's low volley had driven her team into an early lead after a gentle knock down from the slim Somali girl. Victoria equalised soon after, and then the blues snatched an unexpected second. The red defence, sleeping, showed signs of drink and dancing on a Saturday night. They conceded a third soon after, angering their captain who always wanted to win.

By the time it ended, the score reached double figures. He told the girls they did okay, and gave them some tips on defending. Then he headed home to catch up on the day's results which now too had passed into history.

Alex Ferguson's Manchester United had drawn five goals each with West Bromwich Albion, and Arsenal had pipped Tottenham to fourth place in the table, with a one nil victory. Yeovil Town made headlines too, earning the right to play in the championship in the coming season.

'Palace also,' Fergus hoped, 'when they're beaten by Watford.'

Watching the goals, as he whipped up a TV dinner, cliché followed the achievements of the team from the west country through the evening news. Plucky Yeovil, fighting above their weight. The men from England's cider country punch-drunk, and Brentford reeling, knocked out cold.

'Getting pissed with my boys,' Lance echoed the TV sentiments.

Then a second message arrived. Dyana had found something.

'What is it?' Fergus called her immediately, intrigued.

'It's the interview,' she spoke fast, breathlessly.

He'd guessed that much already. 'Yeah, okay.'

'I found something that's maybe useful in the parts they edited and didn't use,' she fought for breath as she spoke. 'When asked about the inspiration for his new album, Demetrius started talking about his research, going to meet asylum seekers and so on.'

'You expect research more of folks like Katy,' Fergus thought and fought again to resist the dissonance in his mind.

'He talked about going to a club where foreign women end up, and about how they're exploited there.' She paused then, catching her breath. 'Spoke of a network, and migrant girls brought from overseas.'

'Network? Makes it sound so systematic, so corporate.'

'Yes,' she spoke quickly. 'This was a big business he reckoned, and the dancing club is just the part of the iceberg that's above the water.'

'So what kind of club are we talking about here?' Fergus asked, though already had a particular set of images in his mind.

'Gentleman's Club on the Isle of Dogs,' she clarified.

Again, he made a guess. 'Posh name for a lapdancing club?'

'I think it is, and I want to go there tonight.'

'You sure that's safe after what happened to Demetrius?'

'I don't know,' she admitted, 'but I have to find out.'

'I'll come with you,' he set a date for the evening.

Maybe this would shake Katy out of his head, once and for all, or land him in a fresh set of desperation stations in the company of dancing girls.

17. Valley of Desire

*F*ergus booked a cab for the journey to the club, collecting Dyana on the Common's edge, flowering and greening in the spring. Across the Greenwich Peninsula, they cut beneath the Blackwall Tunnel, and emerged on the Isle of Dogs, scene of Lance's gangster stories of olden days. Long gone, buried under a fresh century's lights.

Greyhound tracks, distant dreams. Modern architecture—cubes and towers—swirled above a daily dogfight of stocks, shares, interest rates, and investment. Disorienting and futuristic, blurring borders of day and night.

'Las Vegas meets Manhattan,' Fergus supposed.

'Let's just find the club,' Dyana grew impatient.

According to its website, the club's building had a notable history. Former timber warehouse surviving from the days of the old docks. The kind of place Lance's ancestors might have boxed in, Fergus supposed. But those days had long since gone as they travelled down an underpass via Google Maps, and found the club nestled against the embankment.

'*The Bird Cage*,' Fergus read a script of white neon.

For a second, images from The Dictionary flickered through his mind. Songbirds on the streets of Woolwich, and poultry trapped in wire baskets. Then a couple of burly bouncers stepped into the path of his thoughts.

Guardians of the network, Fergus guessed. Low level hired hands. Brawn fronting the brains that went into the business of selling sex. Even from standing in the doorway, he could see a hard sell in the distance. Mirrors and purple neon, long legs tracing the distance between floor and ceiling. Pulsating music had long since replaced the sounds of a timber yard.

'How much is it to get in?' Fergus spoke above the music.

'Ten pounds entrance,' the goons answered in chorus. 'You pay separately for drinks and dancing, and there's no touching.'

'Of drinks?' Fergus joked, but from their expressions these men had never been socialised into the practice of humour.

Then to his surprise, as he paid, one of the goons gestured towards the Charlton membership cards and season ticket in his wallet. 'You're going to see more action here than at The Valley.'

Dyana pushed him on towards the sight and fragrance of female flesh.

Girls moved as boxers in a gymnasium might well have done, swinging their bodies like punching bags from every available timber beam. The place had an air of midnight decadence. The river's liquid dyes had followed them inside, blending into wine-red décor and soft lighting. Exotic girls stepped through beaded doorways. The scene resembled a catalogue photo-shoot for nightwear—affected smiles, lashings of cosmetics, and loose clothing.

'It's loud,' Dyana competed for his attention.

'Yeah,' he turned to face her. 'And wild too.'

'No more wild than a zoo,' she countered.

Through a swirling cocktail of light and flesh, Fergus drank in the piercing Crème de menthe eyes of one dancer, poised like an umbrella on the rim of a glass. With long dark hair and olive skin, she appeared Mediterranean, maybe Middle Eastern. Across the way, he could see a group of eastern European girls gleaming in the shadows like figures in a nativity painting—angels lighting up a dark and cavernous space. He tried to guess the places that the others came from by looks and accents. Most had tanned bodies but cold eyes—like wild deer enclosed in cages.

'Surely this can't be every man's fantasy,' Dyana whispered as they edged towards the bar. 'Though on the surface I see the attraction.'

In her voice he detected a strange marriage of arousal and repulsion. He wondered whether these girls would pass through both their minds if they slept together tonight when their detective work came to a close.

One of the caged birds, with a piercing in her nipple, brought him back to a rainy afternoon and his first venture into a tattoo studio. He thought of Betty Boop and a Millwall devil pimping flesh in the shadows.

Getting closer to the bar, Fergus heard a buxom African girl making smalltalk with an older white man in town for a business trip. She was from the Ivory Coast, she said—the country that had given Didier Drogba, Salomon Kalou, and the Toure brothers to the Premier League.

'Beers or cocktails?' Dyana mumbled in the background.

Fergus scanned the list of cocktails- Docklands' Dogger, London's Libido, Bang in a Battersea Boat, and Surrey Quays Sloe Screw.

In the end he opted for an Asian beer. Dyana had the same, paying and then finding seats near the stage, as a new dancer mounted the pole. Tall and slim, wearing blue boots, rising high enough to meet the red curls tumbling down her backbone. Staring out on the crowd, the girl's Blue Curaçao eyes cut deep as she stripped out of an orange one piece.

'Wounded,' Fergus sensed suffering beneath the eroticism of her theatrics as she bent down off the stage, reached out to a table of whistling customers, and scooped a handful of ice out of one man's whisky.

'More exciting than The Valley?' Dyana asked, uneasily.

'You don't get party tricks like that,' he made light of her question, sensing something not quite right but unable to put his finger upon it.

Men whistled as the girl shook her hips and the cubes stayed in place—one balanced perfectly on the end of each nipple. But still Fergus sensed the same dissonance in the scene as when he'd received Katy's email.

The drunk men kept on whistling, screaming for more of something, although he wasn't quite sure what they actually wanted. To drag the girl down from the stage, rip off the last of her clothing, and paw different parts of her body like dipping into a bucket of KFC chicken nuggets?

'Piranhas,' Dyana suggested, 'feeding off flesh.'

Suddenly Fergus remembered the story of her mother. Reaching out, he caught her fingers, giving his eyes to her and not the stage. Then the truth dawned on him, as if in a thump from across the boxing rings of the past.

'Holy God, I should have seen it sooner,' he realised.

It was the jaw that gave it away. As a boxer that's the aspect of your opponent's face you're most conscious of aside from his fists.

Yes, the girl with the party tricks carried the ghost of a man's jaw. But the piranhas didn't look far enough beneath the surface to notice.

Turning to the stage again, Fergus watched the girl slipping back inside the full covering of an orange one piece and disappearing into a booth, hired for a private dancing session by one of the piranhas.

'Did you notice?' he leaned back towards Dyana.

'Sure,' her sharp eyes dissected theatrics.

Like Katy though, he found the dancer in the one-piece hard to shake. Something about the scene awakened dissonance inside of his system. All his life he'd been taught to hate that kind of person and yet seeing her up there on the stage, he'd been on the same side against the men beneath her.

Up on stage now, a new dancer had already taken to the timber pole. Tall and slim, with small breasts, she brought to mind his Somali girl.

Seeing the fresh dancer's coppery flesh exposed against the brown wood and her flirtations with the table of men below, a series of guilty thoughts ran through Fergus's mind like diarrhea.

'What if one of my girls appeared on that stage?' he wondered. 'What if they looked down and saw me amongst this crowd?'

The tabloids printed such stories all the time. Girls struggling to make ends meet on their university courses come to places like this for easy cash. There's no harm in what they do, he guessed, but it's the leeches, the voyeurs, the fuckers who feed off cheap flesh like the one who'd just come out of a glass booth in a daze after his dance with Nipple Trick Girl.

'I'm not like them,' he assuaged his sudden sense of guilt.

'We came to do a job,' Dyana reached into his thoughts.

'Yeah,' Fergus surveyed the private dancing area.

'Find a girl, and get her inside one of those booths.'

'Then ask if she knows anything about Demetrius?'

Dyana nodded as he rose and prepared for his strange assignment. Kissing her on the cheek, he began his wanderings through the room.

Brushing against Barbie dolls with legs impossibly long

he gazed into the dancers' eyes, searching for somebody with a flicker of conscience. Somebody whose eyes lacked the cold glaze of a zoo animal. He needed to establish human connection to seek out answers to Demetrius being here.

Moving and mingling amongst the dancers and other customers he noticed how the guardians of the network surveyed everything that moved—like stewards at a football match.

'Maybe this isn't so different to The Valley after all,' he slipped into daydreams, before bumping into a woman who spoke suddenly.

'Special offer,' she moved fast and sleek as a panther, using words that again brought him back to his football girls. 'Just for you sir.'

'Sorry,' he had no interest in what she had to offer.

'Only ten pounds a dance, cheapest in the club.'

'Yeah,' he thought, 'and I can fucking see why.'

He could smell her too, a sickly mixture of cigarettes and inebriation.

If the goons on the door acted as the guardians of the network, this was the rump, the cast-off from whatever business they operated—the one who wanders the floor all night, and never gets up on the stage.

With puncture marks in her tattooed arms, Fergus reckoned that if they ever made a movie of Lance's stories, she'd be perfect for one part. She was exactly how you might imagine The Brown Marilyn, though of a different race. South American perhaps but he wasn't going to ask.

The scars on her arms repulsed him. 'Sorry, looking for someone else.'

Hearing his words, her face assumed a hardshelled defensive grin.

'Huh,' she grunted. 'Maybe I'm looking for someone else too.'

Then she turned on her heels and walked away, still grinning.

Fergus's attention shifted elsewhere, to a younger dancer.

'Yes, she has the eyes that I'm looking for,' he surmised.

Bathed in blue, from spotlights above, she wore shiny silver négligée to match the mirror-balls. Her eyes remained full of light and hope, free from that detached glaze of zoo animals he detected in most of the other faces.

'Hello,' Fergus felt his insides shaking as he approached.

As she turned, her eyes glistened like inkwells. He could be certain now that she had enough of a soul to give something away and shed some light upon the fatal discoveries that Demetrius made.

'Yes,' she spoke on the borderlands of a question.

'Are you free?' his words came out oddly.

'Yes,' she said again, and they sat down.

This was like being back in a disco in Ireland's border country, experiencing the smoke and mirrors of teenage seduction. But this was very much an adult world, with goons constantly patrolling the background.

Across the way, Dyana watched, unrelenting in her gaze.

The girl spoke the mantra, the language of all the dancers in this place. 'Special offer, twenty pounds a dance tonight.'

Double the value of the grinning junkie.

'Okay,' he agreed, seeing other predators within range, and catching sight of the dancer in the orange one piece on the far side of the room.

Crossing the floor, Fergus looked away—towards the windows facing out on Canary Wharf's towers reflected in the Thames. Then he was coming towards another kind of window, a glass booth with curtains and a chair.

'What's your name?' he surprised his dancer.

Poised in the doorway, tugging a curtain across the

glass, she finally relented to his question. 'Estrella, Spanish for star.'

'So you're Spanish?' he assumed, as she gestured to sit.

'Colombian,' she brushed his question aside. 'Now forget.'

'Cool name,' Fergus lifted his eyes to meet hers. 'Exotic.'

Her dark eyes clouded, and her voice grew husky and impersonal. 'I play song, dance, and when music done, dance is over.' Then she offered her final instruction in perfect English. 'There is no touching.'

'Okay,' he agreed and passed her a crisp twenty pound note, waiting for the right time to introduce the subject of the musician and ask this young dancer the questions to which Dyana sought answers.

He sought answers too, as Estrella prepared her theatrics.

Gradually, as she edged closer, the music amplified.

'You ready?' she spoke against the opening arpeggio.

He nodded towards the haze of her flesh. 'Yes.'

'The show begins,' she announced in numb voice.

Shining silvery in her négligée, she lifted her arms skywards. A snake-ring glinted pagan on the slender fingers she wove across the straps of her garment, and he felt a sudden thrill of anticipation for her performance. Tightening the muscles of her neck and shoulders, she threw her curls forward to act as a mask on her inky eyes and soft mouth.

But did he come here for this or for answers? He could imagine what Katy would make of this scene, and wondered what Dyana was thinking.

'Relax,' the dancer whispered, detecting his tension.

Then her mask of dark hair brushed against his face, drowning the island in silence, closing off the rest of the world on the outside of their booth. Straddling the chair and seeming to defy gravity, she pressed her body close to his without actually touching. Breathing in the scent of her waxed skin, he sighed—thinking back to party tricks on the stage.

Theatre, disturbance, and the shivery punch of realisation.

Outside Dyana waited, wondering about the direction of answers. Inside, the music played on. Estrella slipped the négligée off her shoulders, and bared the slopes of her bosom like Betty Boop in the tattoo studio. There too the sounds of the outside world had seemed miles from the scene.

Rain. Hull City. The ticklish feel of a woman's fingers on your skin. Shades of black and amber, something solid forming beneath the surface. The short sharp stab of a sword and the dye of white metals.

Music reaching a crescendo signalled time to drop the négligée.

'Wait,' he snapped out of his trance, touching her arm.

'No touching,' her voice came at him in a shriek.

He'd broken Estrella's trance too, like suddenly shouting at an actress in a West End show as she's delivering her lines on the stage.

'Sorry,' he pulled back, trying to calm her.

She gazed on in confusion. 'What's wrong?'

His heart thumped. 'You don't have to dance any more.'

She stood silent, with time ticking away.

'Music only has one more minute,' the dancer finally spoke through soft lips, pulling the straps back up over her shoulders, seeming suddenly ashamed of being almost naked in the presence of a stranger.

Fergus needed to deliver his message fast. One fucking shot like a penalty in a play off final. Already he could feel the heat of a match at his nipples and the terrible fear of failure roaring inside his skull.

'I'm here to find out something for a friend of mine.'

Estrella looked confused. He'd burst the bubble of theatre, and enforced human connection upon her. That wasn't part of a lap dancer's act. These girls played out their nights to a carefully choreographed script.

But if he was to find answers, he had to rewrite, rebalance the scene. Reaching into his pocket he produced a photograph of Demetrius. 'I'm looking for information about this man,' he tried to pass it to her.

'I don't know nothing about any man,' she grew defensive.

'How can you say that until you've looked at the picture?'

Finally she took hold of it in her slender fingers, dropping her eyes and jaw at the same time as she studied the photo. Then she spoke, maybe from instinct or accident. 'But this man is dead, no?'

'Yes,' Fergus edged forwards in his seat. 'You know him?'

Again she backed away, in her *no touching* mode. The music was almost done. Christ—no pun intended—he needed to get answers fast.

'He was a musician. He came to this club not so long ago.'

'Yes,' the admission again seemed instinctive, involuntary.

'What did he do?' Fergus breathed urgency.

'Please, you should go,' she tried to pass the picture back.

'Why?' The fucking music dipped towards closure. 'Why?'

'Please, he come asking questions, and talk my friend one dancer, and he say too much so they want to keep both them quiet.'

'*She*,' he mentally corrected her failing linguistics.

'Take picture back. No let them see this, please.'

Her fingers trembled, whole body shaking. Fergus took the picture, letting his hand linger on hers, breaking the golden rule, seeing terror in her powdered face, and the sudden glaze that caged the hope in her eyes.

'I'm not a police officer or anything,' he assured her.

'He want to find out where girls come from, what conditions we have,' Estrella's voice dipped to a whisper. 'Maybe some talk too much. My friend talk too much because messed up in head.'

'Messed up, how?' he needed to know. 'Coz o' drugs?'

Was she speaking of somebody like the grinning junkie who'd offered him a ten quid dance? What if the answers lay behind that opportunity and he'd missed his chance? Even detectives often miss what's before their eyes.

'Everything's messed up,' Estrella spoke again.

'What happened?' Fergus thought of Dyana needing answers. 'What did the singer find out that made these people want to get rid of him?'

'Please,' she turned towards the stereo.

'Tell me more,' he demanded, forgetting manners.

Driven by a fury to find out who had gunned down the musician on Deptford's streets in broad daylight, Fergus grabbed hold of Estrella's trembling body so tight he sensed the heat of her skin under the négligée. Touching her flesh, burning and freezing at the same time, he could imagine her as a lover, and regretted the incompletion of his private dance.

'I need to know this for the sake of a friend,' he insisted.

Rolling towards an end, the music veered downwards.

'People at the seaside,' she said, 'they give us girls.'

'What?' he demanded more. 'I don't understand.'

'Network,' she said. 'You see old man at bar?'

'Yes, talking to the African lady,' he recalled, and then grew suddenly conscious of the soundtrack to her dancing having stopped.

With the absence of music, outside noise filled the booth. He had to get answers now or never. What the hell was this network? Why was there a connection to the seaside? Who was the silver-headed gentleman?

'Tell me please,' he made a grab for her, sending her

stumbling backwards and knocking over the stereo with a thud against glass.

'Let go,' she released a fully-fledged shriek.

Then silence, as if all music in the club stopped and he'd made the outside world aware of his attempts to elicit information.

'Shit,' he realised, and turned to take leave of his questioning.

Stepping through the curtain, a goon stood before him.

'Not as good as The Valley,' Fergus tried to joke.

'What's going on?' the goon spoke over his shoulder.

'Nothing,' Estrella answered through clenched teeth.

A second goon stepped in. 'We heard a scream.'

'I touched her,' Fergus admitted. 'I'm sorry.'

'Didn't you tell the man no touching?'

'Yes,' Estrella's voice fell to a squeak.

'So why did you touch the girl?' the first goon stepped closer, clenching his fists tightly, not in the mood for any more jokes about Charlton's home turf. 'I think we'd better step outside and discuss this.'

'Come on you're a guy,' Fergus protested. 'You must know how easy it is to forget your manners with such a beautiful girl.'

'Get him outside now,' a third goon stepped into the scene as the silver-headed gentleman watched in the background from a safe distance. 'There's something about this guy that says trouble.'

'Hey calm down, this is all my fault,' the voice of salvation sounded. 'I'm a tattoo artist and I sent this man on a special mission.'

Surely she wasn't crazy enough to tell these fuckers the truth?

'I've been given a tough assignment,' Dyana edged closer to them. 'Designing a tattoo for a professional footballer. Dancer on a pole.'

'Fuck she's good at this,' Fergus thought. 'Maybe too good.'

'I needed somebody to tell me what it was like in the flesh.'

'So she sent muggins here to do her dirty work.'

'And our detective work is done, so if you don't mind we'll take our leave,' she grabbed his hand and turned on her heels. 'If you've a problem, call the police or even the professional footballer's lawyer.'

The goons looked unsure of how to react as she called their bluff. Then they glanced at the old guy who flickered his eyes towards the door.

'Just go and don't come back,' the goons finally spoke.

'What if they'd called the cops?' Fergus asked.

'I knew they wouldn't. Places like this don't,' she insisted.

But they'd outstayed their welcome, and were acutely aware of it. Dancers seemed aware of it too, before returning to their theatrics. The girl in the one piece had returned to the stage more subdued than before, as the old guy slinked towards a room at the back of the former warehouse.

'Maybe she's exhausted all her tricks,' Fergus thought as they made their way out of smoke and mirrors into the cool spring night.

But the smoke had followed them down the underpass as he caught echoes of Lance's stories from the grinning junkie smoking in the shadows—the woman who'd offered him a ten pound dance.

If he'd taken his chance and looked beneath the surface, he'd possibly have got closer to the answers than he managed with Estrella.

'Let's go somewhere for a nightcap and a recap,' Dyana suggested.

Moving back towards the station, they found a late night café, where Dyana slipped a joke over the rim of her cocktail glass. 'So did you see more action than on a Saturday afternoon at The Valley?'

'No, I stopped her during the dance and showed her

the picture. Wait....' The picture. He'd put it down on the seat when Estrella handed it back to him. 'Fuck, in the chaos, I left it there.'

Bad detective work, leaving a clue behind.

'And there's no going back,' Dyana sighed.

'Maybe not that different to The Valley after all,' Fergus sipped his beer. 'Nothing there ever goes according to plan either.'

18. Mental Jungle

*D*ancing girls strutted the stage of Fergus's mind in the dead of night. Rumbling. Rumble in the Jungle of his system. He could see them arrayed upon the beams of the former timberhouse where he'd spent the evening before, walking among the ghosts of gangsters.

Smoke and mirrors, magic lantern shows of the flesh and on the flesh. He caught a disconcerting Blue Curaçao stare from above an orange dress with gold zips glistening against the bones of a strong back. Then the scene changed. A new dancer had taken to the stage, or was she an old one weaving her spell in this magic lantern show?

Through curls of coloured smoke he could see the new dancer's skin white as apple blossom beneath hair dark as Yorkshire soil. He knew the body, stretched out, sighing, pushing against the pole.

He cried out her name in a cold sweat. 'Katy.'

Suddenly the waking world invaded the borders of his dream country. Birds chirped in his garden and sirens squealed in the wings of Shooter's Hill. Parakeets and emergencies. Morning music, Charlton style.

Dancers gone, he reached out and found his bed empty. Bin lorries churning in the background. First day of the working week.

Seven more to go until Bank Holiday Monday and the play off final. Already the Palace fans were getting carried away with themselves. Gloating about the semi-final against Brighton, they called it their greatest victory ever. The London TV news carried interviews with supporters. Their local papers in Croydon promised souvenir pull-outs for the Wembley visit.

'Smug bastards,' Fergus thought as he rose.

After the cold winter, white blossom had finally foamed upon the gnarled limbs of his ancient apple tree. This summer there'd be no gathering of apples before the peeling, slicing, and stewing. Suddenly he pictured Katy standing by an oven, bathed in the soft light of nostalgia.

'Perhaps Dyana bakes,' he fought for focus.

He had to leave the past behind and move towards the future. He was taking a basketball session in the College this morning. Monday classes weren't easy, teaching a group of boys high on testosterone and attitude. Teenage waste men smoked out of their minds on cheap grass. These were the kids who'd spent a lifetime passing through the school system, drifting to the back of the room, sitting there in a daze as teachers ignored them.

Most carried some form of learning difficulty. Criminal records too, picked up for foolish escapades that cost them opportunities along the way. One boy had been a triallist at Charlton. Another played for a couple of non-league clubs. One, a former migrant, spent a season with Bayern Munich before a knee injury ended his career.

'Fine margins,' Fergus thought of the borders between success and failure. Those boys had come out on the wrong side of the margin. 'Maybe Poppy's father was such a boy once upon a time.'

Last night, after catching public transport back to Woolwich, Fergus had left Dyana on the edge of General Gordon's deserted square at midnight. She had to pick up Poppy from the babysitter's.

'You can meet her,' Dyana suggested. 'Some time soon.'

Fergus agreed, though wasn't sure. The child was like a tattoo, a permanent reminder of somebody else's flesh giving shape to new life in Dyana's womb. He'd thought about this on the crowded bus home, clutching a silver pole to stand upright. In his intoxicated mind, every passenger became a lapdancer. He could see them all strutting the stage, stripping off, enacting party tricks with ice like the dancer in the orange one-piece.

Withdrawing from the garden window, and the white lingerie of apple blossom, Fergus shivered as if melting ice cubes had trickled down his spine. Stepping into the shower, he caught a flash of the sword tattoo that had driven Katy out of his life and onto the back of Wagner's motorbike.

Colours blazed blood red, metallic white, and night-river black through suds and steam. The dream of Katy dancing flashed through his mind once more as he massaged shampoo into his scalp.

A past to be deleted like an email.

'Except I didn't,' he tried not to recall.

He'd taken the message out of the trash, placing it unopened in his draft folder amongst other emails gathered over the short space of their romance. Sometimes when drunk, he strayed towards the landmine of their content—letting old words and images explode before his eyes. Even now, with Dyana in the picture, he found it hard to shake off Katy's words. She'd always possessed the knack of getting inside his head.

He'd lie in bed remembering. Baking. Fragrances of bread and desire. Gas flaring. Butter melting. An evening of goblin laughter upon the television infecting their hearts with panic. Frantic rushing to the seashore and making love in a boat. But it was time to script a new narrative with Dyana.

'Just hope the child doesn't get in the way,' he stepped out of the shower, and dried off in front of his tattooed reflection.

Deep down he understood the injustice of his ambitions. Dyana had carried Poppy in the womb for nine months, and brought her into this world. Sooner or later he'd have to meet the child.

'We'll introduce you as *mummy's friend*,' Dyana suggested.

She didn't want her baby growing up in a world of waste men coming and going at the top of the stairs, so wouldn't call him a lover.

'I'm not a waste man,' he'd tried to assure her in the café.

'Good,' she answered. 'I can't afford for you to let me down. I haven't time for playing games. I'm a woman, not a football club.'

Getting dressed, he felt torn inside. These were serious thoughts for a fine sunny morning, as he went downstairs and ate breakfast. Every shiny surface resurrected fresh memories of the night before.

Girls in white lingerie rose from the kettle's crawling steam. They stayed in his coffee and the blonde butter on his toast. Even in the news of a tornado building up in the American mid-west, readying for a storm.

Finishing breakfast and switching off the TV, he ventured outside. The sharp May light cut his eyes, dancing on the cobwebs of a hangover. Passing through the park, he caught a scent of fresh cut grass.

Spring had come to Charlton after a cold winter. Sometimes he walked to work. Not today. Catching a bus he had to stand against a pole and thought of dancers once more—junkies, and ghosts in an orange one piece.

Getting to College, he bought juice from a machine to relieve his thirst. Then—a commotion up ahead snapped him out of his daze.

'What's happening?' he edged down the crowded corridor.

He could see a cluster of girls outside the Disability Referral Unit. Victoria went there, and hated it for the use of that word *disability*, when she was the most able person he'd ever met, at her own craft—football.

Most of these kids, even the teenage waste men, had a smartness they couldn't express—a nest of thoughts buzzing behind their glassy eyes.

A couple of teachers stood at opposite ends of the corridor, grabbing hold of two girls as the goons had grabbed him the night before.

He noticed the window of the Referral Unit smashed. Splinters of glass littered the tiles. One girl had a bloodied fist, and another a bloody mouth.

A teacher spoke. 'This madam produced a knife.'

'They called me fick coz I'd an appointment here,' the angry young woman protested. 'Claimed I was faking dyslexia to get a free laptop. Said I was so useless I wouldn't even be any good at pretending to be stupid.'

Chelsea and Victoria stood in the midst of the crowd, watching.

The principal then appeared, scattering the crowd with the force of a tornado as his voice boomed down the corridor. 'What's going on here?'

As the teachers explained the situation, he said he wanted everybody to come in early Wednesday morning as punishment.

'That's not fair,' Chelsea protested from amongst the silenced pack. 'We was just watching. Passengers not drivers.'

'You were here,' the principal's face burned bright red at the insolence. 'If you're not fixing a problem you're part of it.' Then he turned around. 'Since some of these girls are on your football team you can be the one who gives them a talk on Wednesday morning.'

'Great, fucking great,' Fergus mumbled on his way down the corridor to seek out the sweet sticky scent of marijuana and basketball.

Maybe at least it would keep his mind off Katy Prunty.

'If it really is desperation stations, she'd call me,' he mulled over the situation on his way to class, 'to find out why I haven't answered.'

Finding the boys assembled in the corridor outside the gymnasium, he ordered them inside to get changed, and set about preparing the equipment. Then, as the minutes passed in a haze, the day's game started.

In the midst of it, his phone buzzed. Hurriedly, he reached for it.

'I need your help,' he read the first line of the message and then realised that it had come from Lance as he scrolled further down the page. 'We're running a new project in the community garden.'

Back in the winter of 2011, fresh out of the army and feeling lonely, Lance had hungered for a cause to pass the time. It was the year before the London Olympics and the city's Lord Mayor had made funds available for 2012 growing spaces as part of the Games' legacy.

Having studied horticulture at College in the days before he joined the army, Lance decided to create an urban garden in his neighbourhood. First he found a patch of wasteland at the side of the apartments where he lived. Fergus and Katy lived there too, between the waterfront and the Royal Naval College at Greenwich where their love first blossomed.

As his neighbours embarked on romance, Lance ploughed his energies into tackling the waste ground, left wild and riotous for decades. Weeds and thorns linked limbs in six foot waves, stooped and gnarled from being unable to climb no further. Dead tree stumps blocked the swing of picks and spades. Foxes lurked in the shadows, afflicted in itching sores from mange. Cats prowled the furrows in search of field mice and unfortunate birds.

Undeterred, pushing inwards and onwards, Lance's army of volunteers cleared a path through the undergrowth, levelled the earth, and brought organisation to the riotous chaos. They fed the foxes antibiotics in honey to heal their wounds so they could drift off elsewhere in rude health, and then built a series of allotments in the spaces they'd vacated. Next came social spaces, sheds, and even a bug hotel, a pine box filled with tubes, bark and wood shavings to create a Noah's Ark of insects in the city space.

'And now,' he explained in his text, 'we're going to create a Forest School so that kids from the local Primaries can use the garden. So I'm going to need some help over the next few days to shift things around.'

'Sure,' Fergus agreed, through the fuzz of his hangover.

'I'm also going to a meeting in Woolwich this evening for a chat with folks from the Council,' he added. 'Come and join me for a pint afterwards.'

'Maybe,' Fergus answered. 'Depends how much work I get done.'

He had a hangover to shake off and a speech to write.

19. Shots in the evening

Fergus wrestled for ideas at a desk facing out on the apple tree in his garden, imagining the blossom as surf set against a sea blue sky. This spring after the cold winter, the blossom had lingered more than he ever remembered the froth of any in his lifetime. But then, looking for too long, it changed to Cappuccino, and he found his thoughts whisked towards Katy and her barista riding bikes along the coast.

'Vomit,' he fought to forget the pair of them.

Then he returned to the struggle of writing, speaking in a language outside his own—the language of contemporary youth. He didn't just want to go in and preach that violence was wrong. They'd ask why, if it's so wrong, the world's most powerful places seem to use so much of it.

These were teenagers whose minds buzzed with dreams and ideas they'd no chance of expressing outside of their own circles let alone realising.

Suddenly his phone, and not his mind, buzzed.

'What the fuck am I going to say to them?'

'Lance again,' he realised as a message flashed.

'Come and meet me in the pub,' it demanded.

Rather than getting into a tennis match of text messages tangled up in the crossed wires of time, he decided to call his friend directly. He found him almost breathless on the other end of a phone, at a pub down where the Thames flowed into the silver shells and cylinders of the Flood Barrier.

'You won't believe all that I've just seen in Woolwich!'

'Never heard anybody come out of a Council meeting so excited,' Fergus felt a sudden sense of intrigue. 'What happened in there?'

'Nothing in the meeting. That was boring as fuck,' Lance clarified.

'So what was it then?' Fergus hungered for answers.

Lance proceeded to feed him slow as eating porridge through a straw. 'This all happened in Woolwich DLR station as I was coming home.'

'And what exactly happened?' Fergus pressed for more.

'Come down to the pub and I'll tell you.'

Though he'd no desire for drink Fergus agreed to the suggestion when his friend explained that he had a hell of a story to tell. Going back out the door and through the park where the scent of fresh cut grass had faded, morning time and his dreams of Katy seemed long ago.

Going down Church Lane he passed the heights of *Dark River Dye*, and then moved on across a busy intersection down towards the river.

'This better be some story,' he said as he arrived at the bar.

'Oh it is,' Lance spoke out towards the Thames Barrier that Fergus remembered from the picture of Demetrius in Dyana's press cutting. 'When I reached the DLR station in Woolwich I was greeted by a commotion.'

'That much of a demand to see your gardening

meeting, huh?'

'No,' Lance laughed. 'I wasn't the centre of attraction there.'

'So what happened?' Fergus dipped his head to the narrow margin of sand that lined the shore where the river brushed Charlton's borders.

'Something crazy,' Lance explained. 'I'm not even sure where it begins and ends, or what part of the story I walked into when I reached the station.' He paused then to wet his lips in the foam of a fresh beer. 'I'd cut across the square, and gone through the front entrance of the station. Swiped my card, and started making my way down the escalator to the platforms.'

Around them seagulls barked and mewed in the light of a setting sun. Boats from across the shore in North Greenwich brought Fergus back again to memories of an evening at sunset on the Ramsgate sands.

The string of Lance's voice pulled him back to the present. 'Going down the stairway, I caught something out of the corner of my eye.'

'Hard to see anything at rush hour in London,' Fergus thought of crowded platforms so different to the broad sweep of the river before them. 'Stations are like weekend cattle markets in Ireland.'

'Yeah,' Lance agreed, following the path of a seagull with his eyes. 'And everybody's alone even though there's thousands of people there.'

'Every man, woman, rat, dog, and child for themselves.'

'Exactly, and that's what was so out of place.'

'How do you mean?' Fergus grew curious.

'These guys got off a train and they had another person with them.'

'But why would you notice that as being out of place?'

Lance struggled to define exactly what it was that had spooked him. 'There was something unusual in the closeness of their bodies. Like you'd see at a football match when the players are huddled together for a corner.'

'Yeah but train passengers are always crushed together.'

Lance shook his blonde locks insistently, frustrated by Fergus's failure to detect the full tension of the situation. 'These people were as fucking tight together as defenders trying to mark Messi or Ronaldo.'

'It's rush hour,' Fergus insisted. 'That's life in London.'

Again Lance protested. 'You're not getting this.' Then he raised his voice as his eyes drifted out towards the Isle of Dogs' skyscrapers, grey and sturdy as a pack of wolfhounds in the distance. 'These guys had the woman in their grip, the way you might imagine an executioner in the movies leading the prisoner towards their death. She was carrying a case too, like she had all her belongings packed, and was ready to meet her maker, whoever that was. And by the end of it, I'm guessing he was some kind of surgeon.'

'I'm still not getting any of this,' Fergus still found the scene indecipherable as the unlit neon of the towers in the distance.

'I think they were holding a gun to their prisoner's back,' Lance sketched further details of the subterranean subterfuge. 'Then as they approached the opposite stairway to where I was coming down the escalator, they got caught up amongst a group of Nigerian women going to a wedding.' His voice quickened around an undercurrent of laughter. 'The girl lashed out at the men with her suitcase, and broke free from their grasp. Everything spilled out of the case onto the platform as the Nigerian women started to scream and beat at the gunmen with a flurry of handbags.'

Fergus leaned in closer to the blaze of Lance's eyes, cheering on the mysterious figure as she sought out the mouth of the station's exit, and the freedom of Woolwich with its back roads through the echoes of history.

'She was slim and supple, able to move quickly up the stairway,' Lance moved on with the story. 'The Nigerian women continued to pummel the men with their handbags until they too managed to break free and give chase, by which time it was hopeless because their target had reached the top.'

'So she escaped from them? All's well that ends well.'

'Yeah but then they opened fire on her.'

'Shooting in a station at rush hour?'

'Yeah,' Lance continued breathlessly.

'So did anybody get hurt in all this?'

'Just the goons,' Lance answered. 'Those Nigerian women took as many lumps out of them with their handbags as defenders used to hammer into Clive Mendonca's shins in Charlton's glory days.'

'So the girl got away from them?'

'Got out of the station anyway.'

'Then it all turned out okay?'

'Yeah but it was very odd.'

Lance stopped to catch his breath, as Fergus watched the sun sink lower and paint every boat in North Greenwich marina brilliant orange.

'Sounds more spectacular than odd,' he snapped back to the present, away from memories of love in a boat and a chilli sun going down.

'Yeah but maybe I've missed out one of the key details,' Lance confessed. 'It was only in the middle of it I realised she was a girl.'

'You didn't know the woman was young at first?'

'No, not that,' he continued down a path as cryptic as Katy's emails. 'This person wasn't like those Nigerian ladies on their way to a wedding. The body shape looked out of place. At first glance I could have sworn on the life of Clive Mendonca that the figure being taken captive was a man.'

Suddenly Fergus's eyes strayed towards the Isle of Dogs and Canary Wharf's towers coming slowly to light above the river's horseshoe bend. Before Lance had even explained the rest, he had a feeling of something wrong in the air—the way that fish are said to have premonitory sensations of earthquakes, migrating from the danger before it happens.

'Maybe it was only when the commotion had passed I realised,' his friend admitted. 'Maybe from seeing the contents of her case spilled out on the platform and people walking over them as if they weren't there.'

'What sort of contents?' Fergus anticipated tremors.

'Wads of bank notes for a start,' Lance recalled. 'Then clothes and shoes—an orange dress with gold buckles getting all torn in the rush as everybody tried to get to hell out of there after the gunshots.'

Nipple tricks sent shivers down Fergus's spine. 'Fuck.'

'And all this happened in broad daylight,' Lance added.

'Just as with the murder of Demetrius,' Fergus thought.

But at least the dancer had escaped from this unholy incident—and he was pretty sure this was the one that spooked him in *The Bird Cage*.

He had to talk to Dyana immediately. 'I've got to go.'

'Come on man, stay for a couple of beers.'

'Nah, hard day at the office,' he shook his head. 'Basketball training's always a bastard. Besides, drinking on a Monday makes for a messy week.'

Monday night soon becomes Tuesday morning, and you're carrying a fuzz in your system that isn't fully gone until the hump of the working week.

'Well, I reckon I'll go across to the Rose,' his friend declared. 'Doesn't matter to me how messy the week gets.'

'Yeah, you don't have to teach people.'

'We've got another gardening session at the weekend though,' Lance rose up from his table at the riverside. 'Could do with a few extra pairs of hands. Why don't you ask your black bird if she'd come along?'

'Maybe,' he agreed. 'She could bring her kid along.'

'She's got a kid?' Lance glanced down the street. 'I'd stay away from that. You don't want to get tangled up with another man's child.'

Regardless of his friend's warning, he had to call her on the way home. Danger stalked the streets of London. Like the days of Jack the Ripper, when Lance's ancestors ventured out of boxing clubs and into protection.

Jesus Christ gunned down on his way home through New Cross. And now a dancer chased through a train station at rush hour by the dark angels who guarded the dancing club they'd visited the night before.

Suddenly he felt a terrible sense of fear, like a woman must get when she hears footsteps behind her in a park late at night, knowing that in those moments of isolation there's no law, no guardian to save her from danger.

Maybe for the first time he understood the darkness in Katy's past, but now it was time to call Dyana and hope the darkness didn't close in on them.

'Hey,' he said when she answered. 'I've some news for you.'

'I don't need any distractions right now,' she put the brakes on his story. 'Poppy's come down with a fever. She's a very sick child.'

He tried not to reveal his apathy. 'What's wrong?'

'She's having problems sleeping. Maybe it's a chest cold.'

Having no experience of kids, he could only draw on his own childhood. 'Why, don't you try giving her some hot whiskey?'

'Whiskey!' she exclaimed. 'To get my baby drunk?'

'Just a nip in a glass of hot water or milk,' Fergus suggested. 'When I was a child in Ireland, my father used to make it for visitors or when any of us were sick. We called it *punch* because it sends you spinning into a deep happy sleep where you dream warm safe things all night long.'

'How do I make this punch?' she'd gotten curious.

It was a simple recipe but required subtlety all the same.

'First of all you boil the kettle. Then fill a tumbler to

the brim so that it's piping hot, using a metal spoon to make sure the glass doesn't crack.' His voice softened as he listed out the final instructions. 'Wait a few minutes, then pour out a third of the water, add the whiskey, stir in two spoonfuls of sugar, and toss in a fistful of cloves.'

'Give me time,' she fussed, 'to take this in.'

He allowed her to catch up before concluding. 'Stir the cloves and the sugar around the glass to take away the whiskey taste.'

'Okay,' she said. 'I might try this if you're sure it works.' Then she laughed. 'And you're sure I'm not going to get arrested or anything?'

'I don't think you're in any danger,' he whispered a wish. Besides if a group of Nigerian women with handbags could beat off a couple of goons, they'd stand no chance against a boy from Ireland's border country who was once upon a time going to be champion of the world. Barry McGuigan may have had his night in Shepherd's Bush. Fergus Sharkey might turn out to be Dyana and Poppy's knight upon the grassland of Woolwich Common.

20. Past Portal

*P*erhaps he should blame the radio left on in his room as he tried to sleep. Lying in bed, listening to the news, a story broke about the dancer from the days before, the girl in an orange dress.

The police had now announced her as missing and labelled her as being what he had noticed on the night before. 'Transgender.'

Teenage trialist with Palace who'd had a sex change.

'No, this can't be true,' he protested. 'Another dream.'

He'd never wakened since his visit to the club last night.

'Paying off debts and trying to save for a future in Australia, the club dancer moved far from life as a football player,' the broadcaster's words tugged Fergus between contrasting states of consciousness.

To prove that he was dreaming he would rise and float downstairs. Getting out of bed his feet touched solid ground. He realised then that the news breaking through the web of his half sleep was horribly real.

Going downstairs to investigate further he made a glass of punch stronger than anything he'd ever suggest Dyana giving to Poppy. Then logging onto the computer he began his search for the former footballer.

Somewhere in the midst of team pictures he grew distracted.

'I shouldn't do this,' he thought aloud.

Deep down he always knew this moment would come.

'**Desperation stations**,' the cryptic title scalded his eyes once again.

Blaming the dancer's death, he had decided to read the email that he had lifted out of his thrash and placed unopened amongst the drafts.

He'd made the decision because life seemed a fragile thing.

Clicking on the message he felt a peculiar variation of fear.

'Hello Fergus,' the message began. 'I know we agreed not to talk, but I've reached a crossroads of the heart and there's nowhere left to run.'

Every word felt like classified information in Katy's world.

'When you came to Ramsgate, we used to go for sunset walks,' she reminisced. 'These days I go alone. I've drifted apart from Wagner.'

Why was she telling him this?

She'd anticipated his questions. 'That's what led to this present situation, where I need your help, urgently. There's not much time, so I'll explain this fast, and if you care, not for me, but for those involved, you'll maybe take some action.'

'Probably exaggeration, egocentric vomit.'

But he read on, pushed by rumbling curiosities.

'Lately Wagner's been spending a lot of time away from me. One day he was gone so early and back so late, I joked that he'd taken a boat to the coast of France. He reacted strangely to that, going all hushed and paranoid, the way people do if they're screwing somebody else. So I started following him, seeing what he was doing after work.'

Not so long ago, Fergus might have been satisfied by the slow decay of her romance with the young barista, but the oxytocin had all dried up. She could screw every love rat in Ramsgate on the beach for all he cared.

Despite this, he had a burning curiosity to know the ending.

'One night, when I was working on my book, Wagner slipped away,' he read on. 'After a few minutes, I followed from a safe distance. He went down along the shore towards the marina. There, he got inside a boat.'

Fergus pictured a vessel by the name of *Valkyries* swallowing up his love rival, as a symphony of intense emotion blasted through Katy's mind. Despite oxytocin's absence, he imagined a music of justice.

Her email continued. 'It was a small houseboat, like those you used to see more often on the Thames. I stood on the shore and watched him going downstairs towards a room with a light.'

Now he imagined the symphonies of an overactive imagination growing louder in Katy's mind until they reached sheer fury.

'Nothing happened for several minutes. Then a woman came to the window and pulled curtains across the face of the light.'

'You must have been burning by now,' he thought.

'Their shadows moved to another space, out of view. All sorts of things went through my head. What were they doing? Shagging in the boat?'

Fergus burned too as he read those words.

He thought of disturbance on the shores of Ramsgate, and waves, hot as chilli, in the red light of a sunset. If he closed his eyes, he could imagine the feel of Katy's mouth and the fragrance of her baking.

And now, out of the blue, he had her voice back,

narrating the ending of her latest love affair. 'They stayed there an hour, and I stayed too, frozen by wind and anger,' the composition continued. 'Then the lights went off. I dipped behind a signpost. They came up from the lower reaches of the boat. Finally I saw the face of my rival.'

'So you get to know the feeling,' Fergus thrilled.

'If your man's going to screw another woman you expect her to be beautiful,' Katy raged against their secret tryst. 'But this bitch had hair turning white and was no Playboy Bunny, that's for sure.'

Reading on, Fergus followed his former lover back to the house she'd rented facing out on the shore on the ferry terminal side of town. She'd raced back to her desk, writing at the window when he returned.

'I asked where he was and he told me he'd gone to his coffeeshop,' she explained. 'I knew then that I had been sleeping with a liar ever since we first stopped by a field on that fucking bike of his.'

'I guess you were lying to me too,' Fergus realised.

He should have deleted the message then, but he kept going as if to get the satisfaction of seeing the wheels of their romance buckle.

'As the days passed, I got more paranoid. Finally I went to the spare room one evening, because he had stored a couple of suitcases there. I thought they belonged to the witch, and he was going to run off with her.'

Fergus paused to draw breath, confused in his emotions now.

'I found the cases padlocked, so I got a knife. I'd snap them open, answer my curiosities, and then put them back together again. I didn't know what I'd find and what I'd do afterwards. I had visions of a woman's lingerie, and that bitch upturned like a turtle on its back in the boat.'

'Life in the mind of a jealous lover,' Fergus mused.

'Sure enough, clothes and shoes tumbled out at first. But there was something else buried into the base, hidden like clues to a puzzle.'

Reaching in, she pulled Fergus towards the case.

'First I discovered maps of the London Underground, and wallets full of train tickets. It was like they'd robbed the machines inside Ramsgate station. Going deeper for answers, I found something else too, smooth and leathery on my fingers like the cover of a book.'

Pushing through the lining, the truth came slowly into view.

'Passports,' she started a new line, as if for impact. 'Dozens of them, as I read the gold lettering above the shield of the lion and unicorn.'

The free lion represented England and the chained unicorn Scotland, Fergus recalled as he pictured the words in gold. 'EUROPEAN UNION—UNITED KINGDOM OF GREAT BRITAIN AND NORTHERN IRELAND.'

Now concerned, he kept reading Katy's story. 'They had to be fake, so I picked some out from amongst the bundle and flicked through the pages to be sure. Everything seemed in order. I was scared now. What if Lance is right, and some people are coming here with murder on their minds?'

A new kind of fear gripped Fergus's emotions. This wasn't the fear of hearing someone's voice on the other end of a phone. This was a fear of the receiver going dead, suddenly and forcefully.

'Even though I was scared, I wanted to know more,' he read her words aloud. 'I looked inside the front covers. There, on every one, I found an identification page, and from each page the face of a black woman stared back at me, sad and scarred.'

He paused to draw breath, imagining the passports.

'Oh Fergus, what's Wagner involved in, and what have I got drawn into by a terrible mistake?'

Images of the dead musician and Calais migrants flashed through Fergus's mind. He thought of slave ships and people smuggling. Women, sad eyed and scarred, chained together like Scottish unicorns.

He remembered Dyana's journey from Africa, from one meat market to another, and the fear of sand that had never faded.

'What exactly has this bastard done to Katy?'

But the email's ending offered no answers.

'I'm so scared, but I had to put them back and fix the lock,' she said. 'I'm debating confronting Wagner or going straight to the police, but first I have to meet my editor. She's coming down from Manchester to Broadstairs for the day. I can't miss this chance to discuss my work. I'll put Wagner to the back of my mind, and sort this out later.'

Then he felt a hot tear forming in his eye as he read the last lines. Much as he tried, he'd never been able to hate her.

'Thanks for listening Fergus. Even though everything ended badly between us, you're always good with pragmatic advice. Let me know what you think as soon as you get this, and I'll check my emails on the way back to Ramsgate. Katy, x.'

'Christ,' he realised, 'this was a week ago.'

Calling her, he got no answer. Searching the net for arrests in Ramsgate he reached a dead end. Her words surfed through his head on fresh waves of oxytocin as he weighed up ways of helping Katy, x.

Going onto her social media profiles, he found nothing from recent times. Giving up the ghost, tired from basketball lessons, he decided to sleep on the problem. Waking early, the seed of an idea had entered his mind.

Trawling through cyberspace, he finally found contact details for her editor, the woman in Manchester that she was supposed to meet.

'I haven't heard from her in weeks but that's normal with writers,' said the lady with a husky Mancunian accent after he explained who he was.

'Didn't you have lunch with her in Broadstairs?'

'Yes, that's the last time I spoke to her.'

'Did she say anything unusual?'

'Let me think.' The woman's voice returned after an interlude of humming. 'She was doing well with the book and hoped to make the deadline.' She hummed again. 'Mind you, towards the end she said something odd about making a mess, a wrong decision, a bad choice. She got quite animated and then left. She said she was expecting a phone call. No she said she was hoping for a phone call.'

That was it. She'd crossed Harbour Street and vanished, as if slipping off the cliffs and into the bay. Nobody had heard from her since, as he called her closest friends, one by one. Because he didn't want to share all the details, most of the radical chicks dismissed his concerns.

'It's just Katy. She's a fashion designer. Her whole life's a show.'

'Look Fergus, it's not your fight anymore. Just forget it.'

But he couldn't forget the image of those passports and the chained women. Though it was the twenty first of May, he felt trapped in another time zone, caught up in the hours after Katy's email. Around him the world moved on, readying for summer as another day's headlines got written. He moved on too, going for a run across Woolwich Common before work. There, he shared his space with a couple of army guys carrying rucksacks.

'Baggage,' he thought, glancing up towards Dyana's empty balcony. Then felt guilty and texted her to find out about Poppy, making sure that the people who'd chased after the dancer weren't hunting her as well.

At breakfast Dyana texted back. 'Fergus, you really are a champion. Your Irish punch seems to have worked. Poppy's better today.'

'Great,' he replied on his way towards Charlton Park.

Shortly after she called him up as he walked to work.

'Hey babe,' she sounded happy as that first day in her studio.

'Hey,' he echoed. 'I've something to tell you.'

She needed to know about the runaway dancer.

'Wait,' she stopped him. 'I've something for you first.'

'Okay,' he sidelined his own thoughts.

Dyana took a deep breath before speaking. 'I think the time has finally come for the little woman in my life to meet the man in my life.'

Suddenly he hesitated as images of soldiers weighed down with rucksacks flashed through his mind. But then he thought of the club, Demetrius, the dancer, and the terrifying brevity of life.

'Let's create a plan for Saturday,' he suggested, wondering what she'd make of going to the play off final at Wembley between Palace and Watford—the 120 million pound game, and then deciding that was a bad idea.

This football season had already cost him one romance.

'Any ideas?' Dyana enthused on the other end of the phone.

'How about an afternoon of chilling in Greenwich Park?'

'Children don't just chill,' she joked. 'They need adventure and action. What about we take in as many parks as possible on the same day?'

'That could be a lot of ground to cover.'

'More chance to get to know each other,' she replied.

He already knew Dyana. It was Poppy he had to learn about, the mixed race English girl who was somebody else's baby. Above all, Dyana's baby. She'd always be there in the background demanding her mother's constant attention. He'd never be anything more than *mummy's friend*.

If she grew up to play for England alongside Victoria and Chelsea, he couldn't even stand up on a bar table and shout *'that's my girl.'*

Because she would never be his girl in the same way as if, together with Katy, he had created *Little Georgie Sharkey*.

'Okay,' he defeated his doubts and agreed in the end. 'We'll meet on the Isle of Dogs and make our way across the river.'

One Saturday with somebody else's baby wasn't going to kill him. Probably best to wait until then too to break the news of the dancer.

Telling her now would only cause her to worry. She'd be scared of something happening to her child when there was probably no need.

'Those folks at the club couldn't possibly know who we were,' he weighed up the rightness of his reasons for not telling her.

'Thank you,' she broke into his daydreams. 'There's nothing sweeter you can do for a mother than to spend a day with her baby.'

Again she was *her baby*, always someone else's child.

Shouldn't be a big deal in the 21st century, but this was primal instinct. The same primal instinct left him concerned for Katy's welfare.

Trying to call her, he got no answer. Then he texted three or four times in the break between classes, hoping that each message would be the last. Finally, after a long and agonising wait, a response came.

'I'm okay,' the words on the screen tugged at his heart as he read them aloud. 'Been busy, under presure. There's no need to wory.'

Something about the message spooked him, but he couldn't put his finger on it as he drifted out of one sports session towards another.

Another text message too. From Dyana this time, enthused by the weekend. 'Told Poppy about our trip. She's so excited.'

But his trip through London's parks seemed far away, and out of reach. He couldn't figure out, at first, why he had a bad feeling about Katy. Then, towards the end of the afternoon, the answer flashed through his mind.

You don't see it at first when you read a text message.

'Spelling mistakes,' he returned to her words, rasping out the message in a whisper as he glanced down at the missing teeth of two words.

Strange for Katy because she was such a language and grammar snob. She never made spelling mistakes. He had a sense of something being badly out of place in the natural order of the world.

Suddenly he too was *woried*, very *woried* by Katy's broken spelling.

21. Savage Garden

*W*ednesday 22nd May, 2013. Birthday of George Best who was one day going to give his name to Georgie Sharkey, English football star with an Irish father. The morning began with a dream of Katy and Georgie. Then a sudden awakening from a stab of light through the curtains. Katy's face receded into a spray of sunshine and apple blossom as Fergus reached out for a radio connection to the world.

'Nothing but bad news,' the stories came in quick-fire fashion.

Tales of tornadoes and people camped out on the edges of Oklahoma. Echoes of Calais migrants fresh from another night of riding rodeo.

Meanwhile, thousands of miles away, blizzards of a different kind. Roadside bombings, and mortar shelling of marketplaces in Baghdad.

'Year of carnage,' the broadcaster announced in perfectly measured BBC Queen's English, 'and it's only

May.'

Great city, former citadel of learning, reduced to ashes.

'Depressing,' Fergus felt glad to leave the house early, to go and give a lecture to his girls on the dangerous cocktail of knives and empty rage.

Going down the street he caught shivers of the sun's ascent over the fine white houses of Canberra Road and blood red buses in the distance.

The roads were empty at this time of morning, save for men laying asphalt. As he walked, he watched them going through a series of rituals. Cordoning off sections of the street. Marking the road for a cutting. Laying out their assemblage of tools. An armoury of shovels stained in the black crust of yesterday's digging. A fresh day's work lay ahead.

It was an ordinary spring morning on the plainest of roads possible. Behind the razor wire on the barrack walls he imagined life stirring. He thought of the mounted soldiers of The King's Troop Royal Horse Artillery readying for a morning ride upon their majestic beasts.

Lance had once explained that this was the unit which carried the quick-firing field guns used for the royal salute. Like drummers on the battlefield, he had supposed, but his · former colleague corrected him.

This section of the British military had a purely ceremonial role.

Fergus had passed them several times on a run across the Common. The female riders with their stiff uniforms and practiced emotions reminded him of Katy. She too had been trained in the rules of social class.

'Unlike the girls I'm about to talk to,' he grumbled inwardly.

All their actions seemed based on raw emotion, he thought as he made his way past Kinveachy Gardens on the borders of Charlton and Woolwich.

As the landscape changed to brown-brick and high rises, he decided to text Katy and tell her where he was, by the road that led to Maryon Park. There, they'd spent many days and evenings together. Strolling, conversing, sharing picnics, clearing the woods, and helping with spring planting.

'*Knives Chat Gardens*,' predictive text messed up his efforts.

Ironic—considering the focus of his lecture this morning.

By the time he arrived in College the principal had already assembled the girls in a classroom, sleepy-eyed and cursing the early hour.

'Why are we even here?' Chelsea lifted her face off a desk.

'To learn about why you don't go playing with knives.'

'We're not kids,' his rebellious young team member groaned again. 'And we know that knives ain't for Barbie dolls.'

'Knives are no way to have an argument,' he insisted.

They gave as good as they got. 'Yeah, but sometimes you have to build a reputation quick, and show people you're no pushover.'

'Street violence isn't the way.'

He explained that even Charlton and Millwall had come together in recent years to support a campaign entitled *Street Violence Ruins Lives*.

The initiative had come from Charlton Athletic Community Trust, after the murder of two teenagers on the streets of London. One was a Charlton supporter, a young actor stabbed to death outside a bar, and the other kid, from a family with Millwall connections, had been murdered in a bakery.

Teenagers dying outside pubs and shops for no good reason put all the rivalries within football into perspective, he told the girls.

Again they struck back with a common refrain. 'Yeah, but you're from a different generation, with no idea how it is on the streets these days.'

'I used to be a teenager,' he laughed as he spoke the words, and they offered blank stares to his challenging their discovery of all the exciting things in the world. 'We had sex, drugs, and violence in those ancient days too.'

'Not like now,' a girl in the front row voiced resistance.

'London's always been a violent place,' he counter-argued but they shrugged their shoulders again because history just didn't matter nowadays.

Maybe if he made this human and personal, he'd get better responses. Therefore, on the spot, he began to narrate the tale of Lance's family.

'We'll go back to Jack the Ripper,' he took charge of the lectern.

From there he progressed through the story of two wars and a greyhound track up to the rage of Vivaldi's Henchman. He hoped the story might shake them out of their sense of rage and violence on the streets of London being unique to their generation.

When the tale was over, they left the room in silence.

Then, with a day free from teaching, he started to design a course.

'Maybe I'll work from home in the afternoon,' he figured.

That was his cue to head back to the house, but first he needed to go into Greenwich and see Lance to pick up some materials for his garden.

'My apple tree has a bad dose of woodworm.'

'Yeah, but it's only on the surface,' Lance explained when they met. 'Woodworm's like maggots, feeding off parts of the tree that are dead.'

'So they're not going to strike at the healthy parts?'

'No,' Lance replied with the assurance of a qualified tree surgeon. 'Come down to the community garden and I'll show you.'

'I'm supposed to be preparing lessons.'

'This is a lesson,' his friend laughed as they crossed into the garden. 'An afternoon session in the ways and habits of woodworm.'

Moving towards a section of trees in the corner of the garden, Fergus thought again of time's passing, and Katy's lack of response. He'd a bad feeling in his guts. Those spelling mistakes had stayed in his head since the last message and there'd been no contact since.

'Look,' Lance produced a Swiss army knife and pointed to a patch of dust on the crumbling edges of one weatherbeaten tree. 'When you scratch away the wood on the surface you come to the layer that's still living, and there's no infestation of that part.'

The dead shavings fell like dandruff at the touch of Lance's knife, and once he scratched away the surface layers, he reached the core of a tree that was still alive, drinking moisture and absorbing sunlight.

'Now I'm going to show you how to treat it,' the former soldier said as they moved towards a shed in the far corner where he stored his equipment. 'If I can find the bug spray amidst all this clutter!'

But while searching for the spray, his phone rang.

'My mate from the army,' he said before answering.

Then his face froze over, turning white and hard shelled as the Naval College standing guard on the waters in the background.

'No fucking way,' shock seared his voice.

Perhaps another suicide, Fergus thought.

Several of Lance's colleagues ended their lives in the months after coming back from Afghanistan, unable to deal with the shame and the secrecy of Post Traumatic Stress Disorder.

'That's just down the road,' his eyes flickered out across the Thames. 'Thanks for letting me know. I'll turn on the news.'

Ending the call, he reached out for a radio.

'What's happened?' Fergus wanted to know.

But Lance didn't know for sure. 'Something in Woolwich.'

They caught the same uncertainty as the radio stuttered to life. Confused voices and a news story that seemed more of a fog than a flash. Something about an attack in broad daylight down in Wellington Street.

'Gangs,' Fergus supposed, but Lance shook his head.

'My mate seems to think the dead man is a soldier.'

'A soldier?' Fergus echoed his friend's surprise.

Sitting down in the garden, listening to the radio, parts of the story emerged like pieces of a jigsaw puzzle. They could hear noise from the scene and interviews with bystanders who'd witnessed the attack.

'A man was crossing the road away from two cars coming up the hill behind him,' a woman spoke with breathless haste. 'One's blue, and the other's white. The blue car swerves, and next thing I knows, it has knocked the man off his feet, and tossed him up like a bag of onions.'

'Joyriders,' Lance tried to peel back layers of the mystery.

Fergus knew the feeling, cruising down the highway of life without a care in the world and then—BANG—you've gone off the road, struck something solid, and your life's never again going to be the same again.

But then just as the story started to make sense, a fresh series of interviews contradicted the joyride theory. These were no car thieves or drug dealers who'd lost control of their vehicle as they rounded a corner.

'Two guys got out,' a woman's voice fell away to a whisper. 'Ah good they're going to help the man on the ground, what's it called—resuscitate him. But no, they're out to make things more terrible.'

'Take your time,' the interviewer said.

'They'd started ripping into the guy's body with knives,' the woman continued, 'and it's as if that's all he was, a straw Guy on a bonfire.'

'Fuck this,' Lance gave up on the radio. 'Let's go inside.'

Heading towards the flats, they realised they'd

forgotten to lock the shed but that didn't matter to Lance now. Quickening his pace, he needed to know what had happened to the guy sacrificed in the street.

'Might not be as bad as it seems,' Fergus suggested.

But as they got closer to Lance's studio, a bad feeling about the situation weighed heavily upon both of them. Turning on the TV, pictures filtered slowly into view. Aerial shots of a street they both knew well. Fergus had walked it this very morning on his way to College.

Down in the dip of the hill, a latent image of chaos synthesised. Smashed car. Trees in bloom, full as fists, punching the sky as they swayed. Police and bystanders coming into view.

Everybody in a daze, even those in ringside seats.

'Afternoon slaughter in SE18,' Lance read from the screen.

The camera switched between images of a car smashed up against a signpost and pictures of a body sprawled anonymously on the pavement.

Punctuations of silence. Then a knifeman asking the crowd to video him, shouting, waving his hands, raising a meat cleaver up to the sky.

Crazed and hysterical—shouting about wars in Iraq and Afghanistan, and why the British Army shouldn't be in *his* countries, *his* lands, as bystanders collected snapshots and soundbites for social media.

'They'll be asking for his autograph in a minute,' Lance snarled, before realising the guy was asking the crowd to record his speech.

A devil had risen from the dying furnace of empire. He'd brought dark music to a spring afternoon, flinging himself against the flesh and bone of another human being left anonymous on the roadside, cut to pieces.

And now in the aftermath of this primitive act of rage, the murderer was calling on modern media to spread his message of hate.

Knives Chat, the chat of knives, knife ventriloquism.

The killers couldn't have known who their victim was, though the TV news had now revealed that he was wearing a *Help for Heroes* sweatshirt—a military charity for British soldiers wounded or injured in the line of fire.

Seeing pictures of the murderers and listening to them talking about British soldiers going to *their* lands, killing *their* people, Lance's rage was close to the boiling point of blood in a human skull.

'This is as hard to take as the days after the landmine blast,' he snarled at the screen as the image of a fellow fallen soldier scalded his retinas. 'Right now I'm back there seeing it, smelling it, hearing it, and living it over again.' Rolling up his sleeves, he pointed to the words *Addicted Forever* blazing in bold lettering against the glare of the screen. 'And even this tattoo doesn't seem strong enough to get me through this darkness.'

'You look like you're ready to put your fist through the TV.'

'I'd take this dagger and put it through the clock if I could just turn back time,' spittle flashed across Lance's lips as he fingered his tattoo. 'Or even go walking there on those back streets of Woolwich and stop the bastards while they were crawling the streets looking for a random victim.'

'Such empty rage,' Fergus sensed his friend's pain.

'Something has to be done about it.'

'What are you going to do?'

'Anything,' Lance voiced the same empty rage as Fergus had seen amongst his girls outside the referral unit a few days before.

'Seeing your own neighbourhood on TV is strange,' Fergus reckoned. 'Like the time of the riots.'

Then they had seen places such as Lewisham, Peckham, and Woolwich burning in front of their eyes on the screen. But bad as it was to set fire to empty buildings and loot shopping centres for TVs and trainers, those summer fires had been minor when held against the mirror of this.

'They say the guys who did this are fucking converts,' Lance growled as fresh pictures unfolded of helicopters circling the trees above Woolwich. 'They're the worst kind, the most fanatical.'

'Suppose so,' Fergus answered with a sense of irony as he glanced down at his own tattoo and thought of the horror of an actual dagger piercing the human skin. Not just once, but over and over again, as if stabbing right at the heart of England, with a haunting soundtrack of black crows in the distance. Then he spoke softly, against the tide of history. 'But we're all on the same side tonight, English, Irish, Charlton, Millwall, and even Palace in the play offs.'

Heading home across the emptiness of Woolwich Common, he thought of the legend that if ravens should ever abandon the Tower of London, then the city would fall. Playing the TV images over again in his head, he couldn't help but feel as if somebody had tried to catch and behead London's ravens, before boiling them all in broth. Temperatures had risen on the streets he walked. This was becoming a different country to the one he'd migrated too. Growing angry, distant, foreign. Then again, as with Katy's heart, it had never been his to own.

22. Streets In Grief

*A*fter the young soldier's death, TV crews, both domestic and international, planted themselves on the edge of Woolwich's brown brick margins. Suddenly a backwater of the world, lost in the passing of Empire, became a hot word on the lips of the watching world.

On the opposite side of the street, the Artillery Barracks stood glassy-eyed above a deepening tide of emotion. Grief took the form of symbols, rising up like allotments in spring sunshine from the nothingness of winter.

Football shirts. Teddy bears. Flags of Saint George stained in weeping ink. Small wreathes. Large wreathes. Flowers wrapped in cellophane, tear-soaked tissue, and handwritten messages of defiance.

Lance had gone there too in the night, and wrapped a Charlton Athletic flag around the railings, to add to the insignia of mourning.

At first, the soldier was nothing more than a faint

shadow on the roadside for several hours. Then they gave him the dignity a name, and released pictures of a young man cradling a bearskin hat.

Lee Rigby, a machine-gunner and drummer from the Royal Regiment of Fusiliers—twenty five years of age, born amongst Lancashire's former mill towns, and picked out at random to die on the streets of Woolwich.

The world had turned deadly serious. Even the signs for Ha Ha Road weren't laughing any more, as Fergus went for a walk on the Common.

He texted Katy again, and asked if she'd heard the news. Then he called Dyana who'd caught the story in the evening after work.

'Shocking,' she said, 'that such things can happen.'

Like the murder of Demetrius, gunned down in daylight.

'Do you want to join me for a stroll?' he offered.

'Already been out on the Common with Poppy,' she punctured his hopes. 'There's only so much walking I can do in one day. I'm not a dog.'

'Okay, we'll leave our walking until the weekend.'

He'd walk alone, reflecting on all that had happened on this dark day.

Up close, shadows turned to crows holding tight to trees for fear of falling into the black and bottomless nothing of a murderous night.

From the far side of the river, he could see trails of smoke. Factory chimneys, Tate and Lyle, the sugar and honey people. But he felt nothing sweet in his throat tonight. No peace in the silence, no softness in the light.

Sometimes, during this season, travelling funfairs came to town.

None tonight, no fun. World not fair, no time for sideshows.

'Katy,' he texted again, as he traced a path up towards Shooter's Hill. 'London's sad tonight.'

But he might have as well have been talking to stars in

the sky. She didn't reply as he checked his phone a hundred times on the walk home. Down the road and back to the house, to have a beer, and check out the football supporters' forums. Most abounded with rumour, and deepening anger as the facts emerged.

'We've got to do something,' the supporters argued.

Fergus feared *something* that would make everything worse. He recalled the London riots of 2011 when football supporters had come together to defend their streets. But what started out as a positive act soon got hijacked by others with their own divisive agenda.

Such thoughts resounded in his head until it was time to sleep.

When morning came, the cameras still focused on an ordinary road facing the media spotlight in a daze, without any make-up on.

Fergus walked to work, passing the growing shrine to the soldier where images of past and present flashed through his mind as he paused to look. Flowers, flags, three lions and Saint George's crosses, framed in soothing green hedgerows pushing out through a stark grey cage of railings.

'Africans against extremism,' he read from a placard. The weight of murder had been placed upon an entire continent just as those evil bastards placed Britain's perceived sins on the shoulders of one young guy.

In College Fergus tried not to talk of the slaughter in the street, fresh on everyone's lips. One or two claimed to have seen it in the raw, and others spoke of going there to pay homage. Another fight broke out in the corridor too, over disputes regarding who was to blame.

'Have you learned nothing from my talk yesterday?' he groaned.

Through the morning, he waited to hear from Katy.

'Even a spelling mistake,' he thought, 'would be something.'

Nothing, as the day passed—these days counting down

slowly towards Crystal Palace's play off final that slipped far down the London news. Even Lance had forgotten, preoccupied by a brand new cause. They spoke of it over the phone, as Fergus asked what he was going to do.

'March in Woolwich. You can come join us.'

Fergus refused the offer, having heard of senseless attacks on mosques the night before. Going out on the streets, blaming the innocent, only gave the killers what they wanted.

'Race war, more blood on the streets o' London.'

'Maybe, but you can't just sit back, and do nothing.'

Then he was gone, off to his march that would later feature on the TV news. Fergus understood the desire to express his anger, but not the way he was doing it. Surely a better tribute to the dead soldier would be to do something positive, as the fans' forums had already started discussing.

He had his own ideas about what should be done, but no time to contribute because he had two mysteries to solve. Katy's disappearance and general lack of responsiveness. Then the missing link between Demetrius, the dancing club, and Estrella's reference to the seaside.

'Maybe I should go to Ramsgate,' he thought, alone in the evening.

But to do that, he'd have to disappoint Poppy and Dyana. There was even an outside chance of Lance getting tickets for the final on Bank Holiday Monday. Perhaps, the weekend after, he'd go down to the seaside.

Or maybe the incident with the passports had blown into nothingness. She'd felt embarrassed at talking about her new lover, with the former one. They'd kissed, made up, and rode off into the sunset.

'Surely she must have heard about the soldier's death,' he mulled over possibilities. 'The whole country's talking about it.'

Wasn't she even interested in whether or not he was okay? Didn't she ever think of how the killing was so

216

random, it might as well have been him walking to College? Then the news would have been very different, with the crews of Ulster Television camped in Woolwich.

- Irishman murdered in broad daylight in the immigrant backwater of Woolwich, mistaken for an English soldier -

If she didn't call him now, she never would. Perhaps it was time to let this rest and concentrate on Dyana. Just like countries, people have to redefine their relationships according to the demands of the time.

When Poppy's age he could never have imagined being an immigrant with a former soldier as his best friend and Charlton Athletic as his team. Surely then he could take another step down the changing roads of his life. Changes that started in a tattoo studio on a day when the Tigers came to town and his tribe taunted them with songs about Jimmy Savile.

'I have to make an effort,' he edged towards his new 21st century life, 'and try to accept Dyana's daughter as if she's one o' my own.'

23. Sacrifices and selfies

By Friday evening, Fergus had reckoned with many of the events happening in the world around him. The image of a soldier dead at the crossroads had stayed in the headlines since Wednesday. These past nights, lying in bed, thinking over all that had happened it felt as if the entire country stood at a crossroads.

He hoped something good would bloom out of this present horror. Britain, an island, could retreat into its own shell, or move outwards. This terrible murder could give birth to the disease of hatred, or serve as an impetus for scraping the few bits of dead wood out of its system.

'Call over Friday night,' he tried to take Lance's mind away from anger, 'and we'll put the world to rights with cans of beer.'

It wasn't just England that stood at a crossroads after all. Charlton too, with issues of ownership stirring in the background. Despite their decent ending to the season, stories and rumours on the fans' forums suggested that the club was broke. Unless they found new sources of investment, the momentum of recent seasons would soon evaporate.

Chris Powell's management had established a platform of hope, and resurrected dreams of a return to the Premier League. But it was the hated snakes of Selhurst who now stood at that particular crossroads, and Lance had managed to get tickets in the hope of going there to watch their defeat.

'Are you really going to support Watford?'

'It's not about wanting Watford to win,' Lance pointed out, 'but more about bragging rights in South London, as they say. If Palace get into the Premier League, they'll be top dogs this side o' the river.'

'So who do *we* hate most, Palace or Millwall?'

'That's a question with no fixed answer,' Lance admitted, and was about to elaborate when a sudden knocking struck the front door. 'You'd better get that, or they're going to take the fucking thing off the hinges.'

Going out into the hallway, Fergus wondered who would come calling at this time on a Friday night. Could it be Katy back home at last?

Entering the hallway, he held her face in his mind as if to magic her onto the step. When he opened the door he'd see her eyes, blue-green like the shadow of mountains meeting the sea, and merging into one.

But when he opened the door, Katy wasn't there.

'Victoria!' he exclaimed in surprise.

Drinking in the sight of his captain on his doorstep, he became conscious of a second figure, skulking behind in a cloud of blue denim.

'Chelsea,' he realised. 'What's going on?'

'We have to come in,' they barged past as they spoke.

Lance, surprised by their sudden entrance, put down his beer and cast an accusatory glance at Fergus. 'What's going on here then?'

'I'm as much in the dark as you are.'

'We're in trouble,' Victoria confessed.

'But we meant no harm,' Chelsea intervened.

Lance spoke bluntly. 'What the fuck have you done?'

Immediately they clammed up, as a team.

'Say what you've done and get it over with,' Fergus demanded.

'You're probably going to hate us,' Victoria confessed. 'I'm sure you've heard tell of selfies. Everybody our age takes them nowadays.'

Chelsea chirped in. 'It was my fault, my idea.'

'It was just a game,' Victoria insisted.

'They all think I'm a dyke, and since we became friends, they say nasty things, so we thought we'd show them for a laugh,' Chelsea added.

Fergus had a bad feeling. 'Where did you take selfies?'

'No, it wasn't in a place,' answered Victoria.

'Surely it had to be somewhere,' Lance assumed.

'Yes,' she admitted, 'but not like you go specially to that place, and you say to yourself I'm going to take some pictures here.'

'Okay, we knew we were going there,' said Chelsea, 'but we were messing about and didn't know how close we were to the soldier's shrine.'

'Holy fuck!' Lance exclaimed. 'Selfies there?'

'No, no, it wasn't like that,' Victoria protested.

'Then what the fuck was it?' Lance stood up, embattled.

'We started messing around taking pictures in the sidestreets,' Victoria explained, 'and then suddenly we were right beside all those flags. Next thing we heard shouting, and we recognised some boys from our estate.'

'White boys,' Chelsea cut in on her captain's description.

'Them boys thought we was dissing the dead soldier,' Victoria's words criss-crossed her friend's interruption like a high speed train. 'As they came running, we started running too, down one of the sidestreets where you hit a dead end when you come to a school, and you can't get no further.'

'They caught up with us, and had us cornered.'

'You're lucky they didn't kill you,' Lance spoke bluntly.

'They looked like they was going to,' Chelsea recalled, 'and they started calling us names, pulling my hair, trying to feel me up.'

Victoria helped her out. 'It was horrible.'

'Are you a boy or a girl, huh?' Chelsea imitated their deep voices. 'Hey, let's pull down its pants and see what it is—what it has.'

'It was mostly talk,' Victoria admitted, 'but nasty talk.'

'I grew angry,' Chelsea said, 'took out my knife.'

'You've got a fucking knife!' Lance exhaled.

'Not after all that we've been through,' Fergus chastised her. 'Surely you must have learned something from my talk the other day.'

'Every kid in London's got a knife.'

'You know what her temper's like,' Victoria spoke again. 'She swung out and caught one of the guys on the cheek.'

'Yeah, protecting you, protecting us,' Chelsea cried out as she rose up from the seat, as if to leave. 'That's the thanks I get.'

'Okay, okay, okay,' Fergus tried to take on the role of Mister Sensible amidst the chaos. 'There's no need for more fighting. What you've done is done, and we can't change it. What happened to the boy you hurt?'

'He ain't hurt bad,' Chelsea growled from the settee.

'But as we ran away they said they'd get us.'

'Do they know where you live?' Lance asked.

'Same estate, different block,' Victoria admitted.

'We've got to decide where we go from here,' Fergus reckoned they had two choices. 'Go to the police or go find those boys and talk to them.'

'Not when their blood's up,' Chelsea protested. 'They'd shank us.'

'Jesus what kind of a world is this coming to?' Lance

asked.

'Think we saw what kind of a world it is, a few days ago.'

'Fergus is right,' his team captain rose to her feet. 'It's a bad world, but also a fast world so they'll forget all this in a week or so.'

'So what are you proposing to do then?'

'We need to lie low,' Chelsea reckoned. 'So we was thinking about whether you'd be able to get us the keys to College so we can hide there.'

Fergus laughed off the suggestion. 'I'd get in far less trouble with the principal if I just gave you the keys to my house.'

'Really, so can we stay here?' the separate train of their voices crossed onto the same line once again. 'We'd be no trouble at all.'

'It was a joke. I'm your teacher, remember.'

'Yeah, but we'd even be happy in a garden shed,' Chelsea grew excited at the prospect. 'You wouldn't even know we were here.'

'Sure,' Victoria echoed her friend's argument. 'It's not like it's against the law or anything. Staff are allowed to rent rooms to students.'

Fergus shook his head. 'I need another drink.'

'I'll come with you,' Lance followed behind, as they made their way into the kitchen where a fridge of beer lightened the weight of the situation.

'What the hell are we going to do?'

'Selfies opposite a barracks after what happened,' Lance answered. 'They're lucky they didn't get shot. This ain't our fight, mate.'

'Come on, we've all made mistakes in our life.'

'Maybe they do just need to lie low for a while,' his friend strategised. 'Stay outa sight until the heat's gone out of the air, and let this pass.'

'And what if those boys go to the police?'

'Most of these kids would rather die than grass to what

they call the feds. It's not so different to the old days over on the island. '

'Katy would know what to do, if she was here.'

'She ain't here. She's in Ramsgate, my friend.'

'That's it then. I'll go to Ramsgate.'

The hard part would be explaining this to Dyana, but he'd manage that by telling her he was going to solve Estrella's riddle of the seaside. Even if that meant going to see his former lover, it was all for a good cause.

'Just means we'll have to postpone our Saturday date to Monday,' he explained. 'And just to show you how much I'm looking forward to that, I'm going to give up the chance of going to Wembley.'

'Okay,' she reluctantly agreed. 'But if you let me down, so help me God, I'm going to get me a tattoo of *CPFC—Always True*—on my heart.'

'Best reason in the world to get back quickly then.'

24. Coast Road

Following his joyride, first in hospital and then during his days in prison, Fergus longed for the freedom of open road. He would lie back on his bed and use the ceiling as a projector screen, an imaginary cinema transporting him out of the cell.

The darkness of his auditorium would subside gradually to images of blue and green, a meeting of mountains and the sea. He'd imagine the colours of evening changing through the seasons, and other shades too running through his head like snapshots of a world before the joyride.

Headlamps on tar, lemon juice softening treacle. Bread white clouds hanging in udders above herds of Holstein Friesian cattle. Lambs frisking across the stubble of hayfields with streaks of graffiti on their curly backs. Men and tractors made one in the shadows of a sunset. Hot orange light sinking low, accentuating the verdure of pines lining border roads.

'A few hours and you could cross the whole country.'

Ireland was a very different land from England, in size and history, scattering her people to the four winds rather than absorbing races.

With this in mind, he set out for Ramsgate—several hours from London, a journey that was barely a scratch on the headboard of England, such was the size of this place where he now lived.

The sun had risen over a sleeping city when he said goodbye to his girls on the floor of the living room where they had stayed through the night.

'Fucking crazy,' according to Lance, but such was life.

'Bye sir,' Victoria mumbled. 'When you coming back?'

'Sunday night or Monday morning,' he promised.

He had to get back for his date with Dyana. Thinking of their trip through London's parks he left the house in the cool of morning.

By the end of this drive he would have reached the edge of England and found the answers to Katy's silence and her spelling mistakes.

'Maybe we could even work on the other mystery together,' he thought of the girls in the club and the riddle of women at the seaside.

Remembering that night in *The Bird Cage*, he pictured the dancer Estrella and recalled her words, vivid as neon.

'*People at the seaside, they give us girls.*'

Though he was no expert in the human flesh trade, he could hazard a guess that this was happening along the south coast, the part of England closest to France and the European mainland.

'By the time I get back I'll know the truth,' he mused.

Moving away from the terraced streets of Charlton's borders steeped in morning light, he turned on the radio as he approached the Shooter's Hill interchange that fed into the A2's ancient trackway to England's coast.

Catching flashes of fresh life springing up from every inky green corner of the cool May morning, he listened to the radio presenter discussing reactions to the Lee Rigby murder—the flowers, messages, and pulling together of football supporters in the name of a common cause.

Lance and some friends had decided to organise a football match in the soldier's memory, perhaps a game between former Charlton stars and the soldiers in the Royal Artillery Barracks.

'Maybe we could have it on the 4th of July,' he had suggested. 'We could have a theme of *Stars* versus *Stripes*.'

He wanted to play the match up at Sparrow's Lane and feature legends such as Clive Mendonca if he could get in touch with them. But these days the club was in trouble amidst growing fears of its finances drying up.

That fear was made worse when the focus shifted towards Crystal Palace's game on Monday on the green baize of Wembley.

'Watford are the favourites,' explained the broadcaster. They were on a roll, with Palace lucky to have made the play offs after going into decline in the closing stages of the season. The snakes had been fortunate to overcome Brighton too, fuelled by shit in their dressing room.

Leaving the edges of Greater London behind, as the focus switched to the weather and then back again to the soldier's murder, Fergus was glad to have heard no news of any boys being attacked at the shrine.

Hopefully it would all pass off quietly, and be forgotten—just as he could forget Katy and move on with his life once he knew that she was safe.

Now, as he drove, a picture of her stayed in his mind constant as a Saint Christopher medallion upon the dashboard, a grown man carrying a migrant child across Biblical waters.

Coming out of the city to where roads widened, the countryside was sparking to life, the deeper he drove through the cool green haze of morning—getting closer to all of his answers with every minute that passed.

This was England's brewing country—the place that

fed a million men on match days from Charlton and Selhurst down to Gillingham and Brighton. Land of hop farms punctuated in strange buildings with conical caps. On his first journey here with Katy, he had misheard the name as *oats* houses.

She had corrected him. 'Oast houses, used for drying hops in charcoal fires, now mostly converted into homes or hotels.'

Flashes of old conversations went through his head as he passed a sign for Sevenoaks with its grand trees, cricket fields, and paddocks full of young horses galloping in the breeze. This was a place of lords and land owners, resembling the pasturelands of Ulster's east coast.

'But most of Ireland is so different to this,' he thought of the wilder west side from Donegal down to Clare, land of rugged places and girls' names. 'Places that feel like *home*.'

Driving at a measured pace, he edged across the Kent Downs towards Whitstable where the tides had a habit of washing up relics of ancient times. Fragments of sharks' teeth and mammoth tusks had been found amidst broken pieces of limpet embedded in the very breath of the sea. Layers of history overlapping upon each other. Like the cycle of news stories as he drove, shifting between football teams, murdered soldiers, and the promise of glorious sunshine on this holiday weekend.

Still no word of a stabbing. Good news for his girls.

Getting to Whitstable he drove so close to the sea he brushed against the shadows of trawlers coming in from Herne Bay, and then stopped for fish and chips, the blood of their catch bandaged in yesterday's newspapers.

25. Palace of Answers

*H*aving finally reached Ramsgate, Fergus parked by the marina, facing out on the sea. Belly full, from a brunch of chips stained in news print. A story of the play offs. Soggy potato flesh inked in Palace and Watford colours swallowed with a pinch of salt.

He got out of the car, read a sign, and laughed at the words.

'Welcome *toe* the English coast.'

Somebody had scrawled an extra *e* in tomato ketchup.

'Referral unit for them Monday morning,' he mused.

Not Katy. She rarely made spelling mistakes in text messages—*presure* and *wory* out of place for a girl with dreams of being a writer.

Moving along the seafront he could taste fresh salt on his tongue. Chips combining with a sea breeze rising off the ocean's brutalist architecture. Somewhere beyond a fishing museum, you had France.

Suddenly he thought of evenings walking this shoreline.

Katy's words filled his mind. 'We could loose a boat, and sail away. Feast on wine and cheese as we drift off, and wake up on the edge of Paris.'

Like the owl and the pussycat. Characters from Poppy's nursery rhyme books. Edward Lear's songs and stories of nonsense on Dyana's bookshelf.

Time to move on. He had to cut Katy loose.

Slowly he approached the first stage of his mission. Chalky scrawls of lettering blazed from a sign at the front of a coffee shop. Smells of dark roast, heavy as cigar smoke, clinging to the salty air outside. Fragrances stirred through with seaweed, and the briny echo of fishermen's mornings.

A list of exotic offerings blazed in his mind as he stopped outside. 'Mocha Java Smoothies, Frappuccino, Iced Caramel Latte.'

Going in, fragrances of mint and baking bread greeted his senses. Fishermen smells gone, swallowed up by lines of pastries. Plum & pumpkin galettes laid out alongside red cabbage & walnut tarts.

Looking away from the temptation to eat again so soon after his chips, he could see few customers. A bearded man with a Macbook had occupied a space by the window, facing out on a scattering of boats in the marina.

That was Katy's place. She had gone there to sketch ideas in her notebooks, and been seduced by the young barista.

Today, someone else guarded the line of pastries. Tall and slender girl in her early to middle twenties. As Fergus approached the counter, her black apron formed a stark contrast to her floury skin.

Lifting her head, she smiled. 'Can I help you?'

She spoke with perfect English, on the base of a Slavic accent.

He ordered a Danish roast to steel his nerves for the journey ahead, and started his investigation. 'Isn't Wagner here today?'

'I don't know anyone of that name,' she said.

Fergus probed. 'How long have you worked here?'

'Three weeks,' she answered, swapping coffee for payment.

He thanked her, and then set out on the next stage of his mission. The coffee fuelled his walk to Katy's house. It was a stroll of no more than fifteen minutes, or ten at pace, heading towards the ferry terminal.

This had to be finished quickly. Get it over with. Cut Katy loose, go back to London for Bank Holiday with Dyana, and listen to the evening news of Watford hammering Palace by six goals to nil.

'But where has Wagner gone?'

He could have fled Ramsgate and England, forcing Katy with him. Worse, he might have hurt her to protect his secrets.

Fergus stopped to think, on the brow of a hill, above the ferry terminal. 'Look at the lengths they went to with Demetrius.'

Somebody wanted to leave him silent as this town.

35 miles from the French coast, the port stood as a microcosm of Ramsgate. Both town and terminal had seen better days in decades past.

Once upon a time, commercial ferries connected the English seaside to more exotic places across the Channel. The few that remained were gradually closing, reducing Ramsgate's sea traffic to tugs and trawlers.

Most of the action had shifted down towards Dover leaving a ghost port to stand as a permanent reminder of past glories, alongside the town's grand period houses like the one Katy rented.

Turning his back on the port, Fergus climbed towards that house.

'So this is it,' he thought aloud. 'Place of the answers.'

Maybe Palace of the answers, in the hands of the tomato sauce artist. Katy's palace took the form of a 19th century house rising three storeys above the coast, facing out on a white blaze of cliffs in the distance. She'd fallen in love at first sight, calling it a house of stories, deciding to stay there from the very first week she arrived in Ramsgate.

Finding this house on the seafront, they'd headed straight to an estate agency in the centre of town. There they came across an eccentric and assiduous manager who was also a Charlton supporter and gave them a good deal on account of Fergus's loyalties.

The grounds had housed a commercial boat yard, but the Scottish lady who owned it retreated back to Kintyre after the death of her English husband. Katy had loved everything about the house from first sight, from its location on a hill above the sea to its dressage of colour.

'Such a strange yellow,' he recalled her words. 'You'd swear Van Gogh painted it during his period in Ramsgate.' For a woman perhaps, a writer looking down on the same sea and stone jetties as the migrant artist described with such passion in letters to his brother Theo.

This would have been a fine theatre for such a love affair. Built in the 1820s, Katy's house of imagined passion stood on the border of two architectural periods. Georgian in shape and Victorian in style, her home by the sea carried the fortitude of a castle softened by silky curtains in the leaden windows that always reminded Fergus of Charlton House.

From here, Katy worked and slept, facing out on the sea as she wrote by a desk at a window high enough to imagine the view of a thousand Greek islands stretching out across the sun-seared Cyclades on a clear day. Fergus had slept there too, in those primary nights of his beloved retreating behind these castle walls to write her book.

This was the house where they fled to the shore and made love in a boat on an evening when the sky burned red from chilli fire.

'But that's gone now,' he thought of Dyana waiting for him back in Woolwich Common confused and fearful about his encounter with the past. 'It's time to get this over and done with.'

Lifting his eyes to the writer's room, he could detect no sign of life and noticed the curtains closed. That was odd for the time of day. Usually Katy rose early, to start writing or take a walk on the beach for inspiration.

'There's nobody home,' he reckoned.

But was that cause for relief or concern? Making his way to the entrance, he rattled the door upon its hinges.

Getting no answer, he turned the handle. Going inside, his footsteps reverberated in as much silence as an empty football stadium.

'Too many things out of order,' he grew concerned at the sight of junk food packaging discarded on the floor, and shoes that didn't belong to Katy. 'Maybe she's gone and somebody else is renting the place.'

The more he looked the greater that probability became. She didn't read such magazines, or keep the sports section of newspapers. She wouldn't leave a sewing basket sitting on the kitchen table, and needles scattered. She detested clutter. Another tenant had surely taken charge.

'I should go,' he figured, 'and try to find Wagner.'

But then he heard creaking from upstairs.

'Somebody's here,' he realised. 'Katy?'

Crossing towards the hallway, he hesitated. What if he got up there and found her in bed with Wagner and the passports long forgotten? What if there had been an altruistic reason for him having them?

'Unlikely. He's no Demetrius.'

Moving towards the hallway, his heart thumped, fearful of what he might find. Trying not to be noisy, he began his ascent of the stairs. Again he heard a creak—a small symphony of floorboards brushing against one another like tectonic plates, followed soon after by a tremor of footsteps.

Suddenly the bedroom door opened and a stark figure came into view. The sight shocked him backwards, and he grabbed for the bannister.

'Sorry,' he spoke towards the advancing stranger.

Instead of his former lover, he'd found Wagner's secret from the boat, exactly as described in the cryptic email he hadn't opened at first.

'This bitch was no Playboy Bunny, that's for sure,' he recalled Katy's words, but he was the one caught up in *Desperation Stations*.

The sallow-faced woman had a gun in her hands and the closer she got, the closer he came to a feeling of hot piss in his pants.

'I'm not a burglar or anything like that,' he tried to explain.

'Shut up,' she snapped, 'and get inside that room.'

Backing into the lounge, his host followed behind, keeping the handgun trained on him. He could see anger in her bloodshot eyes, and tightness in the way she clutched the weapon, all the veins and bones of her hands showing. She had a scar on each cheek too, deep in a face devoid of feeling.

'I'm not here to do you any harm,' he insisted.

'Get down,' the woman castrated his protestation.

'I'm only here to find my former girlfriend.'

She flipped the catch. 'Get on the floor.'

'Okay she's not here. It's all a terrible mistake.'

'I told you twice and won't tell you again,' she touched the trigger. Fuck, this was some serious shit that he had stepped into. Comic book quicksand! 'Look, you really don't want to mess me around mister.'

'Okay, okay,' he agreed to get on the ground.

But as she lowered the gun, he caught her off guard.

'Bitch,' he dived towards her with a rugby tackle.

Falling backwards, stunned as a bunny in headlights, she dropped the weapon. A bullet struck the sewing basket, sending it sideways.

Toppled off the table, needles scattered everywhere.

He could see them as he rolled with the woman

beneath him, kicking and scratching, fighting like a cornered cat in an alleyway. She was putting up a good fight, hissing and clawing as they struggled. He could feel her nails and then her teeth sinking mercilessly into his skin.

'Fuck you,' he cried out, as she scratched the length of his face, and then switched her hands downwards in the direction of his groin.

This was no boxing match or lap dance, with rules of *no touching* as she grabbed for the places that cause a man most pain. He'd no choice but to break the gentleman's code of never hitting a woman, ever.

Feeling the sharpness of her grip on his groin, he raised his fist.

'Let go,' he hoped the threat alone would stem the pain.

Instead she tightened her hold, as if to cut the blood.

Dropping his fist, he struck her hard across the face. Less of a Playboy Bunny now, her lip burst open— splattering him in blood. Like Vivaldi's Henchman, he'd fallen from the name of gentleman.

Looking down, seeing her out cold, his heart told him to be gentle, but for once, he listened to his head. Hurrying to the kitchen, he found binding, and tied her up so that she wouldn't come at him again.

'Time to find Katy,' he wiped the blood off his face.

First he decided to take out insurance and call Lance. The phone rang for ages. In the end, he left a message on the answering machine. 'This has got crazy down here, man. I got to the house, and a mad foreign bitch came at me with a gun. I beat her off, and I'm looking for Katy now.'

He picked up the weapon and the sewing basket, placing them both on the table. Then he headed for the hallway, leaving the woman tied up, out for the count, detecting no sign of any accomplices being in the house.

As he climbed the stairs for a second time, he heard chains. Remembering the lion and the unicorn on the face of a passport and Katy's stories of the women, he feared what he might discover.

What if he found a whole gallery of women imprisoned, and his former lover amongst them? Chained up like slaves for God knows what purposes. Cargo bound for meat markets? And what would they do with Katy, the white radical chic girl who'd wandered into their dark underworld?

The closer he got, the more it sounded like somebody trapped. Pushing the door open, he feared a vision of Hell unfolding before his eyes. But as the full picture came into view, he found only one woman.

'What the fuck's going on here?' he couldn't believe his eyes.

He'd discovered his former lover chained to the bedframe in fur-lined handcuffs, as if abandoned fully dressed in the midst of a kinky sex game. But he could see this was no game. She was being held prisoner, as Rapunzel in Ramsgate trapped in a tower above the sea. Her eyes raged and then softened as they met his, visibly hungering for freedom.

'Why the hell have they got you in handcuffs?'

But she couldn't give him an answer. They'd tied a stocking around her mouth—possibly in a hurry when the woman heard his entrance.

'Sorry, I'll get that off and you can tell me everything.'

'The bastards!' she exclaimed as he freed her of the mask, and she took a deep breath to suck in the room's stale air. Then she wanted answers. 'Where's Grace, the woman? What did you do to her?'

'I'll get you out of these cuffs and tell you everything.'

But he couldn't break the cuffs with his bare hands, and could see no sign of keys close to the bed that stank of sweat and piss. Traces of worse smells too, echoes of an away dressing room at Brighton.

'Fuck, these seem to be industrial strength.'

'There's a letter opener in the writing desk. Use that.'

'Okay,' he sprang across the room. 'Where exactly?'

'Somewhere beneath one of my old drafts, I think,' she tried to remember as he searched frantically through the drawers.

Then his phone buzzed and he got distracted. Not Lance, but Dyana wondering how his investigations were going and when he'd be coming back.

'Hurry,' Katy cried out. 'Wagner's here too, and there's more.'

'More, where?' he asked, as he finally found the letter opener.

Turning towards Katy, the answer came unexpectedly. She screamed for him to look behind. He turned but before he had time to react, he caught a glimpse of Wagner's face, and then a flash of something else. A weapon far outside the Marquess of Queensberry rules of boxing.

'Knuckle duster,' Fergus could do nothing to stop its fall.

Feeling a whack of brass across his jaw, he heard Katy scream again. Suddenly the ceiling, then the whole room turned blood red.

26. Final Score

'*A*rsenal 2 Manchester United 2,' the rising cadence of a broadcaster's voice signified a score draw in the evening's classified football results. 'Crystal Palace 0 Charlton Athletic 6. Six zero to South London's finest.'

Attentively, Fergus listened as the broadcaster traced out a path through the divisions and across the map of England. He projected his voice and accent in that cultured manner of somebody educated, like Katy, as he shifted from Middlesbrough and Newcastle down to Brighton.

Gradually the voice rose towards Scotland. 'Heart of Midlothian 3, Hibernians 3. Glasgow Rangers 0, Hamilton Accademicals 5.'

'A team that sounds as if philosophers and writers should play for them,' Katy used to say. 'Today's goals from Roland Barthes, Jean-Paul Sartre, Simone de Beauvoir, Robert Burns, and Walter Scott.'

Okay, so he's in the living room listening to football.

239

Katy's in the kitchen mixing herbs and spices by a murmuring stove. He knows from the sweet fragrance creeping out through the door and into the hallway.

He can hear her humming above the TV, showing the league tables. Then she drifts outside to the garden where the snowy blossom has slipped away and the apple tree stands pregnant with the promise of baking.

She's moving amongst pots full of chilli peppers, and tomato plants anchored in bags, pinned back by a metal frame. He's with her now, out of the living room, away from the last of the league tables, abandoning them in the region of the Scottish Second Division. Bending down towards the budding vines, he tries to help Katy loosen the strings. But they catch hold of his wrists, tight as anacondas, constricting the flow of blood.

Suddenly the tense and tempo changes.

'Let go,' he spoke to the strings entangling his fingers.

But they wouldn't let go and he was dragging a counterweight of tomato plants up out of his dreams into the conscious world. The hard summer's ground beneath his feet began to soften. He recalled a blood-red darkness. Desperately he tried to cling to the fragrance of Katy's baking.

Whispers greeted his wakening. 'He's coming round.'

Fergus detected something foreign and uneasy in the voice. This was no BBC broadcaster listing names on football's spectrum. Opening his eyes, the cold and stark surroundings startled him. Trapped between a firm mattress and a high ceiling, he was bound up like a tomato vine.

'Wha', what am I doing here?' he strained his aching neck.

'You got hit from behind,' a familiar voice whispered.

Turning around, he could see Katy in pink fluffy handcuffs. Suddenly, memories started to hatch through the shell of his daze. Confronting the woman, finding Katy, and getting struck with Wagner's brass-knuckle weapon. He'd gone spinning into deep, deeper, deepest sleep, and surrealist dreams of being back home in Charlton on a Saturday.

Many hours must have passed since then, for it was now dark outside, and half-dark here too, in the pale candlelight.

'What the hell's going on?' he struggled to rise.

Two figures eased out of a blur. First he saw the woman he'd knocked out cold on the floor. She wore a stern gaze, and eyes angrier than before. Wagner stood at her side like a pillion passenger.

'Look, I don't know what's happening but you have to let me go.'

The motorcycle man spoke. 'You're staying with us for a few days. Think of it as an unexpected twist in your holiday.'

'People are going to be looking for me,' he warned.

Wagner shook his head. 'You're only going to be gone a short time. Once we've completed our business, you're free to go.'

'What business?' he fought for answers.

'You already know as much as you need to,' the stern woman interjected. 'Your girlfriend went snooping and found things she shouldn't have. You can blame her for this. Or blame Romeo!'

Wagner growled. 'Once the boat comes in, it's over.'

'Boat, what fucking boat?' he sought answers again.

'Fergus,' Katy hissed, 'don't talk about the boat.'

'She's right,' said stern face. 'The less you know, the better.'

'I grew up on the Irish border,' Fergus protested. 'I'm good with secrets. If you let me go, I'll head back to London and you'll hear no more on this.'

'You've already told your friend who left a message on your phone.' Wagner's words shocked him into silence. 'If we can forge passports, it's not so hard to hack a phone.'

'Then you know people are looking for me.'

241

'Sure,' his nemesis admitted. 'But I've already handled it.'

'What the hell have you done?' he wrestled the ropes.

'Lance said he'd come right away, but I said there was no need. The cops have been called. You and Katy are on your way back to London, stopping off at Herne Bay for a couple of days.' He smiled then. 'Here's the clincher, the certainty that it's you texting.'

Fergus wanted to knock the arrogant grin off Wagner's face.

'You'll be back in time for the play off final,' his rival leaned in close. Then he gazed towards Katy. 'She taught me a lot about you Fergus.' His words carried a competitor's cruelty. 'You're predictable like the football team that you always seemed to put before her.'

'Others are looking for me too,' he refused to chew the bait.

'Yes. Some lady named Dyana,' Wagner's grin grew more arrogant, 'with texts coming thick n' fast all through the afternoon.'

'What did you tell her?'

'Just that you'd gone upstairs, found Katy in the bedroom, and things got a bit heated, but not to worry, you're sleeping it off together.'

'You fucking bastard,' he fought the ropes again.

Wagner laughed. 'I'm pulling your leg, Fergus.'

His accomplice wasn't amused. 'Stop it.'

'I said that Katy had stomach troubles, maybe pregnancy, and you had to take her up to the hospital. Then she asked what her and Poppy would do. I couldn't be sure who Poppy was so I said they should wait for news.'

'That's some bloody story,' Fergus almost admired the plausibility in his fiction, though also hoped it might rouse Dyana's suspicions.

'There's one big hole in your plot,' Katy's voice rose with a fury. 'I'd never be pregnant with your baby. I'd drown us both in the sea.'

'You took her away from me,' Fergus directed his anger towards Wagner. 'So why are you holding her as a prisoner now?'

'We're not bad people,' Wagner circumnavigated answers, 'but we've deals to complete, and can't have anybody getting in the way.'

'She tried to trick us,' his partner interjected. 'Twice she attempted to escape. That's why she's handcuffed, and you are tied.'

'How did I ever make such a fuck up?' Katy scowled.

'You weren't saying that when planning a life together.'

'Fiction,' she growled. 'Pure fiction is all that ever was.'

Fergus had no desire to hear this. 'I need to take a piss.'

'We can't untie you,' the stern woman snarled. 'You're an ex-boxer. Look what you did to my face. I'll have these bruises for weeks.'

'If it wasn't for me, she'd have shot you.'

'Surely you don't want me to piss the fucking bed?'

'Okay,' said the woman. 'Uncuff the bitch.'

'It's not me needs to go,' Katy recoiled from Wagner as he opened one cuff and placed a basin upon the bed. 'You can't be serious.'

But they were, as Fergus felt Katy's touch for the first time in months. Under the gaze of a gun, the smell of hot piss filled the room. Then it was done. Cuffing Katy once more, the guards left the room.

Fergus was about to get the answers to a whole set of questions that he hadn't even expected to be asking when he reached the coast.

27. Trading Routes

The sudden change in surroundings had unsettled Fergus, drawing him into dark silence. Ramsgate had been drawn into darkness too, as he lay alone with the Yorkshire rose who had betrayed him.

'I can't cope with this,' he said as she tried to converse.

Using the ceiling as a screen, Fergus imagined scenes from a gangster movie, a night in a make-believe town, as he used to do in prison. Dream movies he called them, stories to soften the lonely nights.

Cruise liners passed through a vibrant port. Passengers disembarked, transformed to tourists, as drunken sailors mingled amongst the local girls. Scents of rum and perfume laced the breezes whipping in off a lukewarm sea.

Characters from Lance's stories strutted the main drag, seeking out gambling dens and arcades. The Brown Marilyn stood in the doorway of a massage parlour, Vivaldi on a record player in the background. Henchmen lurked in the shadows, smoking cigarettes, running scams and errands.

Fresh sirens sounded down in the terminal. The lights of another majestic boat torched the coastal darkness. Tonight, every dancehall in this old town was going to be full as a bladder in Happy Hour.

Maybe he'd go down later, and seek out a dancing girl.

There he'd find Dyana too, carrying out fresh detective work.

'Aren't you going to say anything?' Katy's voice pierced the crust of his dreams sharply as her baking, once upon a time, had filled them.

Suddenly he was back in a room above the coast in the real Ramsgate where ships no longer stopped on their passage along the North Sea route. They drifted by without a second glance at the seaside town on the sidelines, moving between Scandinavia and the Spanish islands.

'You know when you waken with a bad hangover,' he finally spoke. 'You just want to sleep away the whole next day, and never again see another drop o' beer. That's how I feel right now.'

Struggling to move, he shifted his aching body upwards in the bed. Eventually he could see his fellow prisoner, white as a banshee with even the dazzle in her blue eyes faded beneath a few freckles that were receding too. Her appearance caused him pain and anger at the same time.

'There's no point trying to sleep this off,' she deflated his hopes. 'We can't know how long they're going to keep us. They're waiting on a boat to come, and somebody has tipped them off that they're being watched so they're starting to go ape-shit.'

'How come you've learned so much?'

'Self taught,' she answered. 'Nothing to do but listen.'

Seeing the sadness in her eyes, his anger softened, and his ropes slackened. Then he remembered all the aspects of his life that she had put at risk by dragging him into this. Next he recalled Wagner's mockery.

His anger blossomed again. The ropes tightened. He grew conscious of scratches to his face, and the bruises he'd taken from a knuckleduster.

'Why the hell did you get into this Katy?'

'You must hate me, but this wasn't part of the plan.'

Suddenly he recalled the night that Dyana bared the lump of her life story, hoping he wouldn't run. Strangely, Katy's voice echoed that honesty, mixed into a cocktail of suffering and regret.

'I don't hate you,' he assured her. 'Just tell me what happened.'

'I should have run that morning I found those passports.'

But instead of running she'd come back to the house to pack her things, after her meeting with the publisher from Manchester.

When she got inside, she found Wagner waiting for her, with the woman and a couple of strangers from the core of the smuggling operation.

'The woman's called Grace,' she explained, 'though she has none.'

'Nor mercy, nor sympathy,' Fergus added, 'or any such words in the dictionary that you'd find to describe a decent person.'

Katy carried on with her story. 'She's far better than the others though, and there are two of them on the far side of the sea.'

'The smugglers,' Fergus assumed, and she nodded.

Her voice fell to a whisper. 'One I call Lucifer. He's North African, and very dangerous, psychotically dangerous.' She dipped her whispering even lower. 'There's danger in his eyes. You're cut open as he looks at you.'

'So is this Lucifer in charge o' the whole show?'

'No, he's a small fish too,' Katy's sad voice crackled off the enclosure of high walls. 'There's a woman at the top. I call her The Queen Bee.'

'Grace?'

'She's just a worker bee,' Katy shook her dark head. She's not even on the same level as the North African, though he makes her sleep with him when he comes to stay. He's the brains behind this wing of the operation, and the other guy provides the brawn.'

'The second of the two smugglers?'

'Yeah, I call him The Giraffe,' she smiled at her only means of power. 'He's huge, height ways, sort of guy you'd find on a basketball court. I'd say he's from the opposite coast, somewhere along the Red Sea.'

'And you've had these people in this house?'

'Wagner told them I found the passports,' she returned to the email afternoon. 'They'd come to find out how much I knew, and if I'd told anyone. They'd have killed me, if it hadn't been for Wagner defending me.'

'So they just kept you as a prisoner instead?'

'Yes,' she sighed. 'In my writing studio.'

'Handcuffed to the bed like this all of the time?'

'At the start they left me free in the daytime to read, write and even listen to the radio, while Grace kept guard. I tried to be clever, to build up a rapport with her so I could escape, and for a while it worked.'

'Women have a radar for when somebody's fooling them!'

'Yes,' she agreed, dropping her voice to a whisper again, 'but I got to know her life story, and how hard she's had things. She's been left like somebody who had the heart cut out of her as a child.'

'You sound like you almost feel sorry for her.'

'Partly, because she has suffered at other people's hands. It's not her heart that's been cut out. It's somewhere lower down. At the start I thought she was having an affair with Wagner, but she wasn't,' Katy returned to that night she'd followed them down to the shore and found the passports. 'She's Lucifer's woman, though I wouldn't say she's his lover. She can't feel love, and he's not exactly a loving kind o' guy.'

Fergus assumed that Katy had to take an interest in their lives to keep sane. Their actions, moods, and affairs became part of her daily soap opera, an exotic Eastenders episode played out in Ramsgate.

Again Fergus thought of posters on the London Underground. Glimpses of the girls' tear-starred faces, pleas for financial support, and calls to end a practice with no place in modern England.

'She knew that once a year girls in her village were taken to huts on the edge of a forest, for purification by the female elders,' Katy paraphrased Grace's story. 'Everybody else prepared for a party.'

'Like a Catholic sacrament.'

But these weren't little girls in white eucharistic dresses excited about crisps, juice, sandwiches, and envelopes full of money afterwards.

Katy's words transported him far beneath the London Underground. 'They've a ceremony outside the huts, music and dancing to block out the screams of when the blade falls on each girl.'

He could guess how sharp the cries must sound to a child waiting for their day to come, perhaps the next year or the one after, beginning to understand that all distant waves reach the shore eventually.

'Grace's mother sent her away a few months before she was due to face the knife. She moved to a rundown suburb in Brussels. She went to school with Belgian children, and others from different parts of the world. She felt safe there, and smart—given a chance to learn.'

Katy paused then, smiling, championing the migrant child.

'She said she had big dreams, that she was an old head on young shoulders. She wanted to be a nurse for children. I felt strange, having her tell me that, like I was the nurse and she was the patient.'

'Beware of Stockholm syndrome,' Fergus warned.

'There's no danger of that,' Katy assured him. 'I've seen

too much cruelty in her, but I feel sorry for the little girl who's not there any more and I think you have to understand *her* to know why this is happening.'

'I'm guessing the bitch never made it to be a nurse?'

'What happened to Grace I wouldn't wish on my worst enemy,' Katy's eyes moistened as she spoke. 'It was the summer after she finished her exams for the next level at school. She'd managed to get the best grades in her class. The teachers said she should try being a doctor one day and not a nurse.' Again Katy paused, shivering in the cold candle-lighted room. 'She went into that summer with such excitement, heading towards a new school, new friends, and a new life as a teenager.'

'So what happened to all those dreams?'

'A couple of elderly cousins came to snatch them away. One afternoon, she sensed the whispers she remembered in her village. Walking into an awkward silence, she feared what was coming next.'

'They'd come to take her back to Africa?'

'No, they just drove her to a back street doctor right there in the modern European city she'd embraced with all her heart,' she corrected him. 'Like taking a turn out of one century and retreating into another.'

Fergus imagined the terror of a child as Katy sketched in the details, combining parts of Grace's story with their own imaginations.

Screams of no, and bitter sobs, prayers for a miracle. Secret parts handled like pieces of meat. Slices of bacon to be scalped away.

The man's fingers pinching a child's body, moulding the flesh into place, preparing to take away something that really belonged to the adult. Then the order to stand still and accept the swipe of a blade.

Once, maybe twice. The child hadn't remembered because after the first flash and slicing of her skin, the world turned sanguine, and she felt liquids coming out of every orifice from head to toe, back to front.

She'd screamed and they caught her hands to stop her grabbing the numbness. Then she'd drifted out of her body, and into a scarred mind.

'She said it was the most terrible pain she ever experienced,' Katy's words caused such a scorch of feeling Fergus sensed it in his own foreskin. 'Like a tattoo of blood at the back of her eyes.'

Then it was time for discarding the flesh and washing away the blood. Cold sponge between the thighs, and the stitching of wounds on the surface. Sacred parts of the child discarded like fat from pork, as they laid her out to stare up at a teary ceiling, as her torn body throbbed back into focus.

'The doctor's tools were dirty and the wound got infected. Little Grace spent the summer bed ridden, barely able to walk, permanently scarred. You can see traces of the old wounds even now, in the way she carries her body. She's most beaten out of shape when the North African stays.'

'Where's he now?' Fergus shook the snipping from his mind.

'They've gone across the Channel to the other side.'

'To pick up their human cargo in places like Calais?'

'No, it's nothing to do with Calais,' she surprised him.

'What has it do with?' he sought answers.

'These smugglers are so sophisticated that they bring thousands of people into Europe without ever going anywhere near the places you hear of on TV,' Katy revealed another back street operation. 'This Queen Bee is a lawyer who runs a sideline catering business for cruise ships.' She laughed then with a bitter sense of irony. 'While the media's working us into a frenzy over desperate people living in mud huts behind barbed wire fences, this woman's smuggling others across Europe in the grandest style imaginable.'

'Right under the noses of everyone?'

'Yeah,' she answered. 'They switch their passengers

onto fishing boats or livestock vessels on the coast of Europe's mainland.'

'Treated just like human meat,' Fergus supposed.

'Yes,' Katy spoke insistently. 'They'll kill anyone who gets in their way, passenger or migrant. I heard whispers about them going after a dancer, who talked to that singer who was killed in Deptford.'

'Jesus Christ!' Fergus exclaimed in double-barrelled shock.

'Yes, that's the one,' she declared. 'He got wind of what was going on, so the North African headed up to London and took him out. I know it's a bit sick, but that's another reason to give him the name Lucifer.'

'But surely somebody's trying to stop all this?'

'They are from what I can gather, but it's a mess.'

Again he glanced to the ceiling, conscious of the ropes on his wrist. 'Seems that way from the position we're in now.'

'From what I heard in their conversations on the radio, they're being hunted down by a Europe-wide police force that's hard to organise so every time they pass through a new country, they give the cops the slip.'

'Yes, but aren't migrant camps at the heart of all this?'

'You're repeating what's in the papers and on the TV,' she argued. 'This whole rumble's far bigger than a couple of migrant camps on the French coast. These people are running a network that stretches all the way from Casablanca to Canary Wharf.'

'I'm not sure I understand.'

'These smugglers supply workers to brothels, bars, mushroom farms, chicken factories, and anywhere else that needs cheap labour.'

'Surely it's good that they're being given jobs?'

'Yes and no,' she spoke against a growing backdrop of noise downstairs and the preparation of an evening meal. 'These workers get paid but most of their money goes back to the smugglers, and the companies they work for turn a blind eye to what's happening.'

'So it's like a conspiracy of cheap labour,' he concluded.

'Worse than that. In some cases it's slave labour.'

'Slavery,' Fergus echoed the weight of her words.

'Shush,' she warned him as footsteps sounded on the stairs. 'I don't want to get in trouble with them again. I can still smell what happened before.'

'What happened?' he asked, but there was no time for answers.

The scent of mystery changed to a fragrance of fish, fried mushrooms and coffee as the door opened. Wagner entered, holding a tray loaded in two dinners. Grace followed behind, snipped of emotion.

28. Bedtime Stories

*W*agner placed the steaming plates on the floor beside the bed, and then freed a single arm of each prisoner.

'Tonight's feast,' he announced. 'I'm sorry it's not as good as before, but our regular chef's away, catering for the cream of Europe.'

'He's going to need a high ceiling,' Katy spoke in codes.

Fergus guessed The Giraffe had been the regular chef.

'I hope you'll find my cooking just as good,' Wagner grinned arrogantly. 'They say that the way to a woman's heart is through her stomach.'

'The food's decent,' Fergus interjected. 'Maybe when all this is over, you should cook for the rich on the seas of Europe as well.'

'Be quiet and eat your food,' Grace pointed the gun at Katy. 'You be careful what you're telling people. These walls are thin. I have, what you say, thin patience and you are skiing on thin ice.'

'Skating,' Katy met her stern glare.

'I told you before what I've thought of doing.'

'Grace,' Wagner cut in. 'Just let them eat.'

'You could let us loose for a while, for some exercise,' Fergus pleaded. 'We're hardly going to make a run for it. You've got a gun.'

'We've had our trust betrayed once before,' Grace answered coldly. 'If you want to blame anybody for this, then blame her.'

'Yeah, but letting us loose for five minutes would harm nobody.'

'Don't waste your time,' Katy mumbled. 'They won't let us go.'

Minutes later they were alone again, bound to the bedframe. At least they had food in their bellies to sustain them through the night.

'This whole fucking thing's absurd,' Fergus tugged at his bondage. 'What did you do that made these bastards so mad?'

'I played games with Wagner's mind and thought about killing him.'

'Whoah,' he exhaled sharply. 'I never expected that.'

'I got too ambitious in the days after the others headed off. I thought these two were weak without the North African, and so I tried my old charms on Wagner. I started to talk about good times in our past, even though I closed my heart to him from the day I found those passports.'

He told her about the network, the cruise ships, and the purpose of bringing these poor people to Europe in the back of boats.

'I forced myself to kiss him,' she said, 'even though I hated the bastard who's not even worthy of sharing his name with a Nazi composer.'

Suddenly Fergus felt a pang of jealousy, wondering if she'd have gone further to gain her freedom. But why should he care? She'd made her own bed, and now they were lying in it.

'After the kiss I talked of starting a new life together,

and he told me that he wanted to escape too, that he was just paying off debts,' she said. 'He'd been a migrant once, working his way through the cities of Europe. But then as he was opening his heart Grace walked in on us.'

'Had she heard what he was saying?'

'Every last word of it,' Katy enunciated. 'She told him that I was poisonous and a fierce row broke out between them. She cursed him for bringing me into the picture. Then she wished the North African had taken me away to sea, and dumped my body in the ocean. Wagner got angry and pushed her away. She fell backwards, and caught me smiling as it happened. She picked up the basin and threw it, soaking me in my own piss. Wagner got really angry and said he was letting me shower.'

'You mean, they haven't allowed you to wash?'

'They bring in a tub of water most mornings and let me wash. But that's different from being alone under a hot shower.'

She closed her eyes then, sinking into the soapy heat of memories.

'I must have stayed under the water for three quarters of an hour,' she whispered. 'Then he started banging the door, saying it was time to get out.' Opening her eyes, she spoke angrily. 'But the feeling of freedom had been so beautiful I couldn't bear the thought of being a prisoner again.'

'What did you do?' Fergus fantasised of murder too.

'I slipped inside my bathrobe and savoured the scents of the bathroom because I knew I'd soon be back again in this stinking bed.'

'Yeah. It reeks, and no bloody wonder.'

'I breathed in the fragrances of the bathroom,' her voice fell to a whisper. 'Then he was banging again, and it was time to go. Coming, coming, I called, as I caught a glimpse of the razor in the cabinet.'

'The old cut-throat made of Sheffield steel?'

'Yes,' she hissed. 'I smuggled it into my pocket before

opening the door, fantasising about taking a terrible revenge on the pair of them.'

'Did you try?' Fergus willed her towards vengeance.

'I came out of the bathroom with the razor hidden in my pocket. Clean, and smelling fresh I thanked Wagner, and kissed him on the cheek.'

'You're a brilliant little Judas!' Fergus thought, in silence.

'But as we walked, he noticed the bump in my pocket.'

'What did he do?' Fergus's fantasies turned to fear.

'Jumped me from behind and fought for the razor.'

'I hope you gave the bastard a good fight.'

'He ended up cut,' she admitted, 'and then Grace came along.'

'I'm sure she wasn't exactly pleased.'

'I told you I'd no sympathy for her, no Stockholm syndrome,' Katy spoke coldly. 'She threatened to cut me as she'd been cut.'

'How'd you manage to get out of that?'

Suddenly Fergus had a strange fear that Katy's story of Grace hadn't been about somebody else at all, but was a tale of her own fate at these people's hands. The thought of her suffering filled him with a sudden longing to soothe any trace of an ache in her body.

'I tried to play with their minds again, comparing my dreams to those of migrants out on the sea,' her eyes dazzled as she caught the sympathy in his. 'But that just made them angrier, and she ordered him to get the sewing basket, and a towel to soak up the blood.'

'I hope they didn't end up hurting you.'

'They made me realise what I was up against,' she answered in that same cryptic manner as her emails. 'These are people who trade in human flesh as if it has the value of bacon in a synagogue. They prey on people and sell false promises at every step and stage of the journey.'

'I don't care about them as long as they didn't hurt you.'

'I thought she was going to do it, but Wagner managed to persuade her the spray of piss had been enough and there'd be no need for cutting.'

'Wagner, your knight in shining armour once again!'

'No. You've turned out to be the knight,' she spoke as she used to, before the slow decay of their passion. 'Tell me a story Fergus.'

'How about a fictional gangster tale set in Ramsgate?'

'Isn't this mess enough of a gangster tale already?' she laughed. 'Perhaps you can tell me something about Charlton instead.'

'Why?' he asked, after all she'd said to Wagner.

'Your stories help me to sleep,' she said, 'and not because they're boring. Because they come from the heart and they're my stories too.'

Fergus started out on the tale of a man who came to London and fell in love with a woman and a football team, going full circle from where he was right now. Katy drifted off to sleep, somewhere on the road to his first tattoo.

29. The Grand Finale

*F*ergus missed home, freedom, and routine. He'd left Ireland to forget life in a prison cell, but lay trapped in an upstairs bedroom on the Kentish coast. He'd driven here, afraid that he wouldn't find Katy, but his fears had changed to something more unbearable.

'Never seeing Charlton again, the place or the football team.'

Most of all, he feared that he'd never get to explain this to Dyana. Listening to the smugglers, he'd come to realise the danger of the situation. He'd catch fragments of conversations in the rooms below.

'The seas are too stormy for travelling, but the brutes are getting restless,' Grace spoke of the passengers as if they were beasts of burden. 'You should never ferry more than a dozen.'

'How many are there?' Wagner asked.

'Upwards of twenty,' she rattled the stairs with her fist

as she spoke. 'That's more work on our side when they land.'

'We'll find places to send them,' Wagner spoke confidently.

'If they get here and don't drown first,' Grace countered. 'But if they do, that's not our problem. We've met our end of the bargain.'

Wagner whispered. 'Maybe better they drown.'

Through these snippets of conversation, Fergus put together a mental jigsaw of the situation. Some weeks back, a cruise ship had started out on a journey from Egypt to the Norwegian fjords.

Tracing a path across the Mediterranean, the ship's wealthy passengers explored islands and cities from Greece to Spain's south coast. Along the way, as they wined and dined, their vessel picked up groups of women, sneaked in amongst caterers and cleaners.

Lucifer and The Giraffe then caught a flight to Spain, and met the boat at Cartagena, as the catering shift changed over. Amongst the wealthy customers, the tall man had found renown. Specialising in the cooking of game meats, he'd created a persona beyond any suspicion.

'He's actually the jewel in The Queen Bee's crown,' Fergus reckoned. 'There's probably a thousand foot soldiers like the North African, but this giraffe gives them access to shipping routes.'

The Giraffe and his accomplice stayed on board for the length of a journey around the Iberian Peninsula, along the Portuguese coast.

From there they curved towards the Bay of Biscay, and France. Then, at Le Havre, the smugglers transferred their cargo to a fishing boat, amidst another changeover, and a goodbye to game cuisine.

Things had changed for the migrants too, left behind on a cold shore as the one per cent moved on to Amsterdam's casinos and diamond stores. They'd got used to a good life, feeding off leftovers in the ship's udder, experiencing the luxury they'd dreamed of when leaving home.

Crushed into a cold and stinking fishing boat, they'd rebelled from the start. Lucifer had beaten one of the girls to keep her quiet, for fear of alerting the port authorities. Fergus knew this because Grace had a ferocious fight over their radio in the back room, in broken English.

She wanted to know if he *touched* the girl after he beat her, and screamed about how she didn't want any of their diseases.

'They talk of them as if they're animals,' Katy moaned.

The final stage of the operation, crossing the Channel from France, was supposed to last no more than a matter of hours. They'd set sail under cover of darkness and hope to strike land in the morning.

Unfortunately for the women, and the prisoners upstairs in Ramsgate, stormy weather sweeping down from the North Sea had stalled their plans. The worst of the storm would have passed by tonight though, coming in across the migrant camps of Dunkirk and Calais, striking Thanet with its tail end as it crossed the Channel.

'Then the boat can sail and this will be over,' Wagner came upstairs once again, with tea for his captives. 'You can go back to your lives.'

These past couple of days, Fergus had feared never seeing that old life again. Wagner though seemed assured that the ordeal was almost over.

'Sure won't miss having to answer your text messages.'

Every time he thought of this, Fergus angered at his helplessness, wanting to break free and get revenge for that blow with a knuckleduster. But he was powerless, lying here, listening to news of contact from anxious friends. Dyana's texts had grown insistent apparently, wanting to know the truth no matter how much it hurt.

'I said you are with Katy and me,' Wagner gave voice to a fantasy. 'There are complications with the pregnancy. You're staying to help.'

'And what have you said to the others?'

'Very little. There's just one question from somebody called Victoria. She asked if you'd ever been to Middlesbrough.'

'Why'd she ask that?' Fergus shifted position.

'She's going there for a football game next week.'

'Never been anywhere near it in my life,' he faced Wagner's gaze. 'From what I've heard it's a shithole you'd never want to visit.'

'Okay,' Wagner said. 'No point replying then.'

'What about the boat?' Katy demanded to know.

'They're giving stormy weather for tonight.'

'So another day of this?' she lamented.

'One last supper by candlelight,' Wagner grinned. 'Nice way to close the Bank Holiday weekend and our love triangle.'

Bank Holiday, Fergus realised. Trip to the parks with Dyana.

'Fuck,' he said, and fought the ropes on the bedframe.

'If you don't want supper, you can starve till morning.'

'It's not that,' Fergus answered. 'I was just thinking about the Bank Holiday. It's the play off final. I'd like to listen to the radio.'

'Would you be okay with that?' Wagner leaned in on Katy.

'Sure,' she spoke against the tides of their past.

'Thought you hated football. That's why you left.'

'Everything's different now, isn't it?'

Wagner went downstairs, came back with a small radio, and switched it on, as the frequency crackled from the storm coming in across the coast.

On the other side of the A2's ancient trackway, they had sunshine, glorious sunshine as Palace and Watford took to the theatre of battle.

'Enjoy,' Wagner glanced towards Katy as he left the room.

'Imagine if your tattoo artist could see us now,' she spoke against the *Five Live Football* description of the two teams lining up for the 120 million pound game. 'You inflicting torture upon me in bondage.'

'If Palace win, the torture's going to be all mine.'

Katy laughed, and filled him with a sweetly numb feeling. They'd renewed their friendship, remembering what it meant to *like* one another, without the complications of love. This close, things might have happened between them if it hadn't been for handcuffs, ropes, and the radio. Closing in on kick off, a Scottish soprano performed the British anthem.

'In bright sunlight and shadows,' a commentator sketched the scene.

Here, rain had started to fall, as a storm's whispering crept over the coast. Closing his eyes, Fergus imagined the colours ablaze in Wembley sunshine. Fresh as ink in Dyana's studio.

Watford's golden yellow flags arrayed in hedges of gorse behind the goal. Palace on the other side stamped in twilight shades of red and blue.

'And they're off,' the yellows sparked the game to life.

Battle commenced. One hundred and twenty million pounds at stake. He could imagine Lance watching from the stands, cheering on Watford as they attacked from the start and took the battle to Palace. The snakes though slithered their way out of trouble in this contest for football's biggest prize.

Trips to Anfield and White Hart Lane for the winners. Yeovil, Bournemouth, and Doncaster for the losers. Stadiums without obvious names.

And then The Valley. Banishment and sins inflicted upon exiles. His team rising from the dead, and Mendonca's moment in the sunlight.

'Come on Watford,' Fergus willed the yellow men onwards, as the game came to a halt, briefly, to remove a flotilla of red and blue balloons that had snaked a path out

265

of the Palace ends and down onto the pitch.

'Party atmosphere,' the commentator's voice crackled.

Palace didn't deserve this glorious day in the sunshine. Zaha, scorer of a brace against Brighton, winning the ball, charging down the wing, misplacing a pass. Ha ha, move broken. Watford on the attack.

'Yes, yes,' he followed the ball, swept in behind goal.

Out for a corner. Chance of a goal. Nah, beaten away. Thoughts of 1998 flashed through his head, another game on the radio. Sunderland, also in yellow, versus Charlton in a darker shade of red.

'Where's Watford's Mendonca?' he wondered.

And he'd give anything, love or money, for a Palace Michael Gray. Actually he'd light the match and hold it to the guy's nipples he reckoned as more balloons floated out of the stands and onto the pitch. Heated talk of passes made. Strokes and caresses on the Wembley turf.

'Sounds arousing,' Katy's eyes caught his.

Things started to speed up. The crowd's impassioned roar dimmed skittles of rain striking the window. Eighty two thousand bodies clung frantically to the straps of a rollercoaster dipping this way and that, far from this lonely room where former lovers lay together in bondage.

Zaha had sprinted down the wing, slicing towards the centre. Then Fergus brushed against Katy at the same time as the Palace player made his pass, his push for goal. Despite her body heat, the awkward lunge in handcuffs descended into a sense of chaos, as she swayed out of reach.

Thunder crackled in the radio. Bodies gasped, deep sighs of expectation. Then blockage, as Watford cleared. The chance came to nothing, and play moved on. Together they listened to the radio and the storm. Out of the corner of his eye he could see her mouth damp and red as he remembered—a special Charlton kind of red, a ripe apple form of redness. But he knew then he'd never again look deep inside those blue eyes, and kiss that softly freckled face lying sideways against his own.

Damien Delaney, Palace defender, saved him from distraction.

'He's Irish,' Fergus spoke of the man who enacted a vital blockage on a shot from a striker buzzing in like a hornet upon the enemy goal. 'Forty minutes gone and there's hardly been a decent shot on target.'

With the stakes so high, there was no surprise in that.

'Everybody's scared of making a mistake.'

'You're really getting this, Katy.'

'Watching you getting into this.'

'Better if we could get out,' he rattled the bedframe.

She laughed. 'Once we do, I'll be glad but sad too.'

'Why sad?' he asked, as the half time whistle sounded.

The crowd's gasp disguised the absence of an answer, and then silence. Voices switched from pitch to studio. Glass walls. Expert commentary. Talk of tension, very few flashes of possibility on an afternoon with so much at stake. Damien Delaney's priceless clearance, and Zaha's pace serving as the highlights of a cautious game.

Studio experts played a cautious game too. 'Nobody knows how the day's going to finish, and in whose hands the trophy will end up.'

The storm crossing over Thanet and missing the rest of England distilled its rage on the seas outside. Seeing flashes of lightning, Fergus thought back to the day he'd walked towards Dyana's tattoo studio.

So much had happened since that first home Saturday of the season. Something else had come close to happening in the first half too.

The burning of an itch that requires the cool feel of another. The moment had passed though, and there was no going back.

'I thought of you last week,' she spoke against the voices in the studio. 'Listening to the news of the soldier I wondered if you were okay.'

'Good to know that you were thinking of me, that you

care.'

'Of course I care, silly,' she pushed against him. 'Every Saturday, even when I was with Wagner, I waited for the Charlton results.'

'I realise now that you really are a friend.'

'Shared history's a hard thing to shake off.'

'But it is history,' he knew from her tone.

'Yes,' she said, as the referee prepared to start the second half. 'Doesn't mean that we can't be mates though.'

'That's more of an English thing than an Irish,' he told her, as Palace took their turn to kick off. 'Being mates with an ex.'

'Then we'll break the mould,' she spoke against the passion of Palace's first attack. 'New century, new ways of looking at relationships.'

'Here's to new relationships,' he clinked his body off hers as if they had a couple of glasses—beer for him, and wine for her.

Then they settled down, listening to the second half unfolding. Lightning flashed. Thunder sounded, and the game ticked towards the hour, coming alive like a friendship reformulated and reimagined.

Palace attacking from a ball won by Delaney and eventually reaching 15 million pounds worth of talent in the feet of Zaha, dancing towards the box, before flicking the ball into the path of Stuart O'Keefe. *Fuck no, Lance up there in the crowd, get a match, a fucking flamethrower to his nipples.*

Fergus shared the crowd's breath of anticipation as the young Englishman, with an Irish name, burst towards goal and swayed a shot to the left. The tide had turned from stalemate to a red and blue surge.

Palace, wearing eagles upon their shirts, had developed a cutting edge like Charlton's sword. Creating the better chances, the bastards looked like they were going to steal the bragging rights in South London.

'Cunts,' he could imagine Lance's words from amidst a yellow shield behind the Watford goal, getting nervous at this sea change.

Right about now, he was probably texting furiously, venting his rage. And surely if he was, the lack of response would suggest something out of place. Unless Wagner, far more of a bastard than any man who had ever worn the famous red and blue, texted back with a series of bad spellings.

Lance, in his passion for the game, wouldn't notice.

'We're here to morning,' Fergus felt resigned to fate.

From outside, sounds of the storm enclosed the big old house.

Palace continued to drive forward as the minutes ticked down to dinnertime. Wagner was busy cooking in the kitchen below, fashioning them a last supper together.

Once that boat came in, they'd go in separate directions.

'You think the storm's going to stall things?' she asked.

'Probably,' he turned his head from the radio, feeling mixed emotions.

He might relish one more night of their new-found friendship. But after several days of confinement, he wanted the chance to freshen up.

He knew the sweat of Watford fans watching Palace gather momentum. Yellow shirts beaten against the ropes, unable to control the quickfire punch of Zaha's feet. He was playing the role of a snake's Mendonca, doing everything—creating, crossing, causing a chaos of clearances and corners—but thankfully not getting the ball in the net.

'Sounds like the Watford goalkeeper is having to earn his money,' Katy too sensed the changing direction of the game's tide.

'Extra time,' Fergus breathed a sigh of relief.

No goals in the ninety minutes, Watford's fortress held secure.

'What happens now?' Katy wondered. 'Penalty kicks?'

'Not yet,' he explained. 'There's a short break and then

they play for another half an hour in two periods. If nobody scores, it's penalty kicks.'

'You can hear the storm again, thunder in the distance.'

'Yes,' he agreed. 'The whole stadium's fallen silent.'

82,025 people watching, waiting for the next stage of battle to commence. Players scattered on the sidelines, struggling against cramp and fatigue. Two managers pushing the teams, dead on their feet, towards more.

Three quarters of an hour from now it would all be over. Fergus could picture Lance inside the stadium, raising his eyes to the heavens. Praying for Palace failure, and the preservation of South London's bragging rights.

Maybe Dyana too, watching the game, waiting for his text. Cheering on Palace, and preparing to ink her flesh in red and blue. Cursing the waste man who'd passed across the top of her stairway, staining Poppy's memories. *Mummy's friend* letting them down in the grand finale.

Laces tied, bodies massaged, half-refreshed, players resumed positions. 'And they're off,' the commentator's voice crackled on the radio.

82,025 voices pushed through thunder's growing blitz upon the coast.

'Sounds like it's getting very close,' Katy whispered.

Interference had already started to snatch words from the commentary, as the tide turned again, and flowed in a wave of Watford dominance.

'Just hope the electric holds till the end of the game.'

'Maybe we can write our own ending,' she suggested.

He laughed. 'Where Palace lose painfully as possible.'

But as the minutes passed, the Eagles survived Watford's onslaught in the way they had survived shit in the dressing room. Then Delaney pushed a shot towards the yellow goal in the closing minutes of the first period.

'Close,' the commentator said, 'but not close enough.'

With no goals scored, the match was drifting towards penalties.

But out of nowhere a great cry of 'NO' rose up from

the room.

'Fuck, fuck, fuck,' Fergus rattled his hopes on the bedframe.

Kevin Phillips, veteran substitute, had passed the ball out wide to Zaha. Nothing more than his name mentioned, and seconds later a cry of penalty.

Yellow card for the Watford defender, an Italian international.

'Phillips, creator of the moment, steps up to take the penalty.'

'Miss,' Fergus looked away from the radio, as if a TV.

He thought of goblins. Wicked malevolent laughter and a cruel fate. Thunderous noise in the stadium and seas outside. Gritting his teeth, he prayed. He'd take another week of this prison for the sound of Kevin Phillips striking the crossbar or sending the ball into space.

'Miss,' Fergus rasped again, as the Palace No 9 stood on the spot.

Then suddenly, noise pierced the lower part of the house.

'What was that?' his attention shifted from the radio.

'Lightning breaking glass,' Katy reckoned.

'Or maybe dinner plates smashing?'

Then, in the midst of their conversation, fresh noise followed in two places. From the radio Fergus knew what had happened, even without words. The crowd's roar revealed that Phillips and Palace had scored.

'But what's going on downstairs?' Katy wanted to know.

'Somebody's gone outside,' Fergus heard the door opening and gusts of wind shaking the bones of the house, coming in more fiercely off the sea than before. 'Maybe the place has been hit with lightning.'

'Hopefully fried the wicked witch!'

'At least our radio's still working.'

Kevin Phillips had scored with a clinical strike. Celebrations ensued, as a whistle sounded for the interval.

Then a fast restart. Fifteen minutes for Watford to salvage something, and silence the Palace supporters sensing victory, in fine voice, in the Wembley sunshine.

The bastards had earned themselves a Mendonca moment, and the promise of a Tuesday night party for their homecoming in the streets of Croydon. The gartersnakes would be up off their bellies dancing.

But suddenly, fresh noise interrupted their chants of triumph.

'A woman's scream from downstairs,' Katy spoke breathlessly.

Perhaps a second flash of lightning had scorched the witch's flesh to ashes. Thunder had arrived too, in the form of heavy footsteps on the stairs.

'Police,' Katy breathed excitement laced in a tremulous fear.

'Don't know,' Fergus didn't want to get his hopes up.

Then the bedroom door swung open, just as Watford kicked off the restart of the game in the Wembley sunshine. A man they didn't recognise had entered the room, dressed in jeans and pointing an old-style gun in their direction. A knife scar glistened down one side of his face and his hair was gingery, turning grey, as he stepped into the light and edged towards them. But who the hell was this unexpected visitor?

Could he be a policeman? Off duty and out of uniform? Concerned neighbour? Another member of the smuggling network?

Somebody waiting on the cargo of flesh to arrive?

They couldn't know, as the man stared in disbelief at the sight of their bondage, slipping the gun inside his trouser belt as he approached.

Just for a second he seemed more concerned with what was happening in the game, on the radio, than their predicament.

Then he turned and called out down the stairs.

'They're here. I've found them.'

Watford's fightback faded out of view, as the seconds ticked away in the sound of fresh footsteps on the stairs. Like Palace's trip up the Wembley steps, getting closer with every dying minute of the 120 million contest.

Pressed tight against Katy, Fergus waited for the game's ending.

30. Unexpected Guests

The storm's fury had risen in the space of half an hour, drenching Ramsgate's seafront to the point of drowning. As waves battered jetty walls, the marina's boats held firm against incessant storms. Local TV news said that trees had fallen on the roads out of Thanet, turning it to a proper island once again.

Even if the roads were passable you wouldn't dare leave in this weather. Fergus had listened to the heavens rage as he took a quick shower after his escape. Katy bathed on the other side of the room because they'd nothing left to hide after their nights of bondage.

'Trains have stopped running too,' he caught the news on the end of a report that spoke also of Crystal Palace's one-nil victory at Wembley.

There'd be no going home tonight. There would be no tugs, trawlers, or fishing boats out on the sea either. This kind of weather created storm wrecks, and left widows weeping by the windows of fishermen's cottages.

'Waves are hittin' ten feet,' said the man with the gun.

'Freak storm,' the younger of the cousins agreed.

Fergus listened to their banter, still in a daze. He'd almost believed himself to be hallucinating when his friend stepped through the door.

'Thanks for what you've done,' he said again.

'Just buy us a few beers on the way back to London.'

Timmy spoke in a softer, more polite manner than Fergus had ever imagined the man who'd come close to inheriting his family business before Vivaldi's dark music with the Brown Marilyn.

'Besides kiddo has ended up glad that he sacrificed the Palace game,' the former gangster gestured towards his cousin. 'Bad result for Charlton.'

Timmy had come out of retirement for one last family gathering. Different to how Lance described him back in the day.

Less of a hothead, his ginger hair had faded to grey, and he carried a spare tyre around his midriff. Life as a mechanic probably involved less stress than his days as heir apparent to the family empire. He had to stay vigilant though, always looking over his shoulder for fear of a visit from people with long memories, and scars old as his own knife wounds. Hence, he kept guns.

'But the police won't give me a licence,' he grumbled. 'So I've got to collect antique weapons like this Smith & Wesson Model 29. This one's from the 50s, like in *The Dirty Harry* series.'

'I'm still amazed how you boys managed to rescue us.'

Katy's voice softened the scene, after her bath.

'Victoria's sense of bad spelling helped save you,' Lance explained.

'She's somewhere on the dyslexia spectrum,' Fergus pointed out.

'She reckoned there was something strange in your text messages,' Lance continued. 'We started to realise that most of your communication over the weekend felt badly out of place, so I drove up to Essex, picked up Timmy, and came down here to stay in a hotel.'

'We drove by the house a couple o' times last night,' Timmy added, 'but everything was in darkness, and we couldn't see anything unusual.'

'Yeah, the bastards went to bed early,' Fergus remembered.

'They'd expected the boat to come today,' Katy sketched in the details. 'Probably would have if it hadn't been for the storm.'

'We needed to be sure that somebody else was using your phone,' Lance delighted in his detective work. 'Middlesbrough was the clincher. Victoria would ask if you'd ever been, and hoped for an answer.'

'It worked,' he'd almost forgotten his spontaneous moment of cunning. 'Thank God for Victoria, and thank God for Middlesbrough.'

'When you said you that it was a shithole, we knew for sure it wasn't you, and it was time to move in.'

'Why's that such a code word?' Katy wondered.

'A while back I went up there with my team, expecting a place that was a dump, according to its portrayal in the media,' Fergus explained. 'I expected single mother junkies with needle marks in their arms, but I found a place that was down to earth and cultured in its own way.'

'So whenever we go to a pub or a game and it turns out better than expected, we talk about doing a Middlesbrough,' Lance elaborated.

'Well, I'm very glad you went there.'

'We're glad too that you guys came to rescue us.'

The rescue operation had been executed beautifully. Timmy booted a football through the window, from the front garden—one shot, timed perfectly.

'The one called Wagner came out to see what was going on,' Timmy described the pattern of events. 'We'd taken out the front light, so it was dark, and he couldn't see. Then I clobbered him with a baseball bat.'

Fergus smiled at second-hand revenge for the knuckleduster.

'Knocked him cold without even a shout,' Timmy recalled.

'Then Timmy and me went inside with guns and a fishing net,' Lance pointed to the hallway they'd come through towards the kitchen. 'Because they thought it was kids messing around with the ball, she'd kept on cooking, and didn't notice a fucking thing as we crept up from behind.'

'Caught in a net,' Fergus said. 'That's poetic justice.'

The affair with the smugglers was over, and he needed to call Dyana.

'All signals are down now,' Lance interjected. 'That's why we're trying to fix the big radio in the back room, to make contact with the outside world.'

'The outside world,' Katy voiced the words with passion. Then she moved across the floor to face her former captors tied up. 'How does it feel to have our roles reversed, you evil whore?'

'Let us go. You don't know what you're messing with here.'

'Maybe I could cut you in pieces,' Katy voiced her festering vengeance. 'But there's nothing human left to cut, not even a heart. I'll give you to those women on the boat and let them claw out your eyes.'

'It's tempting,' Fergus said, 'but we're better than them.'

'I'd take them to the marina, stick them in a boat, and shove them out to sea,' Lance said, 'but we've more important things to do first.'

They had to make contact with the outside world. Fergus needed to call Dyana because of what she had been texting.

'I'm asking you to message me the God's honest truth this morning,' she'd demanded at 6am today, her usual rising time. By lunchtime, another had arrived. 'I can't make sense of this pregnancy story. Why are you giving time for a woman carrying another man's child?'

He saw a certain irony in that question, but felt concerned too. Come evening and another flurry, she had reached a final decision.

'Poppy's been so excited about today, and you've let her down.'

'With good fucking reason,' he wanted to scream through the intensity of the storm gathering pace in the streets outside.

Scrolling through several lines of anger, he came to her ending. 'I've reached a decision Fergus. I imagine there's some doubt about the father of the baby, so I've decided to sit Poppy down after dinner, and tell her that mummy's friend won't ever be coming back.'

Three hours had passed since that message and nothing since.

'It's over,' he realised, 'probably even if I get a signal.'

There's no going back over old ground when a child's involved. This would have hurt Poppy a lot. *Mummy's friend* had been a good man and now he was gone. It's always worse when the good guys let you down.

'Could do with a beer,' Lance's words sprang into Fergus's daydreams.

'There's a shop on the corner,' Katy pointed to the side of the house. 'It stays open all hours, and probably even in this storm.'

'I'll go,' Fergus volunteered. 'I could do with a walk.'

'You'll get soaked to the fucking skin,' Timmy said. 'You couldn't even take an umbrella out in those gales. It'd get blown apart in seconds.'

'I need fresh air. Besides I might get a signal outside.'

'Be careful,' Katy warned. 'Remember the others.'

'They'd never have set sail in that storm,' Fergus grabbed a coat from the hallway. 'Old Lucifer and The Giraffe won't have left the other side.'

'Who the fuck's Lucifer when he's at home?' Lance asked.

'He's the fucker who killed Demetrius,' Fergus told his friend.

'Maybe when his ship comes in, he'll get justice,' Timmy flashed the grip of his revolver. 'Who's going to notice where one stray bullet comes from in a firefight between cops and smugglers?'

'No way,' Katy pleaded. 'These are dangerous people.'

Fergus didn't care as he stepped outside to where the storm had reached full throttle. He clutched his hood in one hand, and his phone in the other as he moved down the driveway. He'd no signal as yet. Some parts of town had suffered an electrical blackout, and there wasn't a single spark of light out at sea. At the end of the street, a Black Series Mercedes sat parked in the shadows, engine running, and lights dimmed. Inside, behind the moving wipers, he could make out the silhouette of a couple, a man and a woman. It didn't look like anything to worry about though. Perhaps they'd broken down, or just stopped because of the weather.

He kept on walking, searching for a signal and the corner store. Though frozen and already drenched to the bone, he didn't mind the extreme elements. At least he was alive, and the agent of his own condition, as he approached the store.

Inside the shop, a young girl showed him the fridges. She probably considered him an alcoholic, coming out for six packs on a night like this.

'Keep the change,' he surprised and gladdened the dark-eyed girl as he paid. 'I'm in a good mood. I haven't had a night out for ages.'

Going down the street, just as in the store, he still hadn't found a signal. Giving up the ghost, he quickened his pace.

The black Mercedes remained parked in the darkness as he approached the house, but its lights had been turned off.

Even the wipers had stopped and he could no longer

see people, as he got closer. Perhaps they too had given up the ghost and gone back inside, as when he reached the door, and checked for a signal one last time.

'You're soaking,' Timmy said, 'but at least you got us beer.'

Back in the warmth, they settled down to drink, chatting about football. Palace, fucking Palace, winning the play off at Wembley. Kevin Phillips scoring the goal. 39 years of age. Shouldn't he have retired by now?

Where was the match to a nipple when it was needed?

'Fucking cunts,' said Lance. 'Devil's good to his own.'

'Hope not where this boat's concerned,' Fergus sipped his beer, then almost spilled it as a sudden knock sounded. Same urgency as he recalled from Victoria after the incident with the selfies, which seemed far away. 'There's somebody out there banging the door.'

Timmy rose to his feet, pulling the old weapon back into action. 'Probably broken down or needing a phone.'

'I passed a black Mercedes down the street with a couple inside.'

'Answer the door kid, and be careful,' Timmy barked instructions.

Lance moved slowly, watched over by his cousin's gun.

Seconds later, as the door opened, guns and badges flashed. Timmy hid his weapon, as the house filled up with strangers.

'Police,' Katy whispered as if it wasn't obvious to everyone.

Foreign accents. Guns that made Timmy's seem prehistoric.

'No need to point them at us,' Lance moved to the fore.

Explaining that he used to be a soldier and the series of events that had led them into this mess, he managed to calm the situation down.

'You're still involved in something that you've no part in,' said one of the officers with an accent bordering on

French. 'Now you've got to let us get on with our job, because there's a boat coming in to this shore tomorrow morning, and we're here to arrest the people involved.'

Operation Red Onion, they labelled the assignment—a process of peeling back the layers until they reached the centre, and found The Queen Bee who was a mystery they couldn't quite decipher, brilliantly evasive, well-protected, connected, and able to avoid capture at every turn.

'So we need to work hard,' announced one of the senior detectives. 'Get the Tech Guy to look at the radio.'

'Can we go then?' Fergus spied hope of getting away from this place and back to the green, and probably angry, dazzle of Dyana's eyes.

'No, you have to stay here until this is all over,' a fresh voice boomed from the background, emerging suddenly from the stormy outdoors.

A tall woman came into focus, wearing a coppery tan that seemed out of season, out of kilter with this weather. Shaking the wet off her trouser suit, she drew the attention of Timmy and Lance who looked at one another and nodded approvingly at first. Then their expressions changed, as she announced herself to be the lead detective on the case.

'From now on I dictate everything that happens here.'

Four men trailed behind her, as she pulled the strings and gave each of them particular instructions without introductions. One stood tall as his boss, but more gangly and less dignified, a bald fellow with hangdog expression. Behind the tall man, a second officer emerged out of the shadows, much shorter, older, and more stylish in a silvery suit that matched his hair. Certain aspects of his face, loose skin and wrinkles, had echoes of the man from *The Bird Cage* pulling the strings in the background as a puppeteer of piranhas. But in this foreign detective's eyes, Fergus observed a pristine decency, a sense of incorruptibility. He stood firmly on the side of the good guys as more of his colleagues stepped in from the shivery darkness.

A third member of the team moved busily about the room, handsome and confident, seeming keen to get the job done and go home. Several times he chastised the fourth man, a dull and spectacled chap who appeared as lost in the midst of all this chaos as a spare sock in a laundry basket.

The female detective spoke bluntly in his direction. 'Go make me a coffee and we'll get this show on the road.'

'Be good to know what the show is.'

'The hunting down of a very bad gang,' said the man with silver hair.

'We've been on their trail a long time,' the female detective took charge once more as the dull man returned with a sugarless coffee that she cursed. 'And these past few weeks we've tracked them down.'

'So you could have saved us sooner?' Katy growled.

'Look we're only following orders,' the other detectives spoke in chorus. 'We don't make the decisions. We just play the game.'

The female detective explained that this was a mixed force from across Europe, centered on Belgium where the network was based. Then she set to work, laying out her gallery of suspects in photos on the kitchen table.

Fergus could see images of Wagner and Grace, the Red Sea chef and the North African with evil eyes moving along different shorelines and through new cities as they knitted together their complex operation.

'What if the boat doesn't come for days?' Timmy asked.

'Nobody leaves till then,' the bald man spoke bluntly.

'What are you going to do with *them*?' Katy glanced towards Grace and the bloodied Wagner surrounded by a phalanx of officers.

'The operation is classified,' the most confident of the four men insisted, 'but you can rest assured that this woman will go to prison for the part she's played, and not get out for a long time.'

'And *him*?' Katy couldn't bear to meet his eyes.

'Take him to the room with the radio,' the instructions of another officer answered her questions indirectly. 'See if he'll co-operate.'

'I guess they need one on their side.'

Lance nodded in agreement with Timmy.

Katy fumed. 'It's not fair. After all he's done, the bastard's going to walk away, and we're the ones that are still being kept as prisoners.'

'Just one more night,' Fergus hoped for the best.

Surely something, at last, was going to turn out right.

31. Shipping forecast

Fergus awoke to the cadence of a BBC weatherman narrating the story of the morning's tides. Clock radio dragging him out of his dreams. Deep sleep, jungle thickly forested. Barricades and razor wire, a gallery of women behind the fences. Dreams gone, he concentrated on the voice. Crisp and composed of clear diction like the classified football results mapping out a Saturday afternoon.

Just a few days ago they had entered his dreams too. A jungle of names from Middlesbrough down to Forest Green Rovers. Charlton and Hamilton's academics as Katy lay beside him in the bed, handcuffed.

Now, chains broken, he was free but at the same time felt a sense of loss. Partly he willed the shipping forecast to last forever.

'Once the cargo comes to shore, it's all over,' he realised.

He'd say goodbye to Katy and move on with his life.

Feeling heaviness in his heart, he concentrated on the broadcaster's voice passing through coastal stations and shipping zones. Dogger, Fisher, Biscay, and German Bight. Routes for fish food, human cargo.

Through the night, gales had blown across Dover and Wight, out into the wavelengths of Sole and FitzRoy. Presumably, in their wake, the boat had set sail. Steered by an assassin, a hash-eater with evil eyes.

Before going to bed, Fergus had looked at the pictures of Lucifer.

'Mercenary in Libya,' the female detective told them.

Then somewhere along the way, tired of war, he turned from soldier to pirate. Trading human flesh, he found an easier way to make his fortune. Became part of a network that stretched down to every sun-scorched corner of the Sahara. But he was never anything more than a foot soldier in the Queen Bee's army, as disposable as the people that he ferried.

Perhaps this was why they wanted him alive. Just as Wagner was the one who might lead the detectives to the boat landing on Ramsgate's shore, Lucifer could prove vital to breaking the power of The Queen Bee.

But Katy hoped she didn't face him at the hour of his arrest. He had kept guard upon her one night when she didn't dare sleep.

'Terrifying eyes,' she described what everyone had seen in the photographs. 'Like a couple of irons, scorching hot, that you could feel pressing down into the bedsheets, burning your skin.'

He told her that he'd like to play. Then he came closer, and leaned over her body to whisper that Grace didn't have to know. He said that white girls were dirty. Asked her if she missed sex from being held in captivity.

Then he started to pull on the bedsheets, already assaulting her with his eyes, saying that he liked these games that girls played. She screamed and he grabbed her by the throat, forcing her face down beneath the covers in the direction of his trousers. Refusing to touch him, taste him, she put up a fight until he caught her by the hair, wrenching away a fistful.

'Luckily Wagner heard the struggle,' she explained, 'and came to the rescue. He made Lucifer stop and sent him off downstairs.'

After hearing that story, Fergus felt Timmy's hunger to put a bullet in Lucifer. Stick the Smith & Wesson to his skull. Blow his fucking brains out. He'd probably do the same to Wagner if he got the chance, but the young barista, Katy's knight in shining armour, had swapped sides.

'No justice in the world,' Fergus finally rose out of bed.

The shipping forecast died out as he dressed. Sounds of the Faroes and Southeast Iceland faded into the chattering of gulls.

'Shannon, Malin, and Rockall,' he rolled names on his tongue.

Places that made him homesick. Not just for Ireland, but Dyana's terrain too. The wild and windswept reaches of Woolwich Common, with summer bringing the promise of walks, picnics, and funfairs.

Planning for this, he left the gulls and made his way downstairs. There, he found Katy already active, standing by a stove, baking bread.

'Did you sleep well?' she asked, as he approached.

'Well as could be expected,' he answered. 'And you?'

'Couldn't settle. Got up before dawn to bake.'

'You've enough food here to feed five thousand!'

'There's a lot of police, and the boys too, though they'll be dead to the world until the afternoon, after last night's drinking.' She laughed, then sighed. 'Maybe best to leave some for those ladies on the boat.'

'Any news coming off the radio in the back room?'

'Sounds as if they haven't been able to make contact,' she sighed. 'The smugglers don't seem to be answering Wagner's calls.'

'Crazy the way he's getting out of this so easy.'

'He's not getting off,' she snapped. 'He has suffered too.'

'If they don't send him to prison,' Fergus tested the waters further, 'they'll probably throw him out of the country when this is done.'

'Probably,' she agreed, 'but it's none of our business.'

Then she asked him if he wanted breakfast and he said yes.

'Boiled eggs and soda bread,' she suggested. 'Your favourite.'

'You still remember,' his eyes followed her to the fridge.

'Of course,' she worked quickly, cutting, buttering, and boiling.

A few minutes later, she had his breakfast laid out on the table. As he began to eat, he wanted to ask her whether things could ever have worked out differently if he hadn't got his tattoo of the Charlton badge.

Then, just as he felt the question forming on his lips, a man's hoarse laughter came into focus. Immediately, the moment had passed.

'That was some night,' said Timmy, 'and some headache too.'

Katy rose from the table. 'I'll make breakfast for you boys.'

Disconnected from his former lover, Fergus talked football. Palace, fucking Palace. A victory that weighed heavily on Lance's mind.

'Stupid Italian taking down Zaha, giving away a penalty.'

'It's just a game,' Katy showed no sympathy for their suffering.

'No,' Lance groaned. 'That was a journey straight to Hell.'

Even the sky looked hellish. Clouds drifted across the sea in royal shades of red and blue, forming Crystal Palace flags out of embers left over from the fire of last night's storm.

'Pathos,' Katy said, as she served up an English breakfast.

'Feast good enough for a grand hotel,' Timmy remarked.

'Thanks,' she watched the men dig into their meal.

Palace skies forgotten, they fell silent as they ate.

Then—noise from the back room. A sudden seismic shift in activity.

'What the fuck's happening?' Timmy rose from the table.

Police voices. Half a dozen accents, languages, and actions.

Crackle of a radio. Wagner positioned, poised to speak.

'They're not communicating, but we've traced the path of their vessel,' the bald officer explained as he stepped from the room where the others readied for action. 'They're coming to land soon.'

According to the Belgian detectives, the coastguard had identified the boat coming towards Ramsgate's shore from across the Channel. Journey almost over for the human cargo. Desert to beach, via barricades and seas. Soon they'd get to glimpse what they'd paid for.

'Love to see their faces when they get here,' Lance grumbled. 'Expecting a winning lottery ticket and when they open up the envelope, all they're going to find is a bloody beaten docket.'

Fergus didn't care what they were given, so long as he got a ticket out of here. 'Can we go, now that it's coming to a close?'

'No,' the female officer insisted. 'You must all stay here.'

He tried to protest, but his efforts fell on deaf ears. The mission had to be watertight, nothing left to chance. They wanted no media coverage until it was done. No showing of the dirty laundry until it was washed according to the dull man whose English was not so good.

'Calling the newspapers is hardly our first priority,' Katy argued.

She had a book to finish, and a publisher to contact.

'Once the operation's over, you're free to go.'

Lance was growing impatient too in his suffering from yesterday's beer and football. 'Why don't you just get a couple of gunboats, and blow the fucking smugglers to Kingdom Come?'

'How the hell are they going to do that without killing everybody? Some soldier you must have made cuz!'

'We will handle this our way,' the silvery gentleman returned to the fore. 'Trust us, we know what we're doing. Everything will work out fine.'

After months of investigation, Operation Red Onion was reaching closure. Fergus imagined the sweet feeling of revenge that would come from the sight of Lucifer on the shore in cuffs. Arrested. Taken to trial.

Haunted in his prison cell by ghosts of the high seas.

'Vengeance for Katy, for Dyana and for Demetrius,' he figured.

Very soon this would all be over, and they'd be free to take back their phones confiscated on the night before by the police. That was why he couldn't call Dyana now, and tell her the whole story.

The female officer's voice broke his daydreams as she signalled towards a couple of goons. 'We are keeping these men as guards.'

'What the hell for?' Lance's protestation came immediately.

Despite having been in the army, he didn't like taking orders.

'There's no need to be alarmed,' she spoke more softly. 'It's for your own protection, while we go down to the shore, and complete the operation. Remember these are dangerous people we're trying to corner.'

'Guess it's not that easy to break a network,' Fergus

lamented.

'Let's go,' the female detective led her four henchmen towards the door. 'Stay here and watch, but whatever happens don't make any attempt to step through that door.'

'Why's he with you?' Katy asked of Wagner's presence.

'He's the face they'll recognise,' the answer came fast.

'And what if he runs?' Lance asked.

'That wouldn't be wise for anyone,' the officer said.

Standing in the doorway, Wagner fixed his gaze on Katy.

'Not so arrogant now,' Fergus thought. 'But free.'

After what he'd done, there seemed a terrible injustice in being able to walk out the door, albeit with a gun at his back, as they stayed inside. Katy tracked his movements with a gaze that dazzled in anger. Sadness too, and a sense of longing. Screams repressed in her throat.

'WHY?' Fergus knew what she wanted to ask.

Why had Wagner got caught up with these people? He said that he owed them, but wouldn't it have been better to run? There was probably a time when she'd have run with him if he had bothered to ask.

'Good luck,' she broke in the end and called out.

By then it was too late for him to hear. He'd gone out of view, to keep his appointment with the smugglers who'd stopped answering his calls. According to the detectives, the coastguard had identified the boat coming towards Ramsgate's shore from across the Channel.

'Nothing more sinister,' the laundry man had said.

Now all four of the henchmen were heading for the sea.

'I want to join them,' Katy argued, but the guards stepped in.

'We can see from upstairs,' Lance suggested.

Katy shivered. 'I don't want to go back there.'

'Surely it wasn't that bad sharing a bed with me,' Fergus tried to lighten the load of the past, as they made their way to the big room.

Opening the door, he could smell traces of their captivity. Sweat, piss, wax, and blood boiling in his nostrils from bad memories. Coming back here, he wanted to be amongst the police ranks with a gun at Wagner's back. Nobody would miss one stray bullet from Timmy's Smith & Wesson.

Maybe two. One for Lucifer as well. The thought of that sweetened the stench as they crossed towards the window. Smugglers dying together on the sands of the coast which delivered such false promises.

'What's happening?' Katy strained to see the action.

The European-wide secret mission, Operation Red Onion, was rolling to a gradual end. Layers peeling back, and the naked truth stripped bare. Observed through an upstairs window, it felt both close and far away.

Fergus thought of TV images from the migrant camps in Calais. Then he had been looking at a world of horror through a glass screen, and though it was before his eyes it had never seemed quite real. Now this was all too real, but still seemed far away, beyond touching distance.

'I hope it all turns out okay,' Katy whispered.

'All over in a few hours from now,' Lance predicted, and then laughed. 'We can only hope there's a better result than the play off final.'

'What'll become of the women?' Katy again voiced concern.

'Doubt they care too much what happens to the cargo,' Timmy reckoned. 'They're after the one nicknamed The Queen Bee.'

Looking through the glass, a lone vessel came into view. Seeing it stamped upon the horizon, Fergus remembered the night of Valkyries, but this was no story of love in a boat. This was Red Onion rolling to an end.

'Old reefer ship,' Timmy said.

'Transports refrigerated cargo,' Lance elaborated. 'I remember them from my days of training up in Norfolk.'

Katy angered, pressing her face closer to the glass, staring out on the sea. 'Literally trying to pass off the women as a delivery of meat.'

This was the vessel that had caused their captivity in the bedroom. Ugly fucking thing. Floating tin bucket. Selhurst Park upon the sea.

Selhurst, cancered in rust, crawled towards Ramsgate's silent harbour. Somewhere below deck, women waited for anchorage, and if this bedroom stank, he could only imagine the reek of that old fishing vessel.

Seeing the boat's approach, fresh questions spiked Fergus's mind. 'What if the smugglers already know that something has gone wrong? What if they've already abandoned their cargo as food for the fishes?'

Minutes from now, the last pieces of the puzzle would fall into place.

32. The Final Cut

*L*eaning closer, Fergus watched police take up their final positions on the shore. One group, disguised as surfers, polished boards. Another team had assembled by the marina. Then, out on the frontline, Wagner waited for the boat to drift in. Several times he'd glance back, with doubt and hesitancy marking his mannerisms.

'The boat's getting closer,' Lance itched for an ending.

Fergus felt the same itch, thinking of Dyana and Poppy. Chelsea and Victoria too, so that he could get back to thank her for Middlesbrough. Get back to training and the safe routines of his weekend mornings.

Timmy hungered for a fight. 'Wish I was down there.'

Selhurst appeared to be rolling blindly towards a crash landing. Away from the empty ferry terminal, and towards the surfers on the shore.

'Unmanned,' Fergus guessed, as the rusting hulk wobbled inwards. 'It's like there's nobody actually steering it from the inside.'

This concerned Timmy, keen to get his crack at the man who'd killed the young musician. 'Fuck! Has the operation been rumbled?'

'If it has,' Katy wondered, 'where does that leave us?'

She paused then with her blue eyes dazzling, as her voice fell to a whisper brushing off the window's hard glass like moth wings in the night.

'And what becomes of Wagner?'

'Don't know,' Fergus watched the boat strike land.

Striking the shore, *Selhurst* served as the metaphor for all endings—the shell of a season, the decaying of a romance, and the passage of time.

The police in their guise of surfers grew agitated at the sight of the boat's last stumble, like a drunk girl staggering onto Ramsgate's promenade. Any second now she'd spill her guts in a last rite of sea sickness.

Through the window, the Channel appeared more immense than ever with the cliffs wired together tight as racquets in the mist, volleying surf across the golden clay court of England's shore.

With a series of nods and winks, the surfers signalled for Wagner to cross the base line and finish the job. Furtively, he nodded back to the police officers who nodded in turn to the four detectives lurking amidst the solid forms and colours of boats pebbling the marina's waters.

Life went on as normal in the seaside town as the day gathered pace. Souvenir shops rolled up their shutters for business, selling sticks of rock, saucy postcards, and buckets with spades for kids to build sandcastles in the shadow of arcades where parents jostled with hungry slot machines.

The female detective directed a girl in a bikini away from the beach, and Katy's eyes burned as that scene caught Wagner's gaze too. But with no time for distraction the four detectives, as one, signalled him forwards.

'He's finally going towards the boat,' Katy tracked her

former lover's path with a light in her eyes that betrayed an earlier indifference.

'Getting in,' Timmy kept up the running commentary, stealing glances all the while at the pretty girl in the bikini moving out of the picture.

'After all he's done to me, I still hope he's okay.'

'He'll be fine,' Lance assured her. 'It's a fucking ghost ship. Not even as much as a monkey on board that the natives can hang.'

'What if it's rigged with explosives?'

'Katy, you're just being paranoid now,' Timmy laughed. 'Only things ever blown up in Ramsgate are bouncy castles and rubber dolls.'

She laughed too, glad of their assurances, as Wagner disappeared inside and suddenly the whole seaside town grew silent as the pale chora of cliffs in the distance facing out on the silhouette of France.

In the room too there was suddenly such a silence they could hear the rattle of a rollercoaster in the distance and the excited screams of children. Fergus thought of Poppy and the promises he had failed to enact.

Some day though he'd take her to the English seaside and help her mother recover from the fear of sand in her passage through dark memories. But for now it was best to concentrate on getting this over with.

'Still no sign of life,' Lance breathed steam on the glass.

Katy, half-consciously, drew an arrow through the steam and spoke soft as the beat of moth wings once more. 'If there's nobody inside and the thing's booby trapped, he could be in great danger.'

'Maybe we'll end up with something in common,' Lance gazed down at the prosthesis he had earned from stumbling upon a landmine.

'If it's a ghost ship,' Fergus supposed of the rusting *Selhurst*, 'at least they've got Grace for being an accomplice in the Deptford murder.'

He had answers to who murdered the musician and

who was behind the smuggling of girls to such places as *The Bird Cage*. But questions remained about the reefer, lying silent on the borders of sand and shingle, offering no signs of response.

Wagner had gone in, but hadn't come out again.

'Is he the one being held as a prisoner now?' Katy voiced more fears. 'Detectives were crazy to send him there in the first place.'

'They won't know he's betrayed them,' Timmy assured her.

'Yeah but if they're not on the boat then something's wrong.'

'True,' he agreed. 'I'd say they got wind of it from inside. Operations the size of this smuggling network always have people on the payroll you'd never expect. Just as it was on the island back in the old days.'

'Then he's not safe,' Katy supposed.

With Wagner on the inside, the police officers disguised as surfers began to edge closer and change out of their costumes. Further up the shore, the four detectives watched through binoculars. Their female boss watched too, and patrolled the front of the marina to stop any interruptions from bystanders who had grown curious at this stage.

'He's been in there several minutes,' Lance observed, as the police took up positions, readying for a sudden entrance if one were needed. 'If the boat had been rigged we'd have heard a bang by now.'

Instead of explosive blasts, the sideways, sidelined hulk of *Selhurst* lay silent as a painting on the far side of the window. Though the boat's door had been opened, the action had retreated inside its rusting shell. They may as well have been miles away, watching on TV.

'What the hell's going on there?' Katy's impatience exploded.

'Maybe blood's thicker than water,' Timmy suggested. 'If the smugglers are down there, perhaps he's decided to switch sides again. Maybe they're going to try and fight their way out, if they've got guns.'

'There's no way out of this,' Fergus pointed to the police lines.

But, in the minds of smugglers, maybe there was a chance of escape. After coming through wars on the far side of the world, these were dangerous people with no sense of playing by the rules. Cornered by the police, they'd nothing left to lose. Death might be better than a prison cell, and the gunfight could last for days, with the women used as human shields.

'We're never going to get out of here,' Fergus felt his growing hunger for home subside into the shoreline's deathly silence.

Then—just as yesterday, with the smashing of glass, everything changed. Suddenly, noise pulsed through the ribs of *Selhurst*.

'What was that?' Katy punched the glass.

'A volley of gunshots,' Lance defined the sound.

'They've killed him,' she cried, then turned, and raced for the stairs. 'I've got to get out there, and see what's happened.'

'Sorry we have our orders,' the guards refused to let her pass.

'Just let her go,' Timmy whipped out his revolver.

Fuck, we're on the film set of Dirty Harry, Fergus thought—machine guns facing down the former gangster's Smith & Wesson, in a Samson versus Goliath battle that everybody was in danger of losing.

'Drop your weapon,' the guards spoke as a duet.

'Hey come on,' Fergus intervened, much as it hurt to placate Katy's concern for his love rival. 'Let her go. We'll stay.'

His pleas fell on deaf ears as the guns showed no signs of dropping. 'No, we have orders from our boss.'

'We can have you arrested,' the second guard spoke.

'I don't mind,' Lance gestured to his prosthesis. 'I've

been doing time since the day of that cursed landmine blast.'

'Come on guys,' Fergus stepped between them. 'This is crazy.'

'Certainly is,' Timmy's grip tightened on the antique.

'Put down your weapon,' the guards ordered him once more.

Then—that sound again—closer than within the ribs of *Selhurst*. Glass smashing, awakening echoes of the storm in the midst of the play off final. Consciousness shifted suddenly to the back room, and the realisation that Katy had slipped away to there in the midst of the confrontation.

Timmy lowered his weapon. 'She's broke the window.'

'Look, she's there,' the guards caught a flash of her.

'Racing for the shore,' Fergus willed her onwards.

'Stop running,' the guards turned their attention to the front door as Katy raced down the lane, away from the house.

But she kept on running as if Wagner's life and her own depended on reaching the chaos of the shore. The guards though had their orders and seemed ready to shoot if she didn't obey their cries of *'halt'*.

Regardless of their cries, she kept going like the Albanian migrant who had once been running loose upon the shore of this same town.

Then one of the guards released the catch on his weapon.

'Surely he wouldn't dare shoot,' Fergus grew worried.

But Lance was taking no chances. Projecting his body forwards on his good leg, he grabbed hold of the goon stalking Katy's path in the rifle's sight. 'You're not here to shoot a woman in the back—pricks.'

'Hoerenjong,' the guard swore in Dutch.

Then, in a struggle, the former soldier fell to the ground and guns flashed once more, with Lance in the guard's sights.

The second guard intervened. 'Stop. Our fight's not with you guys, but we want to see no more tries of escape, and no more protesting.' Then he gestured to Timmy. 'Or no more guns. Go upstairs and stay.'

Fergus helped Lance off the ground and they made their way out of the kitchen, leaving the guards at the door and Katy, long gone, out of sight. Once back at their viewing post, they could see what was happening below.

'No more gunshots but the cops are going in,' Fergus observed.

'M1 carbines,' Timmy named their weapons. 'Gloves are off now.'

'Great,' said Fergus. 'Those women leave war zones to get here, and the first thing they see is another set of men with another set o' guns.'

'Should have stayed at home,' Lance offered little sympathy to the migrants. 'You'd have to be fucking crazy to make such a journey.'

'Crazy as Katy right now,' Fergus tracked her path.

Down on the shore, she fought to scramble her way towards *Selhurst*, but the female officer had stepped into her path, trying to push her back towards the jetty walls slick with seaweed in the mid-morning light. Against the odds, Katy fought furious as Grace on the morning of that confrontation.

Then, everything stalled. The human face of migration edged into view.

The first of the women had appeared on deck blinking in the light of a low sun—England's newest migrant finding no grand welcome. Another followed behind, and then more, flanked by the men with M1 carbines.

'They mostly seem to be African,' Fergus commented, 'but there are others too, lighter skinned, more like us, from parts of the Middle East.'

One of the lighter skinned girls had been separated from all the rest, wearing a loose blue dress billowing gently in the breeze.

'Why's she getting such special treatment?'

'And where are the two bastards?' his cousin added.

'There's no sign of the smugglers,' Fergus skimmed the scene. 'And there's no sign of Wagner either.'

The only men on the boat seemed to be police officers.

Swaggering, swaying, spitting, staggering, shadowing the cargo.

'Look,' Lance brought thoughts of Katy back into focus.

She'd broken free from the female officer who had been trying to console her, and started running again, across the shore towards the light-skinned girl getting special treatment. Once more this confused the police force, not knowing what to do in the wake of her escape.

Eventually a couple of swaggering, staggering males reacted to her actions. But she was persistent. She'd grabbed the girl's arm, and held her ground as a couple of officers tried to prise them apart.

'The girl must speak good English,' Fergus watched the policemen fail to divide them. 'They've been talking a long time.'

Timmy's gaze had moved elsewhere, drinking in the bigger picture. 'Stretchers are going into the reefer,' he observed. 'I'd say what's happened is the smugglers shot Wagner, and the cops shot them. That's why it's only the women we've seen so far coming out of the boat.'

'There's nothing now, no sound, no movement,' Fergus noticed.

Selhurst fully unmanned, except for police. Even the gulls had retreated from the beach, taking shelter in the cliffs and the marina.

'You know,' Lance spoke against the tide of his old beliefs. 'Looking at those women, it's hard not to feel sympathy. When you see people as they are in the flesh, they stop being monsters in your mind. You actually want to help them, do something to get them out o' this fucking mess.'

Any second now, the real monsters in the story might appear on deck. Then, as he scanned the scene with sharp eyes, Timmy spoke.

'Door's opening, somebody's coming up.'

The sight of life stirring in *Selhurst* had caught Katy's attention too. Suddenly her focus shifted from the young woman in the blue dress.

Touching her one last time on the cheek, as if to rub away tears, Katy pushed past the police in a desperate attempt to reach the boat. The young woman's eyes strayed too towards the deck as a stretcher appeared.

Through the window they could catch fragments of the scene—a body underneath a shroud, not fully covered, and one arm dangling over the side.

'Can't see much, but too small to be the Giraffe,' Fergus reckoned. 'Maybe it's Wagner or the North African.'

'Could be either,' Lance predicted.

Groups of bystanders had gathered in the space beyond the marina. They too watched and wondered what was happening in the distance.

'Who is it?' Timmy pressed tighter to the glass.

'Wagner,' Fergus knew by Katy's reaction on the shore.

She had started running across the sand to reach him as the four detectives comically gave chase behind her. Then, in her haste to escape them, she lost her footing. One of her shoes came loose and she tumbled to the ground crashing into a child's castle left from days before.

She got up, and ran on, her face freckled golden with sand and her feet bare like the migrant women who might well have crossed a burning desert to reach castles on the shore at Ramsgate.

'Looks like your prediction is going to turn out right Timmy,' Fergus anticipated an unhappy ending to Katy's love affair. 'The smugglers have realised that Wagner double crossed them, and they've shot him.'

'Live by the sword, you die by the sword.'

Fergus turned from the window as Timmy's words echoed through the big room where he had been held hostage and dreamed of sweet vengeance. He didn't want to look at his dead nemesis. Like being a soldier on the battlefield or a boxer seeing an opponent dying in the ring, there was no satisfaction, poetic justice, or fair play. Just a cold sadness in the stomach, and a sense of guilt for the pain that Katy was going through.

Then Lance's words relieved him. 'Hey, he seems to be alive.'

Sure enough Katy had stopped running. Reaching the stretcher she got down on her knees, and spoke to Wagner. For a second she seemed ready to kiss him, until the sound of a van starting up in the background startled her. Turning around, she faced the young woman's sad eyes framed in the back window. Something changed in her at that very moment as the van drove away, and she rose up off her knees in the sand.

Letting go of Wagner's hand she walked as close to the migrant women as the police would allow her to go, and stared for several minutes.

Dazed and shivering, they stood on the shore awaiting transportation.

Fergus thought of that sign. 'Welcome *toe* the English coast.'

Britain's newest migrants had tattooed their vestige upon the sand.

'They look so ordinary,' Lance retained his new found sympathy for these strangers huddled in his midst. 'So different to expectations.'

Down on the shore Katy stood watching these ordinary women, waitresses and cleaners, and future mothers of the next generation of footballers, until the police moved her on. Wagner had gone too, ferried off in a waiting ambulance, but she barely noticed. Instead she followed a well-trodden path across the beach, back to the house.

'But where the hell are the smugglers?' Timmy sparked

up a cigarette to celebrate as they watched a fresh cadre of police approach the hard shell of *Selhurst* to find whatever and whoever else remained inside.

When Katy arrived back in the house, she provided the answers—sparking up a cigarette, even though she had rarely smoked in her lifetime. She wanted to do it now, having reached the end of her crossroads, and absorbed the shock of the young woman's story.

'The pretty girl in a blue dress,' she spoke softly, with teary eyes. 'I didn't even catch her name, but saw something in her eyes that will leave a tattoo in my memory for a lifetime.' She bowed her head then as if in apology, while her voice lowered to a whisper. 'Never thought I'd say this but that look in her eyes was almost enough motivation to go out and get a tattoo, perhaps a symbol of triumph over suffering written in a foreign alphabet.'

'Nike,' Lance suggested. 'God of Victory.'

'What did she tell you?' Fergus sought an ending, leaning in so close to his former lover he could taste the smoke coming out of her lungs and into his, like the bodily fluids that had once passed between them. 'What happened to Wagner? Why did you walk away from him, and where are the others?'

Katy lingered in the silence of her own cool smoke. She appeared to be in a daze, imagining the horrors that had passed before the eyes of the young woman on her travels.

Calcified stones of memory rupturing the emotions of night—bombs falling on villages, turning homes to rubble and cradles to miniaturised receptables of the premature dead. Pictures scattered in the depths of the skull, painted on the retina, sanguine and indelible.

Turning back towards a view of the beach, and vans loaded up with a fresh meat of female flesh, Katy started mapping out the last pieces of the jigsaw. 'When Wagner entered the boat the women shot him because they thought, or knew that he was the guy on the other side of the smuggling operation who had come to meet them.'

'I called the game wrong then,' Timmy assumed. 'The smugglers weren't on the boat at all. They must have escaped along the way.'

'No, they were on the boat,' Katy corrected him.

'But how come there was no sign of them?'

Finishing her cigarette, blowing out the last stream of smoke, she changed direction suddenly. 'It's all to do with that club on the Isle of Dogs.'

'What club?' Lance leaned in closer.

'The one where the young musician went snooping for answers,' she turned to face Fergus, 'as you told me about.'

'*The Bird Cage*,' he named the place in his memories.

'Some of these women, the better looking ones, are sent there to help pay off the cost of their shipment,' Katy explained in a matter of fact manner. 'Others are sent into brothels and massage parlours.'

'But what has that got to do with the girl on the beach?'

'Her cousin was a dancer at the club, who'd came from Nepal and was turned to a drug addict because of that place. She decided to take a terrible revenge on Lucifer for all the women abused by the network.'

Memories from the lap dancing club passed through Fergus's mind. Colombian girl, cocktails, nightwear, and a world of eternal evening. Then a junkie smoking in the underpass as he exited with Dyana who'd offered him a cheap dance just before he stepped into the booth with Estrella.

Maybe she wasn't the exact cousin of the girl on the beach but it was for the sake of such women that she had enacted her revenge.

'So what did she do to the fucker?' Lance pushed for answers, openly cheering on the migrant women in their struggle for victory.

'She tricked him into going downstairs, with the promise of sex. She brought him down to the refrigerated area,' Katy mapped out the motions of the young woman's revenge. 'He always kept a gun on his person, except when he was having his way with one of the cargo. He'd such power they couldn't say no and took his pick every day.'

'Treated like meat from start to finish.'

'Yes,' she agreed with Lance. 'But this piece of meat was smart. She got him stripped down and pretended that she was going to go next, so she asked him to close his eyes and not open them until she said so. He liked games, as he told me, and so I guess the bastard obliged her.'

'Hope she whacked him over the skull,' Fergus willed.

'Better than that,' Katy spoke slowly at first, then quickened her pace. 'She pulled a fish knife from her belt, and stuck it twice in his abdomen as he stood there with his eyes closed. Then when he fell, she finished him off, but not quite in the way you might be expecting.'

'What did she do?' the men asked in chorus.

Fergus detected a naughty smile as Katy moved on with the story. 'As he lay on the ground she put her knife between his legs.'

'Stuck the knife in his cock!' Lance exclaimed.

'No, she chopped it right off down to the butt.'

'One way to cut a smuggler's root,' Timmy joked.

'What about the other guy?' Fergus transferred the subject from Lucifer's slashed genitals to news of the cruise ship chef.

'The women overpowered him when he reacted to Lucifer's screaming, and he got killed in the struggle with a kitchen knife through the heart,' Katy provided as much information as the girl had given her.

Live by the kitchen knife, die by the kitchen knife, Fergus mused.

'The Giraffe had a quick ending,' Katy carried on. 'But the women left Lucifer suffering, bleeding to death slowly down amongst the ice boxes with nobody to hear his screaming on the open sea.'

'Better than any stray bullet,' Lance reckoned.

'Poetic justice,' Katy supposed.

The ordeal was over, and the women were safe. They'd go to holding centres and apply for asylum. The girl who killed Lucifer might face a trial, but no judge could damn her for what she did.

Once the Belgian detectives came back to the house the laundry could now be washed in public and they sketched in the details of the others. Despite a couple of surface wounds to the shoulder, Wagner would live and Grace would face punishment for her part in the network.

The police had picked up the transgender dancer too— in a bar in London's West End watching the play off final that featured the team she supported. They'd put her on a witness protection programme and keep her safe from the goons who'd tried to kill in Woolwich DLR station.

But, most likely, nothing would happen to the club.

'It's for gentlemen after all,' Katy sighed.

There was to be no neat ending in the search for the Queen Bee either. Lucifer was supposed to be the bait with which they would catch the overlord of the smugglers' nest but he had died in a reefer on the high seas.

Fergus hoped that would be a lesson to other foot soldiers but deep-down feared that it wouldn't. There wasn't just one Lucifer in the world. Already some new devil had probably been signed up to take the bastard's place in this dog-eat-dog world of the human flesh trade.

Katy agreed as she went to the window and looked out on the empty sea, pysching herself to get back upstairs and write the next phase of her story. She would retreat inside her castle, looking down on the sea for inspiration, and remember the triumph she had seen in the eyes of the young woman upon the shore. And yet, after everything that had happened in these past stormy weeks, she remained unsure as to whether this was the beginning or the ending of all their stories.

'But at least it's over for us,' Fergus said goodbye.

He could go, and Katy could finish her book. It was time to leave one woman behind and return to another. He stood and faced her for a moment, saying nothing, seeing her blue-green eyes dazzle as they had always done. Then he sank into their colours, somewhere between forest and sea, and edged closer still to share a hug amidst the heaving tide of his emotions.

She felt as warm as the first time he had hugged and kissed her, but this was a day of endings and not beginnings. Letting go, much as it pained him, he turned towards the door with a final parting glance, feeling the hurt of an emigrant taking one last look at the land they'd never see again.

Her blue-green eyes dazzled in his head like flashes of sunlight at the end of a dark tunnel as he shook hands with Lance and Timmy, parting from them too as they prepared for their drive back to Essex.

'See you for some gardening when we're back in London.'

'Yeah,' he answered his friend with a lump in his throat. 'Life goes on and it'll be another bloody football season before we know it.'

Then he held back the tide of his emotions to walk away from the house and back towards the car parked by the shore, several days ago, before the events that had led to his brief captivity with Katy Prunty.

On his walk along the seafront, the beach stood silent—with only *Selhurst* serving as testament to what had happened shortly before. He could see the female detective and her crew of four, clearing up the last stages of an operation that had ended in defeat for them and poetic victory for others.

Out there, on the high seas, where Lucifer bled to death, The Queen Bee still reigned. The layers of the onion remained half-stripped.

But the storms had passed and the sun smiled on Ramsgate's shore. The forecast seemed good not just for today, but for seasons ahead.

He was going back full circle to *Dark River Dye*, and his apple tree in the garden looking down on Charlton's Valley. That was the part of the world in which he had chosen to settle, and which he now drove towards at speed.

Along the way, passing the fishing boats at Whitstable, he stopped for another feast of fish and chips, an English seaside celebration, coloured in the pre-match anticipation of yesterday's newspapers. He'd no stomach for glances across the sands towards today's headlines in the news kiosks. Crystal Palace, winners of gold at the end of a rainbow.

'Maybe next season it's Charlton's turn,' he mused. 'Some wins in the FA Cup or a promotion battle, and a valley of hope, not despair.'

It's hope that keeps human beings going, whether as hostages to people smugglers, love affairs, rollercoaster rides, or English football teams.

Driving down the A2, beneath a foaming blossom of cloud, he thought of another summer of apples leading to another August, and a fresh promotion battle, as he and Dyana taught Poppy to bake crumbles. He would learn fresh recipes from her mother, and forget Katy's fragrances. Whatever happened in the next chapter of his life with the tattoo artist, Fergus was glad of driving back towards the place he'd migrated to, the place he called *home*.

Made in the USA
Charleston, SC
24 September 2016